Table
for One

~

A story about the journey to
self-love

TRISTANA WEBSTER

Acknowledgments

Thank you to friends and family for your support.

I would especially like to thank Julie Bentley and Tiffany Prince for reading the book as it progressed through different stages. Thank you for sharing your thoughts and encouraging me to complete the book and publish it.

Thank you Burak Aslan and Kathy Shafer for patiently listening to me discuss this project endlessly.

Thank you to the talented professionals who shared their gifts to help make this a beautiful project. Thank you Darnella Ford for starting the journey with me and encouraging me to submit the work. Adam O'Brien, you are a talented editor, thank you.

Thank you Olivier Darbonville for designing the interior of the book, it's beautiful! Thank you WizDiz for your graphic artistry in creating the cover art.

To my inspiration Charlotte Bronte, thank you for leading the way.

Thank You.

Dedication

This book is dedicated to my father Pascal Webster, who imparted his love of literature and education to me.

This book is for you, the reader. I hope what I share within these pages helps and bolsters you on the days that you need a little reminder, to be the beautiful and strong person that you are.

Contents

Chapter 1

A Fruit Tree in Winter

Providence has a myriad means to raise
the fallen and support the prostrate.
Sometimes our fate resembles a fruit tree in winter.
Who would think at beholding so sad a sight
that these rigid branches, these jagged twigs,
would turn green again in the spring
and blossom and bear fruit?
But we hope it, we know it!

J. W. Von Goethe

SOMETIMES WE ARE LIKE A BARREN TREE, WITH NO LEAVES, stripped down to bark and buried under ground. Our self-esteem is hibernating beneath deep layers of winter snow. The energy, or spark inside of us, that makes us unique has fizzled. And just, like a withering candle, the light inside us has been blown out, and turned off by disappointment, hardship, unreturned love, lack of fulfillment, lack of appreciation by others and no sense of self-worth.

At this low time, in this winter of your life, you must remember that just like a barren tree in winter, you will be reborn and spring will again visit your heart. Leaves will grow, the ice will thaw and you will be even more beautiful than you were before. Like a butterfly emerging from its cocoon, so too will you emerge from the darkness. You will hear the birds sing. You will smile as you feel the warmth of the sun. You must have faith and know that desolation does not last forever. Goethe so wisely reminds us of this event in his musings. Even in the desert, one can find an oasis. You must rediscover something in you, or your life, that is an oasis and can nourish you back to life.

The path through the desert of one's soul is different for everyone. I cannot tell you how to find an oasis, which road to take and what to do. I cannot even describe to you what an oasis is. What I can do is share with you my story and how I found my way. But first I must tell you where I was and how I got lost. To do this, I must first tell you who I am.

My name is Tristan. I am a woman. I am multi-racial, Vietnamese and African American. I am the adopted daughter of a Caucasian couple. My mother is American and my father is English. My parents adopted many children of other racial backgrounds and had two biological children of their own.

I was born in Vietnam toward the end of the Vietnam War. The country's struggle for independence from foreign rule strangely echoes themes in my life as I have struggled for my independence and to be free of many labels and limitations imposed by others. My little brother and I were abandoned by our parents and left to live in an orphanage. If we had not gone to America, who knows what would have become of us? We were parentless in an inhospitable world where mixed race children were not welcome. This would have sealed our fate in a tomb of sadness and poverty.

Chapter 2

The Beginning

I LIVE IN A SMALL HOUSE WITH MY MOTHER, MY YOUNGER BROTH-er who is one year old, and I am 3 years old, in the countryside of South Vietnam.

I remember one day in particular where my mother is busy packing items onto a cart. She asked me to find my uncle. I run out into the yard and call for him. There is chaos everywhere. I easily get distract-ed and run down the street, calling my uncle's name. "Uncle, Uncle, mother wants you."

I see him. He grabs me and says, "Child, what are you doing here? It is not safe! Go back home."

"Mother asked me to find you."

"I can't come now," he says, "I will see her later. Do you want some candy?"

"Yes!" I burst with joy as my eyes grow big with delight. I begin taking the candy from his hands that he has pulled from his pocket. He laughs as I eat the candy. He lifts me high off the ground and places me on his lap. Then he sends me home. I run through the streets all the way back to my mother's house.

As I run through the streets, I hear the noise of gunfire and see explosions in the distance. Through the haze of the streets, I happen to catch a glimpse of my mother. She has the cart packed with clothes and household items. It appears as though she is in a hurry. I call her name. She never looks back and walks even faster. I run after her calling, but I cannot keep up. I am exhausted and tired. When I finally reach the house she is too far away. In that moment, I realize that my mother abandoned me and that I will never see her again. As I enter the now empty and disheveled house, I hear my baby brother crying and realize that in this empty house, we are all that remains.

Not knowing what to do, I look for my uncle.

I carry my little brother and walk through streets accompanied by the sounds of gunfire and explosions. I try to avoid being exposed in the open and stick to the side of the street. It is getting darker and my little brother is crying. I am tired and grow increasingly anxious as I look for my uncle. I go to the house I last saw him at and knock on the door. When the door opens, I say my uncle's name. The door closes and then several minutes later he comes to the door, opens it, and with a surprised look takes me and my brother into his arms and the house. The house has a lot of men and guns. He finds an empty corner and tells us to sit. We are cold and shivering. He brings us food and water. My brother is ravenous and crying hysterically. My uncle says nothing because he knows what happened. Without me saying a word, he knows my mother left without us. I can tell he is thinking deeply about what to do.

Later that evening, my brother finally falls asleep. My eyelids are heavy too, and eventually, I too, fall asleep. When I wake up, the house is empty. The men, the guns, everything is gone. The house is silent. I have no idea where everyone has gone. All I can hear is gunfire and explosions in the distance. I am too tired to cry. I know my uncle will eventually return, and if not, I don't have time to worry about that.

My brother is soundly sleeping, so I walk back to my mother's house, hoping that she has returned somehow. I see the house, empty and cold, and I know with certainty that she is *never* coming back. Now I cry, the weight of my situation pushes me into the fit of tears, I feel all alone and small. I am just a child, but know I will never feel safe or free again. The sun is slowly rising. I know I need to return to my brother before he wakes up and feels alone and frightened.

In the far distance, I see a woman on horseback riding toward me. She is tall and slender with long blonde hair. I find that strange here. I have never seen someone who looks like her. Suddenly, she and her beautiful chestnut horse are right next to me. She has piercing blue eyes and long bright golden hair. She exudes power, strength, and grace all at the same time. I am aware that a woman can be both exquisite and delicate, a powerful force of energy. She gets off her horse as if she floats off her saddle, gently landing on the ground and walks toward me and says, "My name is Sara, I have been watching you. Your mother has left you. You will never see her again. You can cry and perish, or you can come with me and I will show you how to be strong. You are a warrior at heart. You have faced loss and death over many lifetimes. I will guide you and teach you what you need to know, to be the warrior that you are destined to become. Do not fear. I will always be with you."

She strokes my head and says, "You must be brave for you and your brother. You must trust that you will be okay and that all is well. Come with me."

She picks me up, places me on her horse and we ride away. I feel the strength and force of the horse as he gallops quickly. I feel the wind in my hair. I feel free. The sun is rising and casts a bright light on the stretches of open land. Time feels like it has stopped. I forget about the fire and explosions. I forget about being alone and afraid. I feel embraced by an angel. She is speaking to me as we ride, assuring me that all is well. I close my eyes and find that I have returned to the house where my brother is. I open the door and see him still asleep in the corner. I turn back toward her, and before I can say anything, I see her galloping away, but she turns to me and says, "I am Sara. I am always with you. Have no fear, for you are safe and loved. You are strong. You are a warrior princess." She bows her head, her horse rises, whinnies, and off they go. It is as if they vanish in the air.

I turn back to the open door, walk through it and close it. I sit near my brother and wait for him to wake up. I have to be his rock now and help him to not be afraid. He slowly wakes up, and I squeeze his hand, so he knows that I am here, right by his side. He opens his eyes and sees me, half smiles and closes them again. He coughs. He is getting hot. I find a rag and some water, and place the dampened rag on his head and sing him a song. Days and nights go by, and no one is in the house. We are all alone. I look through the house for food to give my brother. There is very little, and what there is, I give to him.

Late one night my Uncle enters the house and says, "Come with me my child, I have found a new place for you and your brother to live."

He picks up my sleeping brother, and I follow behind him. We walk for what seems like miles. It is cold and dark. Eventually, we come to a building. My Uncle puts my brother on the doorstep and rings the doorbell. He says this has to happen. It is the only way for you and your brother to have a better life. I will come back for you. I will make sure everything is okay. Don't worry my child."

Then he turns and walks away into the darkness. The door opens and nuns in white habits appear. They ask, "What do we have here?" My brother is now awake and crying hysterically. One of the nuns picks him up and says, "Oh this poor baby has a fever. Let's get him to the doctor quickly."

The other nun turns to me and says, "Child what is your name and what is his name, how old are you? Is he your brother?"

I nod my head and say "yes, my brother is one and I am three" as I show three fingers. My name is Tran and his name is Hyuen."

She is writing as I speak, with pen paused in her fingers she looks at me and asks "what are the names of your parents my child and where are they?"

I shrug my shoulders and say "I don't know. "I can only give them my name and my brother's name. I have never met my father. I don't know where my mother is.

She registers what I have said with no emotion, but she understands that is the legacy of war, parentless children. She tells me in a softer voice "not to worry my child, you are safe here. One day you will have new parents."

Then she waves her hand to a passing sister beckoning her to come close. "Sister Mary, will you please take this child and wash her and put her to bed?"

"Of course, Sister Theresa, it will be my pleasure." Sister Mary walks over to me and in a kind voice and smile says "what is your name dear?"

I sheepishly say "Tran."

"Well Tran, I am Sister Mary, it's getting late, let's get clean and ready for bed my dear." She gently takes my hand and says "walk this way."

She quietly and efficiently washes me, scrubbing my face, hair, nails. "Is that too hard my dear?"

I was quiet and did not answer but my eyes must have said yes as she was a little more gentle afterwards. Then she dried me off and put me in a new white dress and sent me to bed.

As she was tucking me into bed and placed the crisp sheet over me, I ask "Sister Mary where is my brother, is he okay, can I see him?"

She stops for a moment and ponders my question. Then in a kind voice she says, "okay you can see him if it will help you fall asleep." She pulls back the covers and walks down the hallway to another smaller room. She points "he is in there, where we put the sick children. Just say hi for a moment, because you have to go to bed and let him rest too." I enter the room all excited; it too has rows of beds with white linens. I see him and walk to the side of his bed. He, too, is washed and in new white clothes. He is crying, and I sit next to him on his bed and sing him a song. "It's okay Hyuen, everything will be okay. Just sleep. I am here. Everything is okay." I fall asleep next to my brother. Sister Mary was compassionate and let me stay with my brother during our first night in the orphanage. Even though she said I could only visit him.

When we wake up in the morning, they give him medicine. Sister Mary, "Tran we need to keep him in a separate room. Your brother is sick and needs to be by himself until his fever comes down. You must play with the other children."

Sister Mary ushers me to a different room where there are many children of all ages and sizes. "Tran, you can stay here with the healthy children and play."

We must have lived at the orphanage for a while, how long I do not know. I remember being comfortable at the orphanage and seeing the nuns and other children. However, one day, while sitting on a green bench with my brother and surrounded by other children, Sister Mary comes and tells me there is someone to see me. She takes my hand and walks me down the hallway to a different room.

Sister Mary then walks into the room and says "here is your guest." As soon as I am in the other room I see my uncle and light up. At first sight, I run straight to him. He laughs, picks me up, and gives me a big kiss on the cheek. "Tran my sweet, how are you and your brother? I have missed you. I am sorry that I cannot be with you every day." He is holding me as he is speaking. "It is safer for both of you to be here with the nuns who are taking good care of you. I brought you something." He hands me a plaid patterned cardboard purse filled with colorful and pretty taffy candies. As he is speaking to me and singing, I am intensely focused on unwrapping the candy.

My uncle says, "Dear One, I have done something for you and your brother to protect you and your happiness. Know that your family will always love you."

As I am chewing candy and looking into my uncles' eyes, I do not understand what he is saying. He then faces a big window and says "look out there in the distance."

"Do you see that thing in the air? It's called an airplane. It takes people to places that are far away." He starts to get a little choked up.

"One day soon, you and your brother will be on an airplane and will go far away from here to a better life. Just know that your uncle will always love you even though I will not be there for you."

With that, we watched the plane get smaller and smaller in the distance. He kissed me and hugged me tightly. Then he put me down and the nun came over to walk me back to my seat next to my brother. I see my brother and share the candy. In the moment we are content, but little did I realize that would be the last time I would ever see my uncle.

Soon after my uncle's visit, my brother and I were on an airplane. We flew far away, never to return to Vietnam, to our birthplace. As my uncle promised, we went to a new country and became part of a loving family.

The memories of Vietnam come to me and feel real and vivid. In reality, I was about 3 or 4 years old. So much of these events are probably a mixture of real events that are exaggerated due to the intense stress of being separated and abandoned by my mother at a young age. My uncle, the candy, the air plane and the nuns I know are real. How my brother and I arrived at the orphanage, only my soul knows the truth. However, this is the recurring dream that I have about life before I came to America.

We were lucky enough to go to America and into the home of Pascal and Janice Webster, a young couple who decided to adopt children after their first child was stillborn. Although privately devastated, the couple buried their grief when they buried their first born, a boy.

Instead, they focused on having a family by adopting children. At that time there were a lot of orphans from Vietnam, so they adopted a boy, and then me and my brother. As they were waiting for a little girl and her brother to arrive, happy news came to the couple, and they were able to conceive. Janice was pregnant with a very healthy girl, soon to be my little sister.

Chapter 3

Woman with a Preppy Past—The Milton Years

I GREW UP IN A SMALL TOWN IN NEW ENGLAND. THE CENTER OF town still has a common area, and now there are local gatherings such as speeches on Veterans Day, whereas in the past, people brought their livestock to graze. The town decorates the few trees on the common with strands of white lights in the wintertime.

This sleepy, peaceful town has Colonial homes, with beautiful green lawns and blooming flowerbeds that mark the passing of time. At the end of winter, as the snow melts and spring is creeping into the air, the crocuses bloom, and their round blooms poke through the snow. This is one of the first signs that the ground is thawing and winter storms are ending. However, for me, spring is officially ushered in when the beds of yellow Daffodils bloom and bow their golden crowns in the spots of chilly New England spring sunlight. The New England garden is composed of many beautiful and colorful arrangements of flowers;

however, the lilacs and peonies steal the early summer show. The garden truly is a metaphor for the seasons of life, and a great reminder to stop and smell the beautiful flowers and enjoy the gifts of nature.

When I was a child, my father, a tall, handsome English man with thick dark hair and blue eyes, smoked a pipe and had little funny sayings that he liked to share. When he tucked us into bed after reading us a bedtime story, he would always say, "Good night…sleep tight… don't let the bed bugs bite."

My mother has blue eyes, light brown hair and is from upstate New York. She is very direct and straightforward. She was very good at keeping everyone and everything on schedule, always writing lists and delegating tasks.

I grew up in a big yellow Colonial home with white pillars in the front, a barn, and a stable. As I was learning English, I also learned how to ride a horse. I had riding lessons every Saturday on a little brown Shetland pony starting at age four. Eventually, the pony came home with me and become a part of our family.

My father called her Dapple. She had a stable in the barn, but was mostly tied to a large shady tree or housed in a corral nearby. Every once in a while, she would break free and run as fast as she could. Her untamed spirit would speed up and down the lawns in the neighborhood, making it impossible to catch her, even by a group of adult men. Only when she was tired could she be caught and brought back home.

In retrospect, I realize that I am so much like her. Always wanting to run, to be free from expectation and judgment, to choose how I would like to spend my time. (She did throw me once when I was little and broke my arm.) My mother always assumed my waning interest was due to fear and would say horses can smell fear. "Do not show your fear," she insisted. But it wasn't fear that caused my disinterest. It was an overly active mind that easily loses focus.

I would brush Dapple and feed her every day. However, if I forgot, my father would still always feed her. We lived in front of a small beautiful nature preserve. The trees created a canopy along a pathway before leading to meandering brooks and paths. It was always quiet and peaceful there. There were partial stone walls, and a small brook that appeared as you descended worn stone steps that were barely visible, overrun with moss and grass.

The wintertime woods are so enchanting, and though beautiful in any season, the winter woods are my favorite place. The snow and ice make everything look magical. One can imagine fairies dancing in the wind or on the tips of icicles that hang from branches when it snows. We would walk and slide across the icy brook in wintertime.

Sometimes we would sled down the extremely steep hill in our neighbor's backyard after a large snowfall. Ms. Fogg, a tall, elderly woman who was educated in England, lived next door in a large, white Colonial home, which sat back from the street. It had two parallel long rows of garden beds that faced each other and were impeccably groomed by her gardener.

In this small town, neighbors visited each other. Every once in a while, my father would walk us to her house to have a nice chat over tea. She would reminisce about her days in England, and my father would learn about the history of our town. Her family founded it, and owned the majority of the land in our town and the next one. As a child, that means nothing to you. Instead, I remember that she had long bony fingers and wore large rings, and while speaking would often knock on the wooden table for good luck, or to affirm something she said out loud.

Every so often, when we would visit Ms. Fogg, her dear friend from her school days, Calle Merriweather, would be visiting her, and we would have English biscuits and candy.

Calle was a petite woman with light brown hair and blue eyes. She had delicate hands and features. She was very kind and invited us to visit her the next time we were in England.

Growing up, I learned the ways of womanhood like most girls. I pretended to cook on a play stove and cared for baby dolls by carrying and feeding them with a bottle. My friends would dream about their future husbands, what they would name their children, describe what they would wear on their wedding day. The childhood friends who talked most of marriage were the ones who married first.

I don't know why I didn't talk about marriage or why I have dated every man who is the furthest thing from a marriageable prospect, despite my traditional, family-oriented upbringing. However, here I am in my thirties and still picking the wrong man. I know my parents taught me better. I even pick people with completely different backgrounds and then act surprised, as if I couldn't logically understand that a man who likes to camp will not be the type of man to surprise me with an exotic vacation somewhere.

I digress. My childhood, like many others, was a mixed bag of fun, innocence, humiliation and self-loathing, all intensified by family dynamics. Being a multi-racial child in a small New England town was an interesting experience. My mother did not know what to do with my hair and would brush it when it was dry, and gave me the stylish afro haircut (which, by the way, was NOT my best look).

My friends were fun and sweet and always looked beyond race. However, sometimes that was hard for others to do. There would be the occasional racial outburst by a classmate, or condescending remark by a teacher; especially if I went by my Vietnamese name, Tran, and not my formal Western name.

In elementary school, you are just a child, not yet understanding the world and the rules of the world. You do not have the protective armor of deductive reasoning, and cannot yet quite spell or formulate a thesis and provide your proof in a grammatically or mathematically correct way. You are just a sponge, being immersed in the history and basic skills of our culture. Reviewing American history in elementary school, especially in your early years, is so strange if you are a bi-racial child, or just non-white. The discussion of slaves and slavery becomes personal and not an objective recounting of facts. And to complicate matters, if you are of the race that was in bondage, you are identified with inferiority, with differentness. You learn that there are different expectations and rules based on your skin color.

This was something that always made me uncomfortable, which I felt was not right and that I rebelled against in my way, by talking about things and proving that there is no difference in the quality of a human being because your origins are that of a slave. So, I believe that we should be kind to every human being from every walk of life, because we do not know when we will be in their shoes, or maybe in our prior life we were the janitor, the slave, the maid—something more humble than we are now. The adage, "treat others as you would like others to treat you," is my personal mantra. Even though it may be difficult to treat someone who is disrespecting you with respect, we should try. It is during the most challenging interactions that we should wish someone well and bless them.

Chapter 4

Innocence

F ROM A YOUNG AGE, I KNEW I WAS DIFFERENT FROM OTHER girls. My skin color was the major differentiating factor. My parents criticized my body, telling me that I needed to watch my weight, which planted the seed of insecurity. I grew up feeling unattractive, so I focused on school and other things.

I was always in the library as a little girl. I loved to read books and would always volunteer to help the librarians put the books away. I would often read stories of Atlantis, the lost city, and the profile of an Aquarius, my sun sign. These books fascinated me, and I read them repeatedly. Also, I was addicted to Greek and Roman myths. I would put the books inside of my actual school book and read them during class. Of course, I would always get caught up in the story and caught by my teacher who could quickly figure out that I was not paying attention to her lesson.

My father and his brothers went to an old Jesuit preparatory school and thought it would be a good idea to provide us with a classical education. Therefore, we attended Milton Academy, one of the oldest New England prep schools.

Founded in 1798, Milton was established as a co-educational establishment. However, for a large part of its history, the boys' and girls' schools were separate entities, sharing the same campus. The girls' school occupied different buildings, primarily Goodwin Hall. Centre Street divides the boys' school from the girls' school, but now that is a historical reminder and not a physical one. As students, we were reminded of the gender separation once or twice a week during the mandatory single sex general assembly. I still have my hymnal, which I had all my years from middle school to graduation. You don't have a desk in Goodwin Hall until you are a junior. Otherwise, you have a locker and sit on the benches that line the wall.

I can still see it as if it were yesterday, all of us and our teachers, standing in Goodwin Hall, singing a hymn, my favorite of which is "Jerusalem", the hymn from Hubert Parry based on a poem by William Blake.

> Bring me my bow of burning gold;
> Bring me my arrows of desire:
> Bring me my spear: O clouds unfold!
> Bring me my chariot of fire!
>
> I will not cease from mental fight,
> nor shall my sword sleep in my hand
> Till we have built Jerusalem,
> In England's green and pleasant land."[1]

---

[1] Parry, Hubert *"Jerusalem" Lyrics* 1916.

Some songs stay with you forever. This one will always stay in my heart because the melody is pretty and the message is intense. The song embodies the mantra of my school. It was my first public association that differed from my family. They were my first family of friends who are still my friends, and reminders of times that we have shared and that I will never forget.

The school motto is *Dare to be True.* Milton's vision of the world focused on education as a vehicle to improve humankind. Creating minds that will help shape the world, or at least one's individual world—is a beautiful endeavor and in essence is the expression of a humanitarian utopia.

I started Milton Academy when I was in fifth grade. In the afternoon, I would have my piano lesson with Mrs. Daley, an elderly lady with silver-gray hair that was always perfectly in a bob with big curls. She had long fingers and would listen to me as I practiced Beethoven or Mozart. She wore a long pencil skirt and a sweater set with a strand of pearls and dark pumps. The building where I had my piano lesson was near a magnificent apple tree, which had fluffy, fragrant pink-and-white blossoms every spring.

After school, there was the Shakespeare club where we would read different works of Shakespeare, act out the characters, and talk about the meaning of the plays. I also enjoyed art class and painted the stormy New England seas. Living in Massachusetts, the sea is a central part of the New England experience and culture. We have Plymouth Rock, where the Pilgrims landed, and many houses that face the sea have the widow's walk where the wives of sea captains would wait and search for their husbands on the horizon. There are constant reminders of a maritime life in the décor and paintings in people's homes, the food, and the local history.

Later, I would also take piano lessons from Jana, the choir director at church. She was very passionate and demanded that I practice more. She could tell if I only practiced a little and was sight-reading and would become enraged. "Tristan, you must practice a minimum of an hour every day to grow your talent. I take music very seriously and expect my students to as well. Because you have not been diligent, you will learn this entire sonata by our next class next week." I would learn that people who are passionate share their emotions without apology, and expect you to share in their intense expressions or stop wasting their time.

My father used to walk me to the James Library, a Victorian building that became the local library. We would walk up the winding staircase to the room with a grand piano. There was a landing or anteroom where parents would sit on the couch waiting for their children to complete their lessons.

My piano lesson days were before cell phones, tablets, smart phones, and constant emails. My father would relax and listen to me play. He always enjoyed this time. He was content sitting on the couch, smoking his pipe, reading the newspaper, or just thinking, as I learned Fur Elise, sonatinas and minuets.

Childhood can be a simple time of peace and exploration of your creativity and the world. I do understand that it may not be like this for everyone, and the peace and innocence can disappear in a flash, as it would for me.

Chapter 5

Trip to England

WHEN I WAS TEN YEARS OLD, MY PARENTS DECIDED TO SEND me on a trip to England for part of the summer. It was exciting to travel across the pond to England and visit with my extended family on my father's side, who had come to visit us at our house many times. I researched all of the places I was curious to see, such as the Tower of London, The London Dungeon wax museum, Parliament, Big Ben, and the site of the Globe Theater, the renowned home of Shakespeare's plays.

We also visited Oxford University, my father's alma mater, where I bought my father the Oriel college tie to remind him of his school days. As I walked through the courtyards, libraries and many stone buildings, I imagined my father as a young student walking to lectures.

Still, as much as I loved traveling I was happy to return home to my family and school friends after my visit. The summer trip made me appreciate home and my usual routine.

On the summer reading list for fifth grade, I met a lifelong friend. I was introduced to *Jane Eyre*, by Charlotte Bronte. The novel left an unforgettable impression on me. I remember going to the library and finding the book on the library shelf. The book had more than 300 pages that I was required to read before school started. I would bring my book to the local swim and tennis club, and after swim team practice, I would lay my towel on a patch of grass and read every day.

I quickly became enthralled by the book. Jane, orphaned after the death of her parents, experienced so much at a young age. She was mistreated and sent away to a strict, harsh school that showed no mercy to its tenant students. Her closest friend died when she was young due to the mistreatment. The experience of being abandoned twice, once by her deceased parents and then by her aunt, who despised her, did not break her spirit. Jane proved to be strong, resilient, honest, and genuine. Even though she lacked beauty or fortune, Jane possessed intelligence and a pure, loving heart that sought justice. She did well at school and was able to support herself by being a governess once her education was completed. Jane learned at an early age that she could not rely on anyone.

I could relate to her story in so many ways. Although our lives spanned different centuries, and the color of our skin was different, I too at times felt like I was Jane. Being a girl with a mixed-race background and having been abandoned by my biological parents, I felt unattractive as I did not have the light eyes or hair of most everyone else around me. I was not petite, as the cultural norm of the community dictates, and generally did not match the American prototype for beauty. I felt that Jane expressed the sadness, the despair, and the loneliness one may feel when labeled as different, when there is no one in your corner to support you. When you live in a world where different somehow becomes equated with inferior, and you do not have your beauty to rely on, you learn that you must develop your mind and talents. If there is no fortune to sustain you, and if you do not biologically belong to your parents, no matter how loving they can be, you can still feel cast apart and separate. Jane also showed how the pure heart and strong spirit can overcome all obstacles and allow one to forgive those who have done her wrong. The strength of her spirit, her non-judging eyes, and relentless fight for fairness, balanced by her understanding that sometimes compassion is what is right, redefines heroism. Jane transforms the notion of beauty. Her character, firm resolve, and genuine heart were more beautiful than any perceived physical flaws. She is a reminder that beauty comes from within, and that everyone is resilient, everyone is lovely.

Chapter 6

Lightening

I WAS RUNNING DOWN THE STREET TO MY FRIEND JENNIFER'S house. She lived in the white Colonial house a few doors down from my house. She was one of my closest friends. After arriving at her house and knocking on the side door that the family used, I was greeted by her mother.

"Hello, my dear, how are you today?" Mrs. Fewkes asked.

"Fine, Mrs. Fewkes. Is Jennifer home?"

"Yes, of course, come in." She opens the door widely to allow me to enter. As I walk into a large hallway, her mother called to Jennifer loudly. "Jennifer, Tristan is here."

The tall, lanky, wiry Jennifer comes running into the hallway from the family room. She has brown hair, blue eyes, and a thin face with a prominent nose. "Hi Tristan. How are you? What do you want to do today?"

"It's such a sunny day today, let's go outside."

We decided to race to the big tree at our neighbor's yard. Meanwhile, my father, brothers, and sisters were preparing to take a leisurely stroll. Jennifer and I could see them toward the end of my driveway from the large tree in the neighbor's yard.

Suddenly, we heard a scream, and looked in their direction. My father collapsed, dropping to the ground. His body grew soft. We ran over to where they were. One of my brothers ran into our house to tell my mother what happened. Understanding what was happening, she called the ambulance. There was sheer panic everywhere!

My mother ran over to where my father was lying motionless on the grass, and tried to talk to him. His eyes were closed, and there was no response.

The ambulance arrived in moments. My mother told us to move away as the stretcher appeared at the rear door of the ambulance. His body was placed on top of it and lifted into the ambulance. My mother went in the ambulance with my father, and we saw the doors close. The rest is a blur. I just remember that everything changed from that moment: my father was diagnosed as having a stroke due to a brain tumor. There were no signs warning of this issue prior to that traumatic collapse.

During the school year, one of my classmates was the first of us to lose his father. The entire class went to the funeral. We all cried, unable to imagine the grief and shock that he and his family must have felt. I had the eerie feeling that I would soon know how he felt, as my own father's health was declining. After chemotherapy and radiology, my father lost all of his hair. He could barely walk and was pale and rail thin.

Treatments for cancer, especially brain tumors, were in a nascent state at the time of my father's diagnosis. Doctors and neurosurgeons were still trying to understand how to eradicate the cancerous cells. Surgery, chemotherapy, and radiology (i.e. poisoning the body), were the only treatments available even at the most advanced hospitals. After his diagnosis, my father's work would never be in the office—it was now at the hospital, the fight to survive.

As my parents spent more and more time at the hospital, I had to be in charge at home. Although my grandmother would spend time with us, and other family friends were around, I had to grow up quickly. I had to help my younger siblings get ready for school and help them with their homework. To my dismay, my role as big sister greatly expanded. Lacking the necessary equipment to fill parental shoes, I felt as though I had fallen into the deep end of the pool and told to swim or drown. I guess that is life. There are some things in life that you simply cannot prepare for, but you must respond somehow and in some way to what happens. No one gives you cliff notes that you can study in advance. Although thrown in the deep end, I somehow managed to tread water and stay afloat.

It's interesting how we will sometimes subconsciously *know* what will happen, even as a child. I dreamt one night of my father's funeral. I saw his face and body lifeless, without color or movement, his closed eyes, laid out in a dark suit. I saw a hearse taking him away and driving him to our church in New England. Flowers were in front of the church doors, placed in front of the pulpit and all over. The pews were filled with people. The small church was packed to capacity as people were standing in the back.

I knew as I was dreaming this event that it was a premonition. It was inevitable of course, but I did not want it to happen. I prayed. I wrote in my journal. I asked God to keep my father alive. I lived in fear of this event; I lived in denial. I never spoke of this to anyone, knowing that to speak it would be to acknowledge its existence, to give death life.

My father eked out a limited physical existence several years longer than the doctors expected. His prolonged life, those extra three years, gave us false hope that maybe somehow he would live, allowing us to continue with our lives as if nothing had really changed. And so, several years after his diagnoses, I went away for part of the summer. I applied and was accepted to be one of the six American girls who attended International Girl Scout camp. I did Girl Scouts after school with all my friends. Since there were a lot of badges and things that you could do on your own, I always tried new things.

We started in New York City and went to the Empire State Building, where we saw a man dressed as King Kong. We then flew to Jamaica; we were all excited to spend a month there.

We camped with the other girls and also had a home stay with local families. I was very immature and unappreciative—an obnoxious and overly dramatic fourteen-year-old brat. I used my overactive mind to make up stories about the other girls in my tent, I guess for the attention and dramatic effect. When they confronted me about making up stories, I of course lied and pretended it didn't happen. But I did reflect on my behavior, stopped the gossiping, and realized much too late that my words were hurtful.

Ironically, my father fell into a coma while I was away. And from there, his condition did not improve. I was lucky that he was awake and able to wish me luck before I left for the airport. I did not appreciate the fatherly advice, because at age fourteen we feel we know everything.

When I returned from my trip, I went to my father's room to say hi and just spend time with him. His room was the formal living room that was transformed into his bedroom where nurses came to take care of him. Veronica, one of the hospice nurses that cared for my father these past several years, said, "Just talk to him. He can hear you even if he does not respond." She then left the room to give me some private time with him. I must have known then that although he was unconscious, and I said no words, that he was able to know my heart and my presence. He knew I was there even though there were no physical signs of recognition or acknowledgement.

Shortly after returning home from summer camp, one late night when everyone was out of the house, my father quietly passed away. It is true, the dying wait for us to return home before they pass. They also wait for those who will take it the hardest to be away from them before they feel free to let go. I would not understand this for many years later, but I have observed this to be true in other situations. I was the last child to return home. When I did, my father's higher self was ready to leave this world. Although we cannot see a soul, it can see us mortals. The eternal part of my father was ready to move on to other lessons, now that his work here was complete.

Chapter 7

A Man for All Seasons

THE BLUE PHOTO ALBUM, WITH THE PICTURE OF MY FATHER ON the cover, contains pictures of him throughout various stages of his life. There are photos with his family, his wedding, steeplechase, and with us, his children and his wife. There are also pictures of when he was in graduate school, and at one of his very first jobs. Also in the blue photo album is his obituary, a beautiful poem he wrote about how fleeting life is and the story I wrote about him, hopeful that he would be able to beat cancer. If we could cheat death and steal time back, I would ask him about the beautiful poem that he penned in French. What was his frame of mind when he wrote the piece, and if he imagined one day that he would have cancer and not be able to hang on any longer?

It is funny how one's life can be neatly surmised in a photo album. That the spirit of someone you love dearly is now only seen in pictures, articles, writings, and poems.

His funeral was in September. He was taken away in a black hearse. His body was prepared at the funeral parlor near our home. Flowers were sent to the funeral parlor, our house and the church. There was an endless parade of visitors offering their condolences. The same visitors who came to our house each week alternated bringing food to help my mother during the stressful time. The friends my family made at our church and neighborhood graciously cared for us for a long time. Each family would bring a dinner each week before his death and during the funeral. It was an incredible act of kindness and grace to help others during difficult times. I am glad that I experienced this so that I know how to comfort others.

At the time of his funeral, I was fourteen years old. My brothers and sisters were much younger. I do not remember the wake at all. I do not remember even walking into the funeral home. All I remember was getting ready for the funeral. I was in a frantic rush. My nail polish wasn't dry yet, and I could not be late to my father's funeral. Sadly, I was late a lot. My mother was yelling for me to hurry up. My mother's friend, Sharon, came upstairs to my room to help me finish getting ready. She hugged me while asking me if I was okay.

I said I was fine. I was in a denial. In that moment, I was crying, but I stopped crying by the time of the funeral. I felt numb. I can't remember if we drove to the church or walked. It was a short enough distance from our home to walk.

The church was packed. It was overflowing with people. The minister gave an excellent sermon. He possessed the gift of an eloquent yet simple and engaging speaking manner. He always spoke in a straight-forward, gentle tone.

The minister recited an essay that I wrote about my father's battle with cancer. Beautiful music was playing and beautiful flowers adorned the church. I know my friends came to the funeral. The rest I cannot remember. I know I cried. I was upset, and that was the end of it. It was the end of him.

The loss of my father was devastating because he was my friend, my champion and my support. I felt like we understood each other. He had always encouraged me to grow and learn more. He gifted me with things that interested me. He fostered my seeking mind. We talked about history and books, and he always told me stories.

His body lies in a small cemetery in a quaint New England town, across the road from the church we attended and where his funeral was held. This cemetery is hundreds of years old. His grave remains unmarked, as my mother could never decide on the right tombstone. I believe that the missing monument is just denial of the finality of the situation, the last little bit of hope that this is all a bad dream.

Have you ever had that strange sensation happen to you? Where for a moment you forget reality and feel and think that life has not changed? I sometimes have the anticipation that I will see my dad when I am home tonight. He is waiting there. You try to trick yourself into believing that reality is just a horrible dream. He is here.

Little did I realize the grave impact that the loss of a dear one has on the soul. It is a toll that I am paying even today. Everyone pays their toll of grief and loss differently. Some marry early, some become workaholics, or alcoholics, and others never seem to find the right person.

Sometimes I think of my father's grave. I wonder if the soul resides in the grave. Or is it summoned there when you go to visit them at the grave? I do picture him lying there, and at times feel a sense of nostalgia and want to visit the grave site. But I do not think the soul rests in the grave, or at least not all the time. I feel that the spirit is free and travels in and out of different realms of being and knowingness.

Sometimes, at night I dream of my father, healthy and happy, and we are talking. Sometimes it's at our house, and others times we are outside in a beautiful nature setting. But I know that I am in the presence of his soul, which feels complete and at peace and looks like him as I remember him. In dark pants, a dark crew neck sweater with his pipe, dark hair, and blue eyes. My father appears to me healthy and at peace. Sometimes with his beret and sometimes not, but I always know that it is him, and we talk and walk as if no time has passed, and there is no sadness. His presence is so clear to me that I know the soul is free once it leaves the body.

I now know that you cannot lose someone because if you pay attention, they speak to you and visit you still. This understanding of loss happened slowly for me over many years.

Chapter 8

No More Music

WHEN MY FATHER DIED, AND I SAW HOW ALONE, DEVASTATED and afraid my mother was, I felt that I was no longer a child. I had to be the support to help her and my family move forward. There was no more piano, dance, or art in my heart. Now I needed to focus and get into a good school, get a good job, and make good money. I no longer had the luxury of being a carefree little girl.

Winter had settled into my heart and bones. I felt ice inside my soul. I had to help my mother carry the burden of the family, which she was not ready to face on her own. She cried every day. She went straight to bed as soon as she got home from work. She was easily irritable, quick to anger, and a moment away from tears at any given time. She would wake up in the middle of the night and come to the kitchen to pour herself a drink. I would be there doing my homework. She would smoke and cry.

At the marble counter top, with glass in front of her. My mother would cry, "I am not ready for this, this isn't fair." Sobbing, "if I didn't have children I know I would be fine. I wish I was single, without responsibility."

I felt alarmed at her words. I felt not wanted. I kept those thoughts in silence.

In a demanding tone of voice, "make sure that you get your graduate degree right after college, before getting married. You will need to make money at least a six-figure salary and pay your taxes." As an adult, I recognize that she expressed to me all the things she wished she had done before now. Now she felt alone with a huge burden to carry on her shoulders, that of family and grief weighing more than the world that Atlas carried.

I felt like Antigone, bound by obligation not to lament the death of her brother. Conflicted by a sense of responsibility and duty, but to what, is the crux of Sophocles's play. Do we obey the law or honor the heart and morality? Antigone is brave to defy her uncle, the king, in order to do what is right and honor her brother in secret; however, she paid a high price to do so. It is hard and scary to let go of your dreams and follow the tyrant of materialism and logic. Leaving behind the artistry of my soul was the sacrifice I made to not feel the pain of loss and to protect myself and others from feeling that pain. My focus was on my classes and getting into a top college. Music and dance were no longer things I could entertain, as I worried the price would be financial ruin.

I decided to select the Literature and the Human Condition English class. It sounded interesting. I arrived to class, located in Warren Hall, on the boy's school part of campus. The classroom is small. It contained simple plain walls and nondescript carpets. There were traditional desks with a cutout for your notebook and pencil, forming two rows along the small room. There was one large window; however, no one's desk was allowed to face the window. The focus of our gaze was Mr. Rourke and his blackboard.

Mr. Rourke was a gentle and kind man. He was soft-spoken with soft brown eyes and spectacles. He had dark hair and wore a tweed blazer and neutral, dark corduroy pants and brown shoes.

He would announce the title of a book and make us read and then share our thoughts, attempting to pull insight from our young minds. The book that stayed with me the most was the Death of Ivan Ilych, from Leo Tolstoy. "Ivan Ilych's life had been most simple and most ordinary and therefore most terrible,"[2] Mr. Rourke spoke those famous words and then wrote "Leo Tolstoy" on the chalk board.

Mr. Rourke turned his head away from the chalkboard, facing his students, and said, "Class, what do you make of this statement?" Mr. Rourke raised this question with a smile. I believe he smiled because pondering these philosophical questions never bored him.

As a class, we debated how being common and living without passion is a curse by the author and universally. I would not understand Tolstoy's and Mr. Rourke's lesson until I was much older and working in a corporate job. "These words," Mr. Rourke said, "are foreshadowing what is to come, the imminent demise of a man who had no greatness, which is a tragedy."

"Mr. Rourke, do you mean that he had no financial wealth, or political power?" a classmate asked.

2   Leo Tolstoy, *The Death of Ivan Ilych* (Bantom Classics: 1981) p.9

"No, class, it goes much deeper than that. Ivan Ilych had no burning love, no passion. When he died, no one mourned him, thus a life most common and a life most tragic."

"Well, why should that matter, Mr. Rourke?" the class echoed.

"Because we all have a divine purpose in life, and he failed to see his. He focused on making money and not on making a life. His soul died, and therefore he died physically."

"Oh," we said in unison, pretending to understand the subtle point. However, as diligent students we took our notes so that we could pass the exam.

I used to speak with Mr. Rourke after class. Oftentimes I wanted to gain clarity and a deeper understanding of Tolstoy, Dostoyevsky, Galsworthy, and other great writers who talked about love, war, betrayal, passion, God, class and redemption. I will never forget that Mr. Rourke told me that beyond philosophy is math, beyond math is physics, and beyond physics is God.

Wow. How did philosophy, math, and quantum physics prove the existence of or lead to God? I would not think of this for many years. One thing I did know is that math is the foundation of philosophy, and physics is the foundation of math...so he must be right?

Junior year of high school was when you are introduced to your assigned college advisor. This person would talk to you about your goals and helps ensure that you have completed your PSAT, SAT, and applications.

The college advisors sat in Strauss Hall, a beautiful building that looks more like a library in a manor house than offices. As I opened the large carved wooden doors, and found my way to my advisor's office. I noticed a stunning poster. It had a formal building surrounded by rhododendron bushes. It looked regal and peaceful at the same time.

My advisor greeted me at her office door and noticed me looking at the image. She told me that it was a poster for Wellesley College, a first-rate school. However, you need to have excellent grades, a top personality, lots of extracurricular activities, and an incredible essay, of course, with strong marks and scores to get into that school. I just knew that I would go to that college. I felt so confident about attending Wellesley that I never doubted it. The poster firmly etched in my mind, there was no doubt, no fear, and no second guessing.

I did all of my exams, sports, volunteer work and worked hard at my grades. I applied to Wellesley and just assumed that I would attend. Although I received acceptance letters by many other respectable universities and colleges, I felt that my heart always knew that it was only Wellesley for me.

Walking in the graduation procession with my other classmates felt surreal. The girls were all dressed in white and the boys were dressed in beige pants with blue blazers and ties. When you're young, time moves slowly. You cannot imagine ever graduating from high school. And as you are walking across the podium to shake the headmaster's hand and accept your diploma, you feel uncontrollable excitement. You feel invincible and empowered to do or create anything. You feel like you have arrived at the threshold of one of the greatest moments of your life. That you are at the doorway to possibility, the portal of your future, as if you are a conqueror who has conquered a territory and are prepared to receive tribute. As Julius Caesar's famous quote says, *"Veni, Vidi, Vici."* I came, I saw, I conquered.

Chapter 9

Blossoming—
The Wellesley Years

THE GREEN LAWNS SPRINKLED WITH GOTHIC AND 70S-STYLE buildings of Milton's campus were replaced by the green lawns and medieval and eclectic mix of architecture of Wellesley's campus. I attended a school with other prim, proper and naïve girls in Laura Ashley dresses.

By the time I arrived at college, I was exhausted and burnt out. The stress of graduating and ensuring acceptance into a good school took a toll on me physically. Discipline deserted me, as I had to change my major from pre-med to political science and history, because most lectures were not at 8 AM.

My drive to get into a good school and flee my mother's house was strong. I wanted to be free. The freedom I desired was liberation from her judgmental, critical eye and sharp tongue. I wanted freedom from a place where I was always wrong or punished. I felt like Cinderella, freed from house chores and the wicked stepmother. Unfortunately, the prince did not fall in love with me, allowing me to escape my reality, but I *was* able to obtain an education and take care of myself and live in the dorm. I no longer called home. I no longer needed my mother's opinion for everything. However, I learned the great price one pays for their freedom. The choices I made impacted me, and I learned that I had no one I could rely on. I needed to problem-solve on my own.

I was assigned a roommate as a freshman in one of the "new dorms," Freeman Hall, which has a 1960s-style building and not the neo-classical architecture of most of the campus. It was not the prettiest building, but it would be my home. My roommate was a tall girl from Maryland. She had brown wavy hair, green eyes, and a straightforward personality. My neighbors were other girls of all backgrounds from the mid-west to New York City.

I took political science, history, art history, literature, and biology my first year at college. I was just going through the motions. At the end of freshman year, my college advisor told me that my grades were low and that I would need to bring them up in order to stay and keep my scholarship. This was a slap in the face. My performance was good in high school—why am I not doing well now?

As I went home that summer and shared the news with my mother, she was upset and angry. In her usual manner, she got her point across by berating and humiliating her victim, in this case me. I had to listen to her screaming and relentless negative, fearful chatter about not being able to support myself and how important college is. She walked me through a visualization of being destitute and penniless if my grades did not improve.

This interaction was a wake-up call. I realized that I would have to put more effort into my coursework. I was never going to stay at my mother's house again and suffer her wrath or her criticism. I would complete my education as well as I could and support myself. I learned early that to take someone else's money and support comes at a high price. They can take a little part of your soul, of your dignity; they take away your sense of self-worth as they constantly remind you that you are a burden and not worthy of their support. I did not realize at the time that she was projecting her feelings and insecurities onto me.

Chapter 10

Resurrecting
the Grades

I N VIETNAM, MIXED RACE CHILDREN ARE CONSIDERED *bu doi,*
which translates into "dust of the earth." Mixed race children are
not purely Vietnamese; therefore, they are considered flawed, less than
an animal. In short, they are dust with no value.

There was no better time to ponder my ethnic background than
college. I had access to other minds and books. The consistent message
was that in multiple cultures, my racial mix is considered less than, not
enough. Therefore, it is no wonder that I eventually fell in love with
political theory, philosophy and history. I discovered academic disciplines discussing and theorizing about the nature of man and the nature of all life neatly categorizing all manner of thought and behavior,
shedding light on the good and the bad parts of humanity.

In history class with my Dutch teacher, learning became fun again, as her passion for non-western history was contagious. She opened my eyes to Frantz Fanon and his book, *The Wretched of the Earth*, Walter Rodney's *How Europe Underdeveloped Africa*, Janet Abu-Lughod's *Before European Hegemony*, and many other fascinating books. All of these books related to political science and the analysis of marginalized groups, subordinate discourses, and political theory. In addition, Philosophy's discussion of the nature and rights of man, the nature of political man, and the nature of thought and power were also represented.

I finally came to understand how the modern capitalist economy took shape and why marginalization and slavery occurred. It is as I suspected all along…a justification for economic exploitation, not because one race was inherently superior over another; but because, in our society, superiority has meant military prowess. The rest of the attributes of supremacy, such as education, human rights, respect, wealth, and beauty are part of the spoils of war that the victor appropriates to their regime. Therefore, I see the connection that my soul made, to help me bridge the gap in understanding. I see why I was multi-racial Dust of the Earth, which is the same as Wretched of the Earth. It is the dehumanization of an entire race, made captive and slaves to the modern economy. By dehumanizing a race, you can do unspeakable things to them. The brutality ranges from physical, social, and economic, to emotional and psychological damage. You remove their history of power from their collective consciousness. You associate them with slave and not as creators or kings. You take away the past and cripple their future, because it is our past that is our landmark, our stories that shape who we are, that remind us of our collective strength and power.

I poured myself into my studies. I became passionate on my quest for knowledge. I studied, read and talked about what I was learning non-stop. I was constantly in the library. I was excited to learn and to see the world, to analyze through all of these different disciplines how the creation of our modern world has impacted society and what that meant. My friends and I would be up all night in the library, chatting about life as much as studying. We took breaks for food, especially to order pizza or Chinese.

One day I was on the train in Boston venturing away from campus. I was sitting by myself and getting off my stop in Harvard Square so that I could catch the bus back to school. A man in a simple white shirt and a black backpack, with light brown hair, hazel eyes, and glasses approached me.

"Excuse me, do you know what time it is?" he asked.

"Yes," I replied, looking at my watch. "It's 3."

"Okay, thank you." He was smiling. "What's your name?" he asked.

"Tristan…what is yours?"

"Oh! Tristan and Isolde…one of my favorite operas," he said boldly. "My name if Manfred. You are beautiful. What is your ethnic background?"

"Yes, my father is English…it is one of his favorite names. I am Vietnamese and Black. Adopted. You have a different kind of accent… where are you from?"

"I'm German," he said. "I am here on a post-doc with Harvard. I am a physicist."

"Wow! That's great!"

"What do you do?" he asked.

"I am a sophomore in college; I go to Wellesley."

"What are you studying?" he asked curiously.

"Right now, I am really interested in history and political theory."

"Do you have a minute?" he asked. "Do you want to have a coffee or tea with me?"

"Sure, that would be nice."

We were in Harvard Square, so we walked around the corner and ended up at Paradiso Café, a busy Italian café overrun with students. We found a table and sat down. We ordered tea and mineral water with lemon. Although hours passed it felt like minutes as we talked about our favorite books and philosophy. Manfred told me that his favorite book was *Siddhartha* by Herman Hesse, a book that I, too, enjoyed immensely. Speaking with him was like looking into a mirror of my passions about philosophy and art. It is a thrilling feeling to find an intellectual match.

Eventually, I had to excuse myself and catch my bus back to campus. "My, look at the time. It's getting late. I need to catch the bus back to my dorm." Sometimes one falls for looks, but sometimes one falls for another's mind.

"I really enjoyed speaking with you and hope to see you again soon," he said as I stood to leave. "I am ten years older than you. On another note, if you want help you with your math and physics homework, I can help you."

"Oh, that would be great!"

"Okay, what is your number? I will call you, and we can meet and discuss what equations are giving you trouble," he suggested.

"Thank you. It was nice meeting you."

He walked me to my bus stop. "It was a pleasure to meet you. I hope to see you again." His whole body smiled as he spoke.

"Thank you for the tea and the pleasant chat." As I sat on the bus, I thought about our conversation, and couldn't wait to tell my friends about him.

Later, when I returned to my dorm, I was at dinner in the dining hall, surrounded by all my friends. I told them about this new person I met and that he was thirty years old. They laughed and said to be careful, and made jokes that he was too old for me.

Manfred called me the next day and asked me to meet him in Cambridge, asked if I wanted help with my math homework.

I did meet him in Cambridge. We talked non-stop. We both had so much to say about ourselves and our families and who we are. We talked more about our lives than we did about my math homework.

"Would you like to have dinner with me this week?"

"Yes, that sounds good." I accepted the invitation and after many dinners and weeks have passed by, he told me he finds me irresistible and wants to get to know me more.

I had to think about this, because I was a virgin and always kept a distance between myself and men. The most I had ever done is kissed someone. I shared my secret with him. He was patient with me until I was ready to share myself in that way.

I am glad that I picked such a caring and respectful man to be my first lover. He did love me, and always tried to make me feel safe, special and protected. Even though at times I was still very much a childish brat, he was incredibly kind, generous, and patient.

We would debate the theories and facts I was learning. He would encourage me as I stayed up all night completing my papers, studying for exams, and researching graduate schools.

Senior year arrived with the pressure to finally make a choice as to what to do next. When you are in school, you are protected from life. Everything is a theory. Now it was time to take action and move forward on a new path, without a safety net.

Sitting in a large lecture room with our Political Science teacher at the center, he told us how to approach the final year of college.

"Students, as you prepare for graduate school this year, remember there are a plethora of schools not in New England. Not everyone has to go to Harvard or Yale. Be open minded, and good luck with your applications. Please make sure you give me your recommendation requests by the end of the month."

Most seniors went to school fairs to decide which graduate school they would apply to. Some of us decided to attend graduate school right away, and some decided to work a few years before going to graduate school. I decided to go to school right way. My mother always said that we should complete our education before marriage and children. Otherwise, you will be too busy to focus on school. Completing graduate school before getting married was the one piece of advice that my mother gave me that made sense to me.

The essays, GRE scores, transcripts, and recommendations were all compiled and sent off in a mad rush of course, just in time to meet the deadlines.

Graduation came at the end of the spring semester. As I accepted my diploma in a black robe and cap, I could not contain my excitement for my next venture. The elixir of youth allows you to believe you are invincible and capable of anything. My friends and I gave each other hugs and flowers, and took pictures with our families.

Manfred and I threw a party at his apartment to celebrate my graduation, and he also arranged a special dinner for me. We went to my favorite restaurant near Cambridge, the Elephant Walk, which served Cambodian and French fusion cuisine. We sat at a small table for two. There were muted murals of elephants on the wall and the familiar smell of wonderful, savory food.

Manfred ordered a bottle of champagne and was a little fidgety, which is unlike him. He told me how deep his love for me is and how proud he is that I graduated from school. He then got up from our table and kneeled on one knee and pulled out a small dark blue velvet box from his inner suit jacket pocket.

"You know I love you, you are my big love. Will you marry me?"

"Yes!" I was both excited and surprised. Manfred was my first serious boyfriend, and we loved and appreciated each other. It only made sense to say *yes*. Manfred took the beautiful, three stone, round cut diamond engagement ring out of the box and placed it on my finger. I realized it was a larger version of a ring that I had admired on a friend.

Everyone in the restaurant applauded and said congratulations. He kissed me and smiled. I looked at my beautiful ring in shock that this just happened. Later that night and the next day, I called all of my friends and family and shared my good news. Everyone congratulated me.

Chapter 11

Breaking it Off

FOR MANY MONTHS, I WAS UTTERLY EXCITED TO BE ENGAGED to the man I loved, but at the same time, I had this nagging thought that eventually many of my friends would echo. Manfred was my first serious boyfriend. I had never been with another man, so in a way, I felt ill-equipped to make a decision that would affect the rest of my life. One can try a pair of shoes before you buy them, or many pairs of shoes before you find the right one. I had only tried one pair. There was no comparative analysis happening. I had no data to compare my choice to.

Being ten years younger than my fiancé, I worried that I would lose interest or just be unhappy as he ages. I also wasn't ready to have children until I was much older, and he would want children sooner. My heart could not decide. My friends were overwhelmed by my engagement and reminded me that I am too young, and have too much in front of me to throw it all away on a marriage. Given that, my interest in planning the engagement party and wedding started to fade away as doubt crept into my mind. Am I too young and inexperienced to make this choice? Am I ready for this big step?

My mother did not approve of my engagement. In her eyes, I went from her house, to college, and lastly to his home without an opportunity to be independent and take care of myself.

I told Manfred that I needed to think about being engaged. I suggested we continue dating.

He was terribly upset by my suggestion. I took the ring off and returned it to him. I just wasn't ready to get married.

"You will never find another man who will love you and take care of you like I do," he protested.

"You will never find another young, beautiful and intelligent girl like me," I said in my defense.

It was like we threw curses at each other. The only emotions expressed were sadness and anger. Fear that the other may be right. I packed my belongings and left to my mother's house for a short time before I left for graduate school.

It is sad and hard to leave someone you love because you are not ready, and just don't know yourself yet. In many ways, I was still just a child. I listened to what other people wanted or thought for me and needed to figure out what I want for myself. I was terrified of being a mother and having responsibility for my children's happiness. I feared that I would be like my mother: unhappy, resentful, and regretful that I did not have a life I desired.

Chapter 12

Goodbye to You

I GOT ACCEPTED TO USC'S SCHOOL OF INTERNATIONAL RELATIONS master's program in Los Angeles, where I would continue my love affair with history, political theory, political science, literature, and economics. Although, it was not my first choice, I was more than happy to go. I left for school at the end of the summer, transitioning from high school, to college, and then to graduate school without a break.

The reasons were simple. I moved across country to go to graduate school as a way to escape boredom, delay having to make an actual career move, and avoid marriage. I bought a one-way ticket to Los Angeles and held my breath, hoping that I would either fall into good luck or pass out, hopefully without pain. However, I underestimated the challenges of being in a new environment. I had no support from family and friends and tried to drown my sorrows in shopping sprees at the Beverly Center. After all, I am part of a generation who grew up with the media circus, sound-bites, and accessible, ready-to-wear clothing lines. The ad campaigns: *If you wear this you, too, will be beautiful.* And *if you look like this, you will get the man of your dreams* is programmed into my fashion junkie mind. Living in Los Angeles made me realize that you will get the man of your dreams—but nightmares shouldn't count.

My mother drove me to Boston's Logan airport. At the terminal, Manfred and my mother were both there to send me off and wish me luck. I cried as both of them hugged me and said their goodbyes.

"I love you, you are my big love. Be safe," said Manfred.

"I love you too," I assured him. "It's just school. I will be back when I graduate."

"Here, I want you to have this," he said handing me a dark blue velvet box. This ring is yours."

"Thank you," I said in tears. "Okay, I have to stop crying and board my plane."

"Okay, call me and tell me when you are safe, and let me know how school is."

"Yes, thank you. I love you. Bye."

I placed the velvet box in my purse. I gather my few carry-on items and wave goodbye to Manfred and my mother, who are teary eyed just as I am. I turn and walk toward the gate to board my plane.

As my plane touched down in Los Angeles later that evening, my eyes were finally dry from crying. Looking out of the window, I was surprised to see a vast, flat expanse of lights. Where are the skyscrapers and densely populated city blocks, I wonder?

I realized that I was no longer on familiar ground. My college friend, Hsinya, one of my friends from my dorm, met me at the gate.

She and her family were graciously hosting me at their house until my student housing was available. If only I had paid attention more in my Chinese language classes, I would have been able use my Mandarin a little more while staying with them, and would have been able to understand the Chinese soap operas that I never knew existed. Thankfully, body language gives the plot away, so between my few broken words and the dramatic acting I could follow along.

Chapter 13

There is No Place Like Home

THE LUSH GREEN LAWNS OF WELLESLEY AND MILTON ACADEMY gave way to the urban landscape of USC. The red brick faded by the sun and stone buildings were plotted on concrete, not on the grass. This busy campus was diverse and extensive.

My graduate classes were small, between eight and ten people on average. There were students from all over the world—Germany, Greece, Mexico, Washington DC and New Jersey. I met people studying all kinds of topics, not just mine, and they all had different career objectives. The years of course work and research was to prepare us for our comprehensive exams, which required a decent mark in order to receive a degree.

When not studying or in class, I met new people and had friends of all ages and backgrounds. Still, between the business of school and an active social life, in those moments when I slowed down, I found myself being sad. I was not aware enough to understand that I was searching for my authentic self. I assumed that I was lonely not having my close friends and family around, or that I was finally grieving the loss of my father.

I would sometimes go to the library with all my books, highlighters, pens and note pads with the intention of studying and outlining my research, and instead be easily distracted and unable to concentrate. For the first time in my life, I felt alone. I had always been constantly surrounded by people, without a moment of peace. Growing up as the oldest sister in a large family, you are never alone.

In college, I had many friends, and we were always doing something together, eating, talking, running or studying. However, here in this city, I was not as close to people. I felt separate. I felt alone. I found companionship only in brief relationships and friendships.

One day, while, in my graduate advisor's office, he asked me how I like USC and Los Angeles.

"How are you enjoying your time as a student here? Your grades are good, but how is your social life?" Dr. Bender inquired.

"I don't know. It's different here. There is no culture, no fine arts, no one reads books. I can't wait to leave this city," I replied.

He just laughed and offered a suggestion, "You should smoke a little pot and relax. And those activities are in this city, you just need to find them. Is there something bothering you, my dear?"

"Yes," I confessed through my tears. "I am sad. I think the loss of my father is hitting me now. I guess I am homesick."

"Don't worry, just relax. As time passes, you will learn to know yourself. When you do meet yourself, and know who you are, nothing can bother you. You are young and still have much to learn."

"Thank you, Dr. Bender. I appreciate your time." I flashed a big smile and then returned my attention to the research at hand.

I walked out of his 70s-style office and contemplated all that he said. *Meet yourself. Know yourself.* What does that mean? My favorite color is blue. I like chocolate. I grew up on the East Coast and love fried food. That is what I know about myself today.

I would discover later that he was right. We learn that it is not what we do, where we live or what we drive that makes us who we are. This realization only came to me when I almost lost everything, and forced me to appreciate what I have and to show me how resilient my soul is.

Until then, we are like zombies, going through the daily motions, not fully alive and not entirely dead. I always wished I was on the East Coast during my graduate school days, as I had a hard time adjusting to my new culture, new school, and new life. If I had Dorothy's ruby red slippers, I would have simply clicked my heels and wished to be home.

Chapter 14

Reflections

THE SNOW SLOWLY RETREATS INTO THE GROUND AND AIR. THE earth, once hardened by the cold substance, softens, becoming moist with the warming of the air. The gray days of winter give way to the stormy rains of New England's April. I look fondly at these passages in my journal, reminding me of the splendor of nature, and oddly echoing of something more. It has been three years now since I left green lawns with sprawling ivy, lilacs and rhododendron bushes with dark spear-like leaves. It has been some time since I left the pristine schools and circles of classically educated people who speak of current politics and literature. Now I am in a place without history linking it back to Europe. A place where people seem to have no roots, where you are not sure if people read at all, but a place where you can dream beyond borders and confines. I feel alone in this modern city, yet out of place in the old seaport town.

I close my journal sharply, causing a few of the stray sheets of paper with scribbled thoughts on them to fall out. As I reach for the vagrant pieces of paper, I make a mental note to myself: *try to stop dwelling on the past, focus on what is happening now.* You need to complete your research and exams and then viola! The future is open. I sigh as my mind finishes that thought: *the future is open.* What does that mean? What do I want it to signify? The master's program has not made that any clearer to me. As I look around my room, the white walls are barren except for one beautifully framed poster of a romantic picture painted by Sir Alma Tameda. The scene is of three Greek women with Victorian demeanors and features, each one gazing at a boat in the far distance. One can only assume by the picture that these women are pining away for lovers seeking their glory in a great battle somewhere. Who knows, maybe in the battle of Troy, and all that these women have to hold onto are memories, hopes, and dreams.

It just goes to show that dating is terrible no matter what the millennium, and despite the advances in technology and attitudes. My mind is off on the tangent of relationships with men. I must stop dwelling on this subject or else suffer the consequences of being labeled a *bitter woman.* I have noticed that in our society, women who speak their mind are not considered thoughtful, analytical or assertive. Instead, we are brash, emotional, and aggressive; all of which is neatly surmised in the ever popular and compact word, in modern society, the word bitch or "biotch," the urban version. Yes, reflecting on the not-so-pleasant aspects of men renders a woman a bitch, no way around it. As a woman, I find I am unable to tell things as they are and have to find subtle and creative ways to prove my point.

I miss the sharp and chilling coldness of winter. I realize that keeping your emotions at bay, locked in ice, insulates you from pain, but cold winter days—even those sealed in your bones—do not last forever. Spring comes, it always does…even in Alaska. It seems that some hearts are like arctic glaciers, impacted by layers of crystallized water with no hope of thawing, even in the warm rays of the sun.

Do we as a species really need to relate and cohabitate with others of our species? Irony is being intelligent, capable and independent, but feeling insecure and unhappy due to the eerie feeling that you are missing something. Lacking something male in your life, I hope I miss something more meaningful. Not to devalue men, but there must be more to life than conjugally sanctioned reproduction. I do not want to be both defined and confined by my gender, or by what others think those of my gender should be doing. Rather, I would like to dream the big dream, the one where you raise your arms above your head and grasp at the stars and find yourself in space, the endless frontier.

The danger with loneliness is not having the strength to prevent yourself from eroding into the sea, as sharp winds whip around the corner and chide you into shame about your bachelorhood. The danger is the potential loss of a sense of a worthy self. The high propensity to settle for less than you deserve, put your dreams on hold or replace them for that of your partner's, for making poor choices.

Why are single people devalued? Why are you somehow "out of sorts with society" if you are alone? I think unmarried people should be celebrated and championed. For unhitched people are possibly some of the most courageous people to exist. Look at Charlotte Bronte's heroine in *Villette*: she was alone, and she dealt with it while maintaining a sense of pride and created a literary career. She never married, but is that a crime? But, I must not devalue men. After all they are attractive, brash and amusing. Men have the most incredible talent: they can focus on themselves and never feel guilty.

Men can serve as an excellent distraction from studies and other tedious things. A potential date is more attractive than reading discussions regarding the positive or negative effects of capitalism on different societies. And men are infinitely more interesting than a debate on which approach is more accurate, grounded in sound theoretical practices and which one is not correct and why.

I am always amazed at the times when I can shut my mind off and read text without procrastinating, without complaining and with my full attention. What makes this so, fear? Lack of interest? Money worries? The worst thing that can happen to a professor is to have a student who does not fear or abide by the deadlines. To have a student who views the difference between an A or B+ and so on, as not a reflection of intelligence, but of diligence.

Chapter 15

Silence of Night

I FLEW HOME FOR CHRISTMAS VACATION, MY FAVORITE TIME OF the year, especially in New England. Snow covers everything and nature looks like a present beneath a pretty layer of beauty and peace.

Before driving home to my family, I saw Manfred. I took a taxi to his apartment directly from the airport. Although he was expecting me, he was not happy to see me and asked me to return the ring. I feel that he expected me to want to stop the break up and commit to our relationship again, which I was not ready to do. Fortunately, I had it with me and gave it to him. He was so upset with me that he could not look at me or be near me. He asked me to leave. I called my brother and asked him to come meet me sooner. My brother arrived not long after I called and collected me from Manfred's apartment. I guess Manfred assumed that I would want to pick up where we left off and was disappointed to see me aloof and indifferent. He needed to let go of the idea of our reconciliation and me.

On the drive through our town, I can see the houses decorated with wreaths in the windows. Some homes have candles in the windows that always remind me of Colonial New England. I can imagine Paul Revere riding his horse and seeing the lights in the windows at Christmas time that maybe gave him the idea for his famous signal for independence from the British: one if by land and two if by sea.

One can see the lights of sparkly Christmas trees in the windows, and garland surrounding the front entryways and pillars. The lights and greenery with ribbons always warm my heart. In Los Angeles, there is no snow in wintertime, but I have eventually come to feel the spirit of the season there as well.

The baking of Christmas cookies and chocolates, the smell of home cooked food. The dining table decorated with velvet ribbons and holly, the sideboard displaying platters of treats amongst garlands of holly, berries, pine, and ornaments are such a beautiful sight, along with the garland wrapped staircase.

The bustle and mayhem as everyone does last minute shopping for gifts and cooking and cleaning for guests, finally slows down in the early evening hours of Christmas Eve at my mother's house. We all go to the congregational church, the white church with a tall steeple in the center of town. The simple white pews face the candelabra and poinsettias that adorn the pulpit and the simple classic wreaths hang on the large open windows.

The choir sings beautiful Christmas carols and seasonal hymns. A senior member of the congregation recites the story of the nativity; his deep voice is peaceful and confident as he recounts the story of Joseph and Mary in Bethlehem. The minister always provides a sermon about the universality of man, and that we should look at each other as family and protect and cherish one another. We are also reminded that it is up to us to create a better and more loving world. He would urge us to carry the magic of Christmas, of giving and of love, in our hearts always and in every season. There is also a special Christmas donation to the minister's fund that helps people who call for anything the church can do. The fund helps to pay the electric bill, to help with food or whatever is needed. The help is a reminder that you are not alone; you are loved not just by God, but your neighbors as well.

The beautiful sermon closes with candlelight as each member receives a simple plain white candle. Each pew receives the light from the volunteer and then within each row the light is carefully shared and passed. After all the candles are ablaze, the chandelier is dimmed, and the church is ablaze by candlelight. We sing *Silent Night,* all verses, and one in German. As the song concludes, we are reminded of the holiness of the human heart when it dwells in *Love* and the house of the Lord, or whatever you want to call that divine place.

As we carefully extinguish the candles, we then greet each other with hugs, happy chatter and questions about what people have been doing during the year. Then my family returns home and are greeted by our friends who are there waiting for us, and we enjoy a tasty dinner together and play White Elephant and laugh.

As charming as Christmas is, it is challenging being home for more than a few days. The petty rivalries and criticism starts after Christmas…and I feel trapped at home. I become frustrated and eager to leave my mother's house and return to the peace of my small dorm room. I bundle myself up in a winter jacket and walk in deep snow to the center of town to the travel agency. As I enter the room and speak with a travel agent. I frantically ask, as if my life depends on his answer, if there is any possible way he can get me on a flight that will leave in the next day or so? I cannot wait for my week-long visit to end, I need to depart now. I laugh now when remembering this petty drama, as there are barely any travel agencies left as we can book and change flights online.

The travel agent is calling and searching, he is nodding his head telling me that it is not looking good. He finally tells me the bad news. There are no earlier flights that are available as everything is booked to capacity. As I hear this news, I burst into tears and start crying. The travel agent is stunned and silent. I am horrified that I cried in front of a complete stranger. I apologize for my outburst and wipe my face and leave the office.

As I walk home in the snow, my mind is racing with anxious thoughts. All I can think of is that I just want to leave and be at my new home. I am upset that I am going to be subjected to criticism much longer than I can handle. I finally calm down and count in my head how many days remain until it is my departure day.

I must face the next week and be tough. This is only temporary, I remind myself. Why did I feel lonely when I was in Los Angeles? What is happening? Have I been romanticizing my family life? Apparently, with my emotional outburst in public still fresh, I realize that I have been idealizing my childhood. In the loneliness and newness of change, my mind had edited the harsh, judgmental, and critical voice of my mother, showing only the lovely memories.

With each subsequent visit home, I would shorten the length of my visit. I got tougher and learned not to take everyone's insults and not to internalize them although this is a long journey.

As the weeklong sentence finally ended, and I knew I would return to my quiet little existence, I felt better. As the plane flew over Los

Angeles, and I could see the familiar landscape of flat land and endless lights, I slowly started to realize that this was my home. I will not live in Massachusetts again. Over time, each return flight to Los Angeles becomes more and more welcome, until the city is my home.

I was grateful to be in my new home, so elated as if I had never lived in a small dorm. Much like a sailor's happiness to be home on land after years of toil on the endless sea where there is no land in sight, no frame of reference until you are on solid ground again.

Chapter 16

Love Yourself

I THREW MYSELF INTO MY CLASSES AS BEST AS I COULD. I WAS constantly in the library researching and trying to get through all of the required reading. In college, you are given weeks to complete a book. In graduate school, you are given one class to complete books' worth of reading assignments.

Since I was easily rattled by my mother's comments, I decided that it was time to examine my emotional past. I decided to go to counseling during the spring semester to help me sort it out. Flashbacks of "You are stupid," or, "Your body doesn't look good in that outfit," were part of my normal interaction with my mother.

It was time for my counseling session at the school's health center. I was assigned to Dr. Lisa, whom I had a weekly meeting with since the beginning of the second semester. She was doing her hours while studying for her state exams to be a licensed therapist. She had short, spiky brown hair and blue eyes. She was white, tall, pale, thin, and dressed in a boyish nondescript and unfeminine manner.

I had been anxious and sad and wanting to figure out the emotional rut I am in and how to get out of it. Waiting in the lobby decorated with functional and unattractive chairs, I contemplated what I would talk about in today's session.

We began as usual with our general greetings and conversations: How are you? How is your week? And what is troubling you?

I guess I feel alone," I confessed. "I have some friends but no close friends. I haven't met anyone that I am serious about dating, not that I want to be serious with anyone just yet since I have recently broken my engagement and am not ready to get married. I guess I do not know what I want."

"You need to love yourself," said Dr. Lisa. "Try reading the *Story of O*. You will learn how to love yourself and give yourself an orgasm. You don't need to wait for a man to do it for you."

I sat there stunned. After all, I am a prudish girl from New England. I am the only girl on campus without an exposed body part. However, it did sound intriguing. Maybe, the source of many of my problems is my inability to "love" myself. Many of my girlfriends have been "loving" themselves for a long time and prefer it.

In a rushed tone one takes when being polite but not sincere, I said "Okay, sure. I will check out the book and see what the author has to say."

Dr. Lisa emphatically said: "Read the *Story of O*. But also experiment with pleasuring yourself. It will be a good way for you to get to know yourself. This exercise will help you because if you do not know how to please yourself, then how do you expect anyone else to be able to do so?"

I wondered if this recommendation came from Dr. Lisa's own personal story. I looked out of the window, which showed the busy pathway of students rushing to class. While others loitered, I wondered to myself, *how did we get on this topic? What did I say to trigger this response? Why am I here?*

Noticing that I was lost in thought, Dr. Lisa said, "Another thing I would like you to be mindful of, Tristan, is that you have difficulty saying goodbye. Next week will be our last session. My internship will finish soon. So, I want you to process that before our next session."

She said that almost with more sadness than I was feeling. "Yes, of course I will think about it," I said sheepishly. As I said this, I thought to myself, *saying goodbye, that is ridiculous.* I am great at goodbye. I am a survivor. Staying has always been a problem for me. I can't wait to say goodbye, to try new things, to replace whatever or whoever I do not like, that is my nature. Goodbye is easy for me.

I smiled outwardly, but inside I felt a dagger waiting to spring forth in a cloud of spite.

"Yes, don't forget your homework," she reminded me one last time. "Read the *Story of O* and prepare for my leaving. I will see you the same time next week Tristan."

"Okay, thank you!" I couldn't wait to leave her small office, and would have sprinted through the door if I could.

I picked up my backpack and walked out of her 70s-style office with modular furniture and grey and brown colors while smiling and waving at Dr. Lisa. Thinking to myself, *how does one feel stronger?* One's spiritual growth can resonate deep inside you while all external affairs appear to be falling apart. I have been working on my spiritual practice through talking and reading spiritual materials from deeply passionate and enlightened people who guide me and show me the way. I considered that everything happens for a reason, I have met people to help me unravel my personal puzzle. I believe that angels are guiding me. This experience is a curve ball to stop my facade of superficiality and struggle for achievement, causing me to wonder, who am I?

As I passed all of the students in the functional waiting room, nervously tapping their feet and flipping through magazines, waiting for their turn to unload their emotional burdens, I realized that this ordeal is almost over for me. I came to Dr. Lisa's office after having an anxiety attack that felt like a heart attack. I am twenty-five, slim and in good health, so what was bothering me?

Walking out of the waiting room and out of the building into the glorious sunny afternoon in beautiful Southern California, USC's campus, I realized that the answer would reveal itself in time.

Chapter 17

End of Days

I NEVER READ THE *STORY OF O.* I WAS NOT MOTIVATED TO DO THE homework suggested by Dr. Lisa, but I understand the little pearl of wisdom that she shared with me.

When I reached my last two semesters of course work, I panicked. I had intense anxiety. I would cry uncontrollably or procrastinate, which stressed me out and made me cry more. I was not ready to leave the cocoon of school and enter the real world, and I could not focus and apply to law school. I just could not complete my research and was forced to get an extension.

I got a job on campus, which kept me in the cocoon a little longer. But I knew that I needed to finish my research. I finally finished all my research and handed it in, as well as studied for both sets of comprehensive exams which I took back to back, a suicidal move and further indication of my classic procrastination habit. If there was an Olympic event for procrastinators, I would surely win the gold medal. Most people did the general theory exam first year and the concentration exam their last year. But because I am the Queen of Procrastination, I had to complete all of my remaining papers, study and take both exams all in the same time frame. Studying for my exams is when I discovered coffee, the miracle substance that enabled me to stay up all night and study and function during the day.

I started having dreams of lectures, research, and debates about the differences between the Kennedy Round and the Uruguay Round. Thankfully it all paid off, and I completed all of my research papers and passed both exams and did well! After this success, I was ready for a career.

While I was wrapping up my degree, I decided that I would try management consulting instead of going to Law School or completing a different degree. I just wanted to have a career, make money, and have that so-called normal life.

Chapter 18

Mental Atrophy

My acceptance into Andersen Consulting, now Accenture, as an analyst was exciting. I received my FedEx package of my acceptance letter with my salary and signing bonus. I went to training for a month in a town outside of Chicago and felt incredibly grown up.

Little did I know that I would not utilize any of my analytical or writing skills from graduate school in the next phase of my life, my working career. I went from complex multi-layered sentences comprising complex theories to bullet points. It was a tough, yet necessary, transition from scholar to worker bee.

It's ironic that your whole childhood and academic career stressed the importance of original thought, of quoting and acknowledging the originators of our famous theories that we reference today. That to not acknowledge with the proper notation another's thoughts would lead to your being expelled from school and signal the end of your academic career. In the business world, you are told not to think for yourself, to leverage and reuse what others have done. No original thought quoting is necessary as we repurpose content constantly. It is an odd change in direction that takes some adjustment.

I was eager to do well, and placed all of my energy into pleasing my various bosses from project to project. My career took all of my attention and energy. We worked hard and were rewarded well, which kept me wanting more.

People pleasers do well in a corporate environment as you never want to look bad or do poorly, and you care what people think of you and your work. Since I never learned to say *no* to my family, I naturally had no boundaries at work. I would work non-stop and did not think it strange that I would spend Monday-Friday on the East Coast and fly home to Los Angeles Friday night.

Of course, what we want comes to us not according to our plan, but to that of the universe. As I started my new career, I also started dating a new man. He was an actor/model type, which meant extremely good looking and charismatic person who waits tables or bartends, and believes that he is the next A-list movie star and demands your full attention.

My boyfriend did not appreciate my physical unavailability. However, he did appreciate my financial support. As I learned to overcompensate by giving too much in my childhood and fulfilled the needs of others at the detriment of myself, I maintained that in my personal relationships. Just like at home when I was growing up, I never asked for what I wanted, I never demanded or expected to receive from others, but I was always there to give.

So, I paid the majority of the bills. I paid for gifts and trips since my boyfriend made very little money. For the first several years of our relationship, I did not require him to give me a gift for my birthday or Christmas. I always made an excuse for him. I never expected more for myself.

Eventually, I grew tired of being there for him and others, of playing the saint. I slowly wanted more balance between giving and receiving. Although he would intimidate me and refuse to let me leave him, eventually I did. I risked being alone and without a boyfriend than to be in a relationship without healthy boundaries. I guess I started to evolve and love myself. I started to have expectations of reciprocity of others. Like most favored nation status for monetary trade policy, I needed to create my personal trade policy and only give to those who gave to me. Now I will impose tariffs and sanctions in response to unfair treatment and lack of giving and receiving. If warranted, removal of all relations would be imposed. If countries protect their balance of trade, I will learn to protect mine. I could no longer pretend to be happy with being a caretaker in anyone's life but my own.

Chapter 19

Independence

WHEN I LEFT MY BOYFRIEND, I TOLD MYSELF THAT I WILL never live with a man again unless he proposes marriage first or is a male relative.

I did not want my relationship to influence my housing situation. Where you live is so important because it is your safe haven from the world. A good home should be peaceful and feel light and airy. You should gain energy and a sense of relaxation when you are home.

I ended up in an adorable large studio in Westwood with a balcony, fireplace and dishwasher. I was so happy to be there and loved decorating my place. Since I traveled and worked a lot, my kitchen was immaculate, as I never cooked. These were my carefree days. I was renting and made great money, so I had plenty of money for shopping, trips, dinners, and the spa.

I was thin and active. I was never alone and was always going out. In my neighborhood, I could walk to a few shops and one day, I discovered a ballet school on my Saturday walk in the neighborhood. I decided to live one of my dreams and take dance class like when I was a child. I started dancing every week, taking several classes. I bought my black leotard, tights and shoes. At first, I had no idea what I was doing. Everything is in French and you need to remember the combination of moves, the foreign terms, and the number of repetitions of a move per direction. Contorting your body into the angles and positions required is extremely difficult and painful. Eventually, with dedication, I went from no turnout to a decent turn out. I would never be a professional dancer, never be Odette in Swan Lake on any stage. Nevertheless, the dream of dancing is so beautiful and invigorating that I cannot imagine not dancing (or in my case attempting to).

I dreamt of my pink pointe shoes, hoping that one day I would be able to pirouette with grace and do my grand jeté with turn out in those pink pointe satin shoes. When I was not dancing, working out or going out with friends, I turned my attention to my other favorite pastime, shopping.

Shopping is not a replacement for love, but it works for me every time. It is not solely about purchasing or fulfilling materialistic needs that represent the desire to fit in or status symbols. Although these characteristics are components to what drives/motivates us to shop, for me and countless other women, shopping is so much more. It is the thrill of newness. It allows you to reinvent yourself again and again. Not knowing what you want makes you unable to choose properly in life, but not for your wardrobe. You may have challenges picking a great guy, but you know how to pick a great outfit that accentuates your assets and makes you feel beautiful. Magazine fashion layouts give you a blueprint of what you can look like and what you will be perceived as, if you wear any arrangement of fabulous clothes.

My perfect day would be ballet class, going for a quick run, getting my hair and nails done in Beverly Hills, and then shopping for shoes or jewelry at Saks Fifth Avenue, followed by a very late lunch somewhere. Then after being out all day by myself, I would meet my friends for dinner and drinks somewhere fun.

I started to reward myself and give myself birthday and Christmas gifts. Those were new habits that felt good. I vowed to stop being saddened or frustrated by what others did not do for me. Then I was able to appreciate their gestures without bitterness. I even threw myself a glamorous birthday party one year. I rented a large cabana at a popular swanky hotel and had flowers delivered and served appetizers and had a champagne toast. I invited everyone via fabulous stationary. And although I received a lot of gifts, and everyone had fun, I slowly started to feel unappreciated. My little voice started to question my motives for entertaining.

Chapter 20

An Attitude of Gratitude

I WENT FROM ONE LARGE COMPANY TO THE NEXT. AS I ACCEPTED a new offer and received my signing bonus, I would reward myself with a fabulous gift. Since I was independent and single, my philosophy was to take care of myself and gift myself since there was no one there to do it for me.

I was all about working long hours, getting promoted, and making good money. I enjoyed working in a corporate environment where you are part of a large machine. There are intangible things that draw us to work somewhere—such as the prestige and history behind the company you represent. You have opportunities to meet interesting people, to work, to travel, and to learn from people all over the world. I replaced my identity as a student with that of the company I worked for at the time. I began to think that the project objectives were more important than my own.

I was so busy working that I forgot to take care of myself and stopped focusing on relationships. My biggest relationship was the one I had with my career. When you are young, making good money, traveling, and without responsibility for anything other than yourself, you begin to lose perspective on what is important and even who you are. You become a robot, and you know that you can be easily replaced when you are no longer in peak condition. That fear keeps you striving to stay in the game.

Slowly over time, I became unappreciative as I continued in my work-centric world. I became immune to success and bored with my life. I became noticeably judgmental of myself and others. I started to lose that spark, that joy of life inside me. I was getting worn down with deadlines, expectations and thoughts of achievement. Eventually nothing made me happy. Little treats of chocolate get replaced by bigger and bigger rewards, spa treatments, fancy dinners, trips, designer clothes and jewelry. Even the sensation of "retail therapy" gets dulled if you are out of sync with your soul's true desires and dreams.

Dreams keep us alive. But for a long time, I thought it was shoes, purses and jewelry that fueled my fire. When you have a habit, it becomes difficult to break it. I became dependent on material things and people to give me that false sense of happiness. All of a sudden, I looked around me and realized that all these people I called *friend* were selfish and did not really treat me as well as I treated them. But, of course, they told me how much they adored me and valued my friendship. I was blind to the fact that they valued my "sponsorship" more than my friendship. As I started to reflect internally, I started to evaluate many of my friendships. The huge number of friends I had would slowly over the years dwindle to a small select few, those friends who have always been there for me. More importantly, I slowly had to learn to be there for myself, to comfort myself when I am sad or counsel myself when experiencing something difficult at work. Others cannot always be there for support, and some people's objectivity is questionable. As your list of friends diminishes, the burden for protection and cheering up falls more on your shoulders, you can no longer escape by distracting yourself with other people's dramas or opinions.

Chapter 21

Unusual Messenger

S OMETIMES, THE TRUTH IS THE ITEM GLARING US IN THE FACE, and we pretend we do not see it. When we constantly ignore the truth, the universe will find ridiculous ways to remind us to move on, to face the issue, or to call the play and admit the game is over. The play is called, the other side won, and there are no more time outs or over time. This was the case on this unusual day. I was rushing to catch my plane at the Sacramento airport, a small airport where you can check in and pick up your baggage at the same location. This disheveled, drunk, loud man helped me lift my suitcase onto to the rental car shuttle. Interestingly, I did not ask for his assistance. As an independent woman, I have learned to schlep my stuff around, and have become a more discriminate packer due to that fact. (How many pairs of shoes do I need for one week out of town?) While waiting at the terminal to catch my flight from Sacramento to Los Angeles one Friday evening,

I sat next to an older man. He smiles and turns to me and slurs, "Hi there, how are we doing today?"

"Fine thanks," came out cautiously but politely. I flash a polite smile as I assess him. He clearly has already started happy hour.

"My name is Rick. I am a fireman from Hollywood but was here for an event. What's your name?"

"Hi, my name is Tristan. I live in Hollywood, where is your fire station?"

"It is near Mulholland off of Cahuenga."

"Wow! What a coincidence, I live close by near the Hollywood bowl. I know exactly where that is."

We both smile politely.

"You are a beautiful woman, what is your mix? You look so exotic."

Inside I cringe every time someone uses the word exotic to describe me. I feel as if I am some unusual attraction at the Natural History Museum. I imagine a tour guide saying to his group: look over here at the "exotic" flower found only in the heart of the Amazon. So, I politely smile and answer his question "thank you for the compliment, I am half black and half Vietnamese."

"Beautiful." He pauses. I can tell what his next question will be by the pause.

"Do you have a boyfriend?"

"It's complicated."

"Oh, I am intrigued now. How old are you? "

"I am thirty-three."

"Tell me, we have plenty of time before our plane arrives for boarding."

I contemplate if I really want to get into my business in the middle of a busy airport terminal. Common sense would say not today. However, I guess I had been feeling frustrated and decided to share with a stranger."

"Well, I was dating someone at work. He was unattractive, abrasive, and not my type at all. He pursued me and would ask me questions about my interests and then at the next day talk about or gift me with the item I was interested in. We talked about philosophy and he gave me an incredible book. So, although I was not looking at him as a boyfriend, he won me over and we started dating for a year. He was so into me. Then eventually the roles reversed and I was into him. Then I had a project in Europe and after me being away for 3 weeks he did not want to pick me up at the airport, so I ended it while I was still in Europe. If someone won't be there for you for the little things, then one cannot expect them to be there for the big things."

"Why did he not want to pick you up from the airport? Most people in relationships would want to meet their significant other after a long trip."

My eyes grew wide when he said that and I emphatically responded. "I know! I agree with you. He said he rather play tennis with his new friend that was more important."

With a puzzled expression, he asked "why are you regretting your choice? He clearly is selfish. You were not expecting anything extraordinary."

I sat for a moment and looked at the ground while I contemplated his question. "I guess it was how I did it, I did it in anger and realized that my words have consequences. I wonder if I should go back or ask him to try again."

He shook his head vigorously. "No never look back, you did the right thing. Wanting to return to an ex is laziness. He's low-hanging fruit. There are plenty of great men out there. Move forward."

As he finishes the thought, I know he is right and that I need to let go of any remorse about the breakup. Sometimes though, it is the stranger that we speak to who helps us the most. I know the message was sent to my ears.

"Your ex-boyfriend is nothing more than familiar and easy sex. Eat healthy, rest, have fun and enjoy your life, you are young and have your act together. Move on from your ex, it will only bring you trouble." His words burned me, because I knew he was speaking the truth. Although my ex and I care about each other, as lovers/partners our course had run its path and we emptied into different channels.

Chapter 22

Love Through Food

WE SHOW OUR LOVE AND NURTURING THROUGH FOOD. WHEN my father was ill with cancer, friends of the family would show their support by bringing casseroles and lasagnas. Now when a friend is seriously and/or terminally ill, I have learned to do the same. When you want to show someone far away that you care, it is thoughtful to send chocolate or something nice.

Many of us also eat or prepare food for others to provide a sense of comfort. Food is an especially great treat when I am unable to use retail therapy, which is my favorite form of escapism; food is always a great reward. A cupcake, a piece of cake, a piece of candy, or for those of us who like savory items, a gruyere tart or rich piece of cheese, enjoying good food is a way to enjoy life. Often, food is a reward for a job well done or a way to console a stressed out or unhappy person. Taking that moment to savor every delicious bite stops the worry or sadness for a brief moment, even if it is just for a course or two. There are some people who eat just to survive, who do not take pleasure in food and its many varieties and sensations. I cannot imagine such a utilitarian, sterile view of food. I enjoy the mix of flavors, the textures, the colors and smells of food. Garlic roasting in olive oil always warms my heart and makes me feel at home. The smell of fresh baked cookies, cake or pie always leaves me with eager anticipation of a sweet treat. Food roasting on the grill always tastes more interesting somehow.

I admire people who cook often and do so from a place of love. The colleague or sister who bakes a variety of Christmas cookies and shares with others, or a friend who brings you delicious and adorable cupcakes, makes me smile inside and out.

Chefs who create savory items and present them so beautifully and creatively always inspire me to rethink how to display an item I prepare. Sharing a meal or any occasion to have food together truly bonds people together as you relax in each other's company and share food and have a conversation.

How interesting the cuisines of all cultures and how many different ways to prepare chicken or vegetables. It is also interesting to think that many items we eat have been around for centuries. That the way we prepare certain dishes may have been passed down for many generations, that we share something with some of our ancestors. In that way food represents a sort of longevity with time itself, a certain link to the natural world and to others that share this experience both now and in the past.

Chapter 23

You Left for a Reason

WE FEAR CHANGE. IT IS SO MUCH EASIER TO STAY IN A HOLD-ing pattern, even if you are miserable and hate every moment of it, than face the uncertainty of what is new, what is unknown. Regardless of breaking up with a significant other or leaving a psychotic boss, both actions can bring the unpleasant side of yourself that you were trying to suppress. We need to remember that we made these choices in the moment of sanity, not fear. We fear being brave. That is why men have difficulty breaking up with women, and we pretend that the horrible boss is normal, or that our parents are great when we know the truth.

Christianity speaks of Purgatory, somewhere between heaven and hell, sort of like a waitlist to the college of your choice, or a flight you wanted. Christianity has a proactive prescription for avoiding Purgatory. Pray, be a good Christian, or if it is too late, your loved ones will have to pray for your soul until there is an opening in Heaven. Or else you are doomed to wander aimlessly about Purgatory, never home, never settled, for eternity, to contemplate what you did wrong.

I believe there is a Purgatory on earth, which appears when you move on to something *new* without moving to something more fulfilling and understanding your choice, when you react based on old wounds unexamined. Leaving your lover because of childish manners and not being able to deal honestly with yourself and your feelings. Or leaving a job for what is a great job on paper, but not fulfilling your passion or your soul. These actions are a fate that condemns one to wander aimlessly about, unfulfilled by anything, especially money. Learning when and under what circumstances one should walk away is an art one picks up as they get to know themselves. I wish I would learn it already.

Chapter 24

Great Music Can Always Make You Feel Better

NATALIE COLE, FRANK SINATRA, MOZART—BEAUTIFUL, SOUL-ful music can hide anyone's scars and make your heart smile. I always need to remember this point. Great music can immediately lift your mood, your vibration. Let's remember this next time we are feeling sorry for ourselves, or feeling stuck, sad, disappointed, overwhelmed, or just plain in a bad mood.

One of my favorite things to do is drive along the Pacific Coast Highway to Point Dume in Malibu to go for a walk with the ocean as my landscape. I always play beautiful music on my drive that helps me feel relaxed.

If I am lucky I will see dolphins, seals, and even sometimes whales in the water as I walk along the sandy pathway of Point Dume. When I feel lonely or am contemplating something, these walks help me to forget about my worries and leave me feeling light and refreshed.

Chapter 25

Breaking the Pattern- Kissing the Last Toad

I S THE STORY ABOUT THE PRINCESS KISSING THE FROG THAT turns into a prince misleading? I think it is because it tells you that you can change someone into what you want.

News Flash! You cannot change another person in any real consistent and meaningful way. It's rare that a person will change and be able to sustain that change. If it were that easy, everyone would be thin and fit.

If you want fabulous and they are not, guess what honey? They aren't changing...ever. We are who we are unless something happens that creates a profound shift in one's awareness.

For example, some of us are born with an innate ability to coordinate outfits effortlessly and look stylish, while others aren't. No one is better, but you can't change one into another easily—we all have default settings.

At the end of the day for me, it doesn't matter if I meet a prince or not. What matters most is that I believe I am a princess, not because I am beautiful, or thin, or have a great job, but because I am a good and caring person. I believe that I am worthy of love, and the best life has to offer. I will be happy whether prince charming gallops beside me or not.

Smile and breathe deeply…all is well with my fantastic, sassy world. Did I tell you that I have the cutest shoes on?

Shopping, meandering around the counters of shiny objects at Saks Fifth Avenue, I find myself in the jewelry section admiring many pieces.

"Hello, may I help you with something?" a sales lady asks.

"Hi, how are you? Yes, may I please try that ring on?" I request.

"Yes, of course, it is a gold ring from Antonini, hand crafted in Italy. It is a custom-made piece, so if you like it, we have to order it."

"I adore this ring! I think I have an addiction to jewelry."

"That's good! There's nothing wrong with that."

"I want a man to buy me jewelry instead of me, is that bad?"

"You will feel better buying it for yourself. The jewelry will last longer than a man," she says.

Her comment made me laugh out loud with its accuracy.

"You are so right."

When she made that comment, I had an epiphany that everything happens for a reason. She said that because it is true. It was a statement that was true for my situation at that moment in time the statement resonated with me.

I am learning not to get too attached to what I think I want or how I think something will happen. It's ironic that we would think we can control every facet of our lives, especially how someone feels about us. We think we can control what percentage raise we will receive. When you think about it, we can't even achieve all of our errands within the time frame we desire. If nothing is in our power and everything is in our power at the same time, what does that mean? We can create our vision of our world if we truly believe it to be true, and we cannot control what ultimately will be our destiny. Is life half fortune and half what we make of it, as Machiavelli suggests? There are many contradicting directions given regarding our ability to create our life or fulfill our dreams.

I know that the next job I receive an offer for will make me choose certain things that will bring a certain reality into place. I have always been career driven, and am still searching for the next career that is right for me. Why after submitting the application do my thoughts go toward my ex-boyfriend? I see him once in a while, and we both care about each other, but we are not technically dating again…which technically means that he is not into me and does not want me. Why would my thoughts turn to this? I have dated other people. I have accepted our break up, accepted my tears, and accepted that we will never marry. Does the heart always love, even when the body is not there? I realized for the first time it does. One expects to love their deceased parent, sibling, grandparent, relative and pet still. But, does one expect to still love the one you are not with, the one who broke your heart, the one whose heart you broke? Also, if the one you are no longer with also had his or her heart broken before you dented theirs. Does your painful action echo more loudly?

Why was I so sad? Why was I in so much pain? Now I am able to see, touch, kiss my ex-lover and not cry. I can laugh and can remember how I felt both good and bad. Or maybe I am simply romanticizing what little feeling remains.

Chapter 26

Archaeology of a Soul

C AN ONE DECONSTRUCT AND FIGURE OUT WHAT KIND OF PAST lives you lived by analyzing the personality traits, preferences and interests that we hold today? Have you ever wondered what other lives you have lived? What other perspectives you have gained? Why you are partial to things or people that you logically would not know about?

I believe or hope that the items we choose to collect serve as a mirror to yourself and others, key elements about your personality, background, friends, woes and quirks. I glance at the black and white photo framed by glass and matted with white paper. *New York City Snowy Evening in Central Park* is the title, the outline of barren trees lightly dusted by snowy powder, accompanied by a glassy pond that shimmers almost by dullness. It is funny how one appreciates things when they no longer exist. I used to curse the cold snow filled days when the mornings are pitch black, your hair freezes, and your car door is frozen shut. But the lack of seasons in California has come to mean humorlessness to me. I miss the changes of weather. They are clues to you that life is constantly transforming, that things will get better. Each season has its rhythm, its hopes and dreams, its individuality. Winter is the time to relax to dream of the past and to be wistful and introspective. Winter is the time to lay to rest the bad and unplug your battery for a brighter day. Winter is comforting to me like a big soft blanket you pull over yourself when watching television.

Chapter 27

Messy Affairs

M Y NEXT PROJECT HAD ME LOCATED IN COLORADO. THE CLI-ent site was over an hour from Denver International airport. It was a typical project implementation with a decent-sized team. We were in the typical political environment and tasked with delivering the project on time and within budget for the final delivery. I slowly became acquainted with the small team that was in my charge. The majority of the team comprised women, with one man. Many of them had worked together on previous projects and were already comfortable with the type of work and each other's work style. As I met with each person to establish our project guidelines and expectations, the man in the group, Bill, slowly started to share more than documents with me.

He explained his marital situation. I am used to men flirting with me, so at first I did not really pay attention. As he kept telling me about his life, how unhappy he was, how interested in me he was, I eventually started to listen. At first, I kept my distance and said no to every request for a date, and spurned every advance. Then believing he was sincere, I started to become romantically intertwined with him. I somehow started to believe what he said. I believed him when he said that he fell in love with me, that his current life was over and he wanted a new life with me.

After dinners, late nights at the bar, gifts and compliments, we decided to take a ski trip to Aspen together. It was supposed to be the beginning of our relationship together. I was no longer on the project, but flew to Colorado one more time for this ski adventure.

It was early evening on a Thursday in March. I finally packed all of my ski gear and headed to the airport. My black down faux fur lined ski coat, black cashmere scarf, black jeans, and black boots packed away in my suitcase signaled that I was ready for the snow even though it was 80 degrees in Los Angeles.

In a busy airport, I saw a partner from my firm talking on the phone in the terminal. We said our hellos and acknowledge each other's presence before continuing our separate ways.

I was excited and nervous to meet Bill. I convinced myself that I am in love with this man. I, of course, ignored the fact that he is not free to love another, even if I was.

I boarded my flight and sat in my seat. My thoughts were racing through my head, happy thoughts preoccupying my mind. The flight took what seems like an eternity to arrive. I practically run off the plane, I'm so excited to see him.

I practically floated through the airport and arrived at the baggage claim where he was waiting for me. He hugged and kissed me, my tall, dark, and handsome man. He put my luggage in the trunk of the car and opened the door for me.

"Hi stranger, I am so happy to see you," I said.

"Me too, I miss you, sexy. You are such a beautiful woman," said Bill.

"Ah, thanks sweetheart," I said.

"Let's have dinner and go back to the hotel tonight, and then tomorrow we will drive to Aspen."

"Sounds like a plan to me!" I confirmed.

Bill kissed my hand and gently caressed it as he drove to downtown Denver. We parked and went to a trendy part of town for dinner and drinks. The next morning, we drove to Aspen. We booked a swanky hotel for the weekend. It was late after checking into the hotel, so we had dinner and drinks, and went to the hot tub.

The next morning, the phone rang in the hotel room. I answered the call. An angry woman was on the other end, asking to speak with Bill. I immediately handed the phone over to him and realized what had happened. His wife noticed the credit card charge for the hotel and was on to him. He answered the phone and placates her. "Hey baby, no, I am in the room by myself, she's my coworker, nothing is going on." He paused. "Yes I will see you next weekend. Okay, bye," and then hung up the phone. Then he angrily turned to me. "Don't ever pick up the phone again in this room. Now she's all upset with me."

"I thought it was the hotel calling about the loud fan, I am sorry. I thought you told me you told her about us?"

"I haven't done that yet. Let's talk about it later."

Now I understood that he was not serious about a new life at all. As he hung up the phone, he angrily chastised me for picking it up in the first place. He knew that his cover was exposed in both relationships, which lead to no other choice but face the facts of the situation.

Breakfast was an icy event.

"I thought it was over between the two of you! I don't appreciate being the mistress. I cannot be a mistress," I said, angrily but not loudly.

"I know…we are not really together, just legally. I told you I am working on tying up loose ends."

We sat in silence, aware that the truth had been discovered. The lie we had allowed ourselves to believe cannot overshadow what was really happening. We left breakfast and went to the slopes after first picking out our skis. We were ready to put the drama behind us and enjoy the fun day we had planned.

We skied all day and returned exhausted but laughing. We sat in a rustic, elegant hotel lobby, chatting. We both knew this would be the last time we would see each other for a while.

The next day we left the hotel and headed for the airport where he dropped me off. We talked about being married and having a life together. The next week he called me, after I had returned from our ski weekend, and informed me that our plans would never be. It was too expensive for him to get divorced. He worked too hard for his money and would not part with half of it.

Sad and disappointed, I told him it was over. It was never my intention to get in the middle of someone else's relationship, to be the other woman. It was all or nothing for me. If he was not divorcing her, there was nothing more to discuss. He did not try to change my mind. We parted at that point, and a lot of tears fell, but I had to face the facts. He made his choice, so I needed to be clear about what I would accept. Second best is never a good long-term strategy.

This relationship debacle was a huge reminder about karma. There are reasons why people should not interfere with other people's relationships. One reason is that the couple have unfinished business to attend to before anything new can start. I had always strictly enforced this policy of not dating a married or unavailable person before; however, somehow, I slackened my boundaries and was easily manipulated. In reality, I came to understand that it is a no-win situation. As the other person, you cannot compete with a couple's shared history and shared assets. I also see that cheating is the cowardly way out. It is important to end something before beginning something new. Now having fallen into the "I don't love the person I am currently with" trap, I will never catch myself there again. You are not getting a prize when you are with someone who is cheating on their significant other. Instead, you are getting toxic negative karma, and there is nothing romantic or sexy about that.

Chapter 28

Turning Point

SOON AFTER WE ENDED OUR MESSY BUT BRIEF AFFAIR, I REALized that I was very late. My cycle had not arrived. Out of sheer panic I bought a home pregnancy test. The results were devastating—I was pregnant. I went to my doctor as soon as she could fit me in. I told her that I thought that I was pregnant, and after some tests she confirmed my suspicion. She and her nurse were excited for me and encouraged me to keep the baby, since it was a good time for me to do this before I got further into my thirties.

Terrified of being pregnant, I cried every day. I knew that I could not have a career like I currently have. I felt that there was no way I could work long hours, and travel Monday through Friday, without a husband at home. I was keenly aware that the husband was not about to appear in my life anytime soon. I was not ready for a small child. Honestly, I never imagined myself without my career, or having children. It was just an assumption that I would get married one day, but I never filled in the details like so many people do. I never imagined when I would have children or how many I would have. More importantly, I did not imagine myself unmarried and pregnant.

I had the unpleasant task of calling Bill to tell him my news.

"Bill, it's Tristan," I said cautiously.

"Hi," he replied in a stony voice.

"Are you alone?"

"Yes, what's going on?"

"I don't know how to tell you this, but I missed my cycle and went to see the doctor. She confirmed that I am 4 weeks pregnant." I said as calmly as I could.

"Are you joking? Are you seeing someone else? I can't believe this is happening to me. No offense, but I barely know you. I can only assume you want something from me." He accused me of having an agenda, assuming that I was lying about this.

"Bill, we are on the same project with the same client, how would I have time to see someone else between work, seeing you, and flying home to LA on the weekends I wasn't spending with you? A month ago, that was our trip, remember?"

"I'm not trying to make your life difficult, and I'm sorry for making this time in your life harder than it needs to be. Unfortunately, I know women who have lied about these things in the past to achieve some agenda. I'm not saying you are…it just has a familiar ring, especially with the methods we employed," he responded coldly.

"Well honestly, I am only informing you of what is happening. I have decided that I will keep the baby. I do not need anything from you since I have a career. I will raise the child myself. You are not going to be involved with this at all. The child will have my last name. I do not need child support," I said sternly.

"Telling me that you wish me to have no relationship with my child is not comforting, and again is against my beliefs. I've told my wife about you," he paused, and then carefully continued. "The truth is that I like you as a person. I don't know you that well. I cannot take everything and anything said to me at face value. As a father, trust is not a luxury that I have. I'm sorry to be the cause of any suffering to anyone. I will be contacting you in the near future to find out what the facts are and what responsibilities I have," he said firmly.

"Listen, Bill, this doesn't change anything. We are not together, and I do not need you. You will not be involved."

"Well, I disagree." His voice slightly agitated.

I was devastated by his response to my news. I knew I was not going to receive the warmest well wishes, but to be accused of lying was out of the question for me.

My response to Bill was simple. I told him, "Please leave me alone. Your comments are hurtful. I will take care of this situation. I want to put you behind me and move forward. I should never have placed myself in this situation in the first place. You are right: we know nothing about each other, and we should keep it that way. Please respect my choice. Okay, I am done with this conversation. Goodbye."

"Goodbye."

We hung up the phone angrily, and I was in tears. I knew that I would do this on my own, but did not want to feel judged or wrong.

As the weeks moved along, I was slowly adjusting to the idea of being a mother, and felt comfortable knowing that all the new changes in my life I would face alone. I started planning and thinking of the real logistics of how I would pull this off. I knew that I would need to live closer to my family, to a support system that I could trust. I realized that my expenditures would have to change—no more designer purses in the budget, so that I could afford day care. Also, I would need to find a slower-paced job. I started researching and asking friends with children how they balance career and family life. Each friend gave me invaluable advice.

I had to do all of this planning in secret; no one at work knew that I was pregnant. It was hard not to have the support of the father. It was difficult hearing about colleagues and their baby showers, planned maternity leave, and sheer joy.

However, the stress of doing this alone, the horrible behavior revealed by the father, and the stress of my job exhausted me and drove me to tears every night. One night, as I lay in bed sobbing, I heard a little voice say, "Don't worry mommy, everything will be okay."

I heard the little voice repeat itself. At this point I felt like I was pregnant, sad, and going insane. I asked the voice, "Who is speaking to me?"

The little voice said, "It's me, your child. I am here with you."

It was so clear, so soft that I felt calm once we introduced ourselves to each other.

The little voice said: "My name is Max, I am your son. I want you to know that I love you and that everything will be okay. Just trust. You are not alone…you have me."

As the soul of my unborn child was talking to me, I realized that I knew exactly who he was. He was the beautiful child I sometimes see in my dreams.

I did stop crying, and started to relax and said thank you. You are right. We will be okay. My eyelids drooped, and I fell into a deep sleep.

Now, every night when I went to bed after a long day at work, I felt and heard the presence of the little voice. I felt a strong connection with the voice, which reminded me that there is so much more to life than one's career or petty dramas. Unfortunately, the stress of the situation was too great for me, and I sometimes wished for an ending of the situation so that I would not have the father tied to me for the rest of my life. Ironically, I got what I wished. I know that I was not ready for motherhood, and that I did not want to be involved with someone who was so controlling and difficult. Thankfully, my wish was granted, although it would leave me with mixed feelings.

I went to see my doctor. She did an ultrasound to find the baby's heartbeat. She couldn't find it, and expressed concern. She told me to go to another doctor for a second opinion. I was told not to worry that if the baby is not growing then it means that there is a genetic abnormality, it is just nature's way of ensuring a healthy baby.

I saw the second doctor, and he confirmed my doctor's diagnosis. There was no heartbeat, and the baby was too small. The doctor referred me to an outpatient clinic that will conduct the dilation and curettage procedure on Monday. At this point, I am crying uncontrollably. I am somewhere between awareness and unawareness. On one hand, I am sad and wonder how this could happen to me after the first trimester. On the other hand, I know that I prayed for it in an indirect way, and was surprised by my intense grief.

In a way, I was relieved because I knew life would be difficult without a father figure for the child. I was also not as prepared as I would like to have been for a child at this moment in time. I felt that I needed to be in a career where I could balance motherhood, have more savings and a home for this child. Also, now I had added marriage as a prerequisite for me in order to feel comfortable having a baby, as a partner can be your emotional support during this chaotic time.

I had the unpleasant task ahead of me to call the father and tell him the news. He barely said anything. I thanked him for our brief time together and wished him all the best in his life. He said he would call me later. I knew that was just a way to end the unpleasant phone call. I told him it was not necessary. We did not exchange harsh words or parting shots. Instead, we quietly said goodbye.

I never looked back. I never called again. We never spoke or saw each other again, as it should be. Sometimes funerals happen without anyone being buried in the ground; instead, they are buried by memories. The closet, cabinet, or door to the past of your mind engulfs the situation, thereby ending it, annexing that experience into the vast emptiness of your past.

This experience forever changed me. I now know what is truly important, and the type of things one should prioritize in life. I was selfish and afraid of changing my self-centric life. I also realize that I was not ready for the gift that I received. If there is a next time, I will be better prepared—or at least try not to cry all the time. I respect the countless women who welcome their unplanned children into the world without the drama and tears. I am in awe of these brave and fearless women who do not cry, but rejoice at the little miracle inside of them and trust that they will be able to face the challenges ahead for their unborn.

Chapter 29

Transition Gracefully

AFTER THE LOSS OF MAX, I PLUMMETED QUICKLY INTO A DEEP depression. I did not realize what mixed emotions I would have at the loss of the pregnancy at three months. I felt like a failure, and was disappointed with myself for not being able to control my emotions and fears during this time. I could barely get to work on time and could not focus. As a management consultant, companies pay a lot of money for my time and expertise; there is no room for non-productive, non-diligent people. People who do not perform are simply let go. This pregnancy should have been a time of happiness and excitement for me, not one of arguments, stress, and sheer panic.

As I shared my sad news with friends, someone suggested that I meet with a life coach to help me get through this hard time I was experiencing. I agreed that I needed some help, so I decided to drive to Marina del Rey to meet Timothy, a life coach.

I arrived at his apartment in Marina del Rey. I was dressed in all white, with a white mini Vernis Louis Vuitton purse. I knocked on the door and to my surprise, I saw when he opened the door that he too was dressed all in white. He was wearing white pants and a white caftan. "Hi, Timothy, I am Tristan, your appointment. I see that we are both dressed in white. We must have called each other last night and told each other what to wear," I jokingly say.

"Welcome, Tristan, please come in." He gestures with his hand for me to enter his apartment and smiles. "White is the color of rebirth, a color I like to wear often. Please have a seat on the couch."

Somehow, I felt that I was supposed to meet this person and listen to what he had to say. Could wardrobe synchronicity equate to destiny, I wondered?

Timothy was a tall, tanned man with long, dark hair. His charisma and big smile were friendly and unassuming.

"Before we get started, let me tell you about myself. I am part Mexican and part Native American Indian. I am a shaman, a healer who has learned the old sacred ways of medicine, of spirit. I counsel families, and focus mostly on men and how they can be better fathers. I counsel men and their sons throughout Los Angeles, and hold a special retreat every year for them. So, tell me, Tristan," he says while looking at me and finding a place to sit, "why are you here? What do you hope to accomplish in your session or sessions with me?"

"Well Timothy, I was referred to you by Mark. He said you helped him immensely when he was going through an emotionally difficult time. I recently had an unexpected pregnancy and a miscarriage, and feel unbalanced and depressed. There is no relationship with the father of the child, but I am not upset over that. The miscarriage has affected me much more strongly than I had imagined. I would like to return to my normal state of calm and focus. I have a demanding career as a management consultant and cannot afford to be unfocused or not energized." Tears well in my eyes as I explain my current state of mind.

"Yes, that is an extremely challenging experience. Loss impacts us in many ways." After saying that, he studied my face and then, with a quizzical look, said, "Tell me what my middle name is. I have the sense that you are deeply intuitive and can tell me this." Somehow, I knew the answer. The name Michael appeared in my head immediately.

"I think your middle name is Michael."

He smiles as he says "Yes. You are right, and I was right about your intuition."

"Your intuitive channels are opening up, and you are capable of so much more than you think, and I will show you that you can indeed heal yourself."

"Really? Okay, that sounds interesting. I do agree that my intuition is opening up. Somehow I can know things, but cannot explain why or how or when I will know things."

"The mind is very powerful. I see that you are a busy person, so meditation will help you to quiet your mind and listen to the wisdom of your soul. Your soul has all the answers you need and will guide you to the answers you seek."

As he talked about the power of the mind and the need to meditate in order to listen in between the chatter of the ego to get to the silence, I realize that I have heard this point before. In the silence, one can hear the wisdom within which is the source of knowledge. He told me that the answers I seek are housed within me, and that I need to learn, and practice connecting to the quiet place within through meditation.

Timothy then prompted, "Tristan, tell me about your childhood."

"Well I am half black and half Vietnamese; I was born in Vietnam and adopted as a child. My parents are Caucasian, English and American. I went to prep school and college on the East Coast and completed my graduate degree here at USC. My father passed away when I was fourteen which was hard for all of us, my mother and my siblings."

I could see him processing the information about my childhood and observing that I was bi-racial. After I finished speaking, he looked at me with a direct and serious gaze, and said, "I believe that the source of your sadness lies with the issue of abandonment. The original abandonment from your birth parents and then the death of your father, to be exact, is what is causing the discord. I feel that is the source of your deep routed pain, which was activated by the loss of your unborn child."

Immediately I gave my counter point. "I see the point about my father, but I do not agree with the original abandonment analysis because I have never had anger toward my biological parents. I don't have an emotional tie there, so I do not feel that part is correct."

He was shocked by my quick response. "I see that you are a quick thinker, which tells me that your reasoning skills are very advanced. I think that in time you will understand my points. Once you deal with all of the forms of abandonment, then you will be able to transition gracefully to the next chapter of your life."

"What do you mean by transition gracefully? How do I do that?"

Unfazed by my question, he skipped over the need to respond and said, "Let's meditate; you will need to meditate every day to help yourself."

Although I followed his direction, I noticed that my questions were unanswered.

Timothy's mantra was "transition gracefully." Although the idea was incomplete, it was a starting point as to how to leave a situation or state of being, and how to enter a new one. As a student, I needed to know how to transition gracefully. Exactly what did that mean? What does "transition gracefully" look like in concrete terms? Ultimately, I would leave my sessions with more questions than answers, and eventually I stopped going, but Timothy did help me think of some new things. He helped me to understand the value of meditation and planted the seed about abandonment and transitioning gracefully. I would search for the *how* to transition gracefully. I kept looking in books and talked to people about it: "How do you move yourself from depression and chaos to happiness and peace? How do you leave a situation where you are unhappy, but that is familiar to you and brave a new job, relationship or home, and how do you do it as smoothly as possible?"

Chapter 30

Growing Up

SOMETHING FUNNY HAPPENED WHILE TRAVELLING: I STARTED to dream of creating my home and making it cozy, not just a place to unpack my suitcase. I decided to buy a place, and fortunately, one can buy property no matter their emotional state. I bought a condo in the Hollywood Hills with two bedrooms, one bath, and a wraparound balcony. As I processed these experiences, the miscarriage, and ways I was abandoned, I withdrew into myself. I became depressed and sad. I was in inner turmoil. Fear ran rampant in my mind. I stopped caring about my work, and daily life held no interest for me at all. Things just did not seem to be as important as they once were. I would arrive to work later and later. I would not complete items in advance of the schedule. It took all my energy to focus at work. I constantly felt physically and emotionally drained. I never told anyone about my personal ordeal, so no one knew that I was barely getting by.

Now I turned my attention to what meals I knew how to cook, decorating my place, and preparing myself, in a way, for when I would have a child.

I had to leave my consulting job, as I no longer had the drive for it. That career is about the relentless drive to achieve. It is set up as a series of goals or tasks. You must be one hundred percent dedicated to your job, because if you slip, the label of average performance is not only a curse, but grounds for termination. You cannot have room in your life for others except in a cursory way. You are too busy for love, for children, or even yourself.

After my experience of loss, I was no longer interested in being a robot or a machine. The carrot of money and title appeared hollow. Freedom seemed more important, more alluring. Not just freedom in terms of time, but in terms of one's own mental ability, freedom to create for yourself.

It was nice to finally not travel each week. As I had more time, I slowly began to feel more things. The emotions started to seep in like water leaking on the floor, spreading further, diminishing my focus and cast iron will.

I eventually got my energy back, but soon I would realize that it was too late, my depression and carelessness had set the wheels in motion for events that were *truly* depressing and overwhelming. I had a hard time adjusting to a budget once I had a mortgage. I was more limited with my money and forced to balance my expenditures. I had not adjusted to my new situation properly. The combination of depression leading to overspending and not being able to stay in my fast-paced career would prove to be deadly. I was forced to find a new job which was close to home, but I took a significant pay cut for that pleasure.

It was as if I had taken two steps backwards. One should feel thrilled by accomplishment when moving into their home. However, I felt like the purchase was a burden and not a joy. Instead of happiness, I had a bad attitude, and all that I feared came true. Although still many years away, I could not help but notice that forty was approaching and not only was I unmarried, I was completely single! Yikes! You just don't imagine that for yourself. Now exhausted, in a job that paid me much less, I felt like the debt was piling up; at that moment, I did not know how to respond to what was happening.

Chapter 31

Unwanted Visitor

I RECOGNIZED THAT I WAS STILL DEPRESSED. DEPRESSION IS LIKE an unwanted house guest that overstays their welcome. My mood was below normal healthy levels. I was not motivated to do things I normally do, such as work all the time or allow people to tell me what to do and how to do it. My thoughts were changing. I knew that I deserved more.

I felt that my career as I had known it was dying. I no longer wanted to tend to it. I no longer cared for it as I had so intensely all these years. I had already been neglecting it the past year. I decided I must make a change. I could not live for others as I had been, was no longer willing to sacrifice my personal life for that of my career.

I wrote my resignation letter and provided the requisite two-week notice to my employer. I went to the downtown office in Los Angeles. I said goodbye to my friends and the executives that hired and mentored me and thanked them for my time at the firm.

It was terrifying to jump without a plan. The day before my final day I cried. All the same, I knew that I needed to let go of a fake identity and sense of security, and dare to find me.

Although my spirits were high on that final day, I was physically exhausted. I had to remain calm and remember that God loves me and provides for me. My dad and the angels are always here to help me and guide me. I have nothing to fear.

I found a temporary job right away and continued interviewing for a position at a different company. I did receive an offer, and although I had to take a pay cut, at least I was gainfully employed and not required to travel every week. I did the unimaginable—I jumped without a safety net, without a plan, and to my surprise, I landed on my feet. I did not fall apart and did not break any bones. I took a risk and learned that sometimes you have to get off your current road and explore other options.

Sometimes we find ourselves in situations for a short period. I feel that I was at the next company to meet someone who would be an incredible teacher to me. I did not learn this until I was leaving that company.

Elise was a colleague at the small start-up pharmaceutical company that I went to briefly. She had a strong personality, very direct gaze and demeanor. In defiance of blonde stereotypes, she was a no nonsense, non-frivolous person. She was incredibly detail-oriented, articulate and responsible. She would be the other person beside myself in the office working late every day.

Elise shared her wisdom and own personal experiences with me. Helpful and encouraging, she gave me books, DVDs, and activities to help me transition to a new situation. She helped open my eyes and taught me to seek spiritual information and learn. We would talk end-lessly of the power of thought in creating our reality. We would talk about the power of intuition, and about how to claim one's power. All of our conversations would be the guideposts that I called upon when going through troubling times.

Elise and I would discuss the overwhelming workload that kept us in the office late every night. In addition, we both shared our frus-trations about being undervalued. As I continued in this new role. I uncovered many mistakes from my predecessor. However, my current boss considered my predecessor as a living God and did not believe me, even if I received confirmation about the mistakes and issues. Elise was experiencing her own challenges and we would be at the office late, able to commiserate and discuss how to deal with these problems.

Eventually, everything would go wrong. I was unhappy at work, bored of what I do and tired of always taking on so much, juggling many projects while everyone else had two projects. My car was not working well, and I kept sinking more and more money to fix my aging but beautiful BMW 3 Series sedan. My need for furniture for my new place, keeping up with my friends, going out and paying for others out of habit, would eventually lead to my mini-economic collapse. Unfor-tunately, there was no bailout available for me to access.

It was the perfect storm of bad decisions that lead to a depleted savings account and 401K. All these bad decisions eventually needed to be rectified. I ignored the calls from creditors. I was in denial, over-whelmed. It was curious that I had money issues as I made a good liv-ing and was single. I began to consider money an energetic vibration. We associate it with attributes of either plenty or of lack. Ultimately, it is our thoughts and feelings about money that show up in our lives.

Although I had no reason to experience lack, I did as I equated it to childhood fears that I never acknowledged, let go of, or replaced.

I was overwhelmed and in denial about needing to stick to a budget so that I could pay my mortgage, property taxes, and homeowners association fees on time. I fell behind with my mortgage and then set up a payment plan to catch up. And just as I got squared away with *that*, a ghost from my past came back to haunt me—taxes! My paycheck was garnished by the state, forcing me to pay my past due taxes at a much faster rate, thus breaking my payment plan with the mortgage company. Like dominos, the payment plan was broken due to the tax garnishment, and then I was in the new, unfamiliar, scary territory of serious financial problems.

I called the bank and set up a loan modification (which is a tool that mortgage companies provide to you when falling behind in payments—i.e, an update to your original loan terms). The loan modification reduced my mortgage payments, making my ability to repay the mortgage easier. Finally, everything seemed to be moving forward. My mortgage was being repaid and the loan modification would eventually add on the missed payments to the overall loan. But I wasn't out of the woods just yet. In fact, disaster was lurking right around the corner, and when I least expected, disaster hit!

I came home one day to find "intent to foreclose notice" with my name and address written on it tacked to my front door, this sent me into shock and uncontrollable sobbing. The threat of losing my home was the most frightening wake-up call that I had ever received. I felt confused, fearful and paralyzed. I thought that my loan modification would prevent something like this from happening, but, unfortunately, it did not. I called the bank while crying hysterically as the understanding of what was about to happen started to sink into my brain. I imagined myself homeless and living on the street, my closest family 3,000 miles away on the East Coast. I called Steve, someone I was dating, to ask for his advice. I never call my mother; I know she would not help me so that was not an option. She always said, "Once you go to college you are on your own. My job is done."

Crying, I jump right in when Steve picks up the phone. "Hi, it's me; I came home to a foreclosure notice. I called the bank and they said my payment plan broke, and there is nothing they can do for me."

He pauses and says calmly, "I am sorry to hear this news. You should find an attorney who can help you. Just go online and look for attorneys that specialize in this area."

Still crying, I respond, "I just don't know what I will do; I do not have $30,000 to pay off the balance immediately. I thought my loan modification would prevent this."

"This is hard news, but you will get through it. Find an attorney, they can tell you how to help you."

"I guess you won't want to date someone in this predicament," I offer.

"Don't think about that right now, focus on what you need to do. Okay, I have a dinner with a client. I will talk with you later."

"Okay, thanks for talking, goodnight."

"Goodnight, beautiful."

After we hang up the phone, I realize that I am completely alone without anyone to seriously help me. I wasn't looking for a bailout. However, it would have been nice to have an offer of help that was more than advice. If I were in the position to help someone through a difficult time, I would. Needless to say, I later realized many other ways that Steve was not there for me, and that words alone are empty without action to back them up.

After months of phone calls, research and negotiations, I was able to obtain my approved loan modification and stave off the foreclosure proceedings. I could finally breathe with a sense of peace that I would not lose my home.

Several months later, the bank would ask me to reapply for a loan modification program. As that happened several more times, it appeared to be a positive outcome for me. It made me reevaluate my expenses and how I spent money. It forced me to look at my behavior and attitudes about money so that I could clean up this situation. I started to pray, and focused on making more money so that I would feel more abundant. I kept this secret to myself and barely told anyone. It was a huge weight around my neck. If the eyes speak, mine must have been telling a horror story.

Chapter 32

Search for the Holy Grail

A GOOD, EMOTIONALLY AVAILABLE MAN IN THE TWENTY-FIRST century is as elusive as the Holy Grail. Some say the Holy Grail is a chalice, a vessel, a cup, the head of John the Baptist, or even the bloodline of Jesus and Mary Magdalene. In Dan Brown's book *The Da Vinci Code*, the author elegantly summarizes all of the interpretations for us about this ancient artifact.

I have one more interpretation to add to the list: I say that the Holy Grail is the perfect man. The perfect man, this mythical creature, has rarely been seen, and is not tangible. Sightings of this being go unconfirmed, as when captured or identified, the entity disappears into thin air. It is rumored to exist and has been searched for by countless women throughout time. It is this elusive ideal creature that urges women to wait, to hope for more. All women wish that the man in front of them is that perfect being. Women hope that the myths of his valor, integrity, strength, chivalry, nobility, romance, and generosity are true. The definitions and many examples of man as a perfect specimen would indicate that this myth of man is indeed real.

Part of this mistaken identity is due to the folklore of man, the tales of King Arthur's knights. Part of it is because, in the movies, the man says the perfect thing, has the perfect timing at the end of the movie. We do not see what happily ever after looks like, we just see the hope, and the promise delivered in the kiss that he initiates. Our imagination takes over the rest of the details. There is no follow-up, no "where are they now" documentaries detailing how the relationship stayed its course and how everyone was honest and loyal.

This might sound quite bitter, but is mostly poking fun at the archetype of man: that perfect ideal, the mythical creature that we are seeking. No doubt many men say the same thing of women. However, I have witnessed many an amazing woman. I feel that beautiful, strong, intelligent, kind, honest, generous women exist, and there are many to choose from in all shapes and sizes.

After many dates and different potential partners, love still eludes me. I am beautiful, successful, and independent, but still without the man who loves me. I question my quest for the perfect man and wonder if I would have more luck finding a lost treasure or civilization. I believe that I am more likely to find the lost city of Atlantis than finding the ideal man. Or is this because I live in Los Angeles, a virtual wasteland when it comes to relationships that last more than a week?

Chapter 33

Don't Look Back

S CROLLING THROUGH MY EMAILS AT WORK ONE MORNING, I RE-
ceive an email from someone I had not seen or thought of in a
long time.

The email reads*: Hi, is this Tristan Webster from USC-School of International Relations? I don't know if you remember me, but this is John.
I want to say hi.*

As I read who the email is from, I am reminded of this person. He
was an older student in my program who finished the year I started.
He was always nice and very intelligent, yet rebellious. Naturally, I was
curious about his life and what he has been up to. I, of course, assumed
that he had a family with children, and did something related to our
field of study.

I reply confirming his question and ask how he is, what is he up to,
where is he, and mention how nice it is to speak with an old classmate.

After several emails, he tells me he has an upcoming business trip in Los Angeles and would love to meet me for dinner. He lets me know when we will meet and asked for my address. He arrives at my building in a Porsche convertible. He is wearing a navy blazer with brass buttons, a crisp white shirt and dark pants. When I approach the car door, he tells me that I look exactly as he remembers me, beautiful and youthful. Sitting at dinner with cocktails and champagne while hearing about what someone has been doing for many years while you have been out of touch is like watching a mystery unfold. There are clues about ended relationships and who hurt who, but it is vague, and odd pieces that do not seem to fit together lurk about in your conversation. There is that eerie feeling that someone is listening or watching, that there is another person in the conversation. Later you realize that there is another, the ghost of a woman or women where it did not work out, and the knowledge that he wouldn't be sitting across from the table now if things had not disintegrated. The unspoken words resonate like an echo in a cave, but you pretend that you have a sunny heart in front of you, a man that is available and searching for lasting love.

The series of dinners with my old classmate were fun and exciting. However, just as quickly and out of the blue as the email and dinners appeared, they disappeared. I came to realize that the connection or reconnection was more a brief dalliance down memory lane of sorts. I quickly realized that there was no depth of feeling. I guess it was curiosity and mild boredom that led him to reach out to me. As soon as I realized that I had met a Peter Pan with expensive toys, I was able to put everything in perspective. I learned that not everything or every action has depth of meaning, no matter how much you may think you want it to. Also, sometimes a man who looks good on paper, who has the education and assets, is not the right balance for your heart. This type of experience forces you to look at the truth of someone's actions, including your own, as a true barometer for what is real. I questioned what my motivations were, what his motivations were, and what I was willing to accept to be with someone.

I eventually began to understand that the person who will rescue me, who will love me, who will be my support…is me. If I cannot do it for myself, how can I appreciate and recognize it in others? If I cannot value myself, why would I expect another to? It takes learning to love yourself on a deeper level. To love yourself goes beyond, gifts, vacations, dinners and things that you allow yourself to have or experience. It moves into the territory of kindness, nurturing and non-judging. Self-love teaches you to provide yourself with self-acceptance and time to reflect on your actions and feelings without having to be right or wrong.

Some men show a flash of a romantic cloak. It surrounds you gently and feels good. It is a suggestion, the innuendo of more, the charm of thoughts of what love is that they share with you. They fool themselves just as much as they fool you. They are not trying to be malicious. They just get caught up in their fantasy of love, a sentiment or ideal that they share like the tide. In certain situations, if the mood catches them, they cast a spell of romance on your delicate psyche. However, like the tide, they will reel in their feelings and desires and say no more of romance. Instead, they vanish into thin air, leaving you to question what you experienced. Like the phases of the moon, the retreat into reality occurs and the spell breaks until the next full moon of his heart. Thus, the push and pull of his emotions is like the ebb and flow of the tide.

The romantic dreamer is a dangerous man in that he is sincere, and he is charmingly deceitful, both sides of the romantic coin at once. One must be brave and focus on the action and not the words. The focus on action is how you protect yourself and recognize that your dreamer is just dreaming. He never wants to wake up from his beautiful world, and that is all it is, a beautiful world in his heart, nothing more than words.

A year later, on a trip to San Francisco to watch the San Francisco Ballet perform the Nutcracker, with my fiery redheaded girlfriend, Julie, we planned a busy weekend full of activities, dinners and shopping. We stayed at the Parc 55 hotel near Market Street, a great location in the heart of the city.

I hurriedly walked out of the hotel toward the mall on Market Street. I needed to buy some heavy armor—Spanx—to contain my ever-encroaching bulge. The air was brisk, but I was warm in my black fur trimmed coat and hat. Shortly after walking into the mall, a woman with long dark hair and a lot of shopping bags approached me. She walked up to me and said, "I am a psychic and I have something important to tell you about your life."

I was surprised, but, of course, curious. Who doesn't want to hear news about one's life? Who wouldn't want to know pieces of information to help you continue on your path? I immediately asked her how much money she would charge for a psychic reading.

"I charge $20 for a reading," said the Gypsy woman. "Let's go somewhere so I can tell you what I see." She then looked for her daughter and said "Sweetie, follow mommy."

We walked toward some tables and chairs in the food court. We sat down. She was surrounded by her many shopping bags.

"I see that money comes easily to you, but love does not. Many times, love has come to you, but you are closed off, and it doesn't stay. Men are always around you, but there is one now for you."

"Is it the one who just contacted me out of the blue?" I asked curiously.

"Yes. I see that your home will be in New York, not here. You will be married in 2-3 years, and will have two boys."

"So, this man is the one?" I ask again for clarification.

"Yes," she confirmed, "but you have a choice, and you may not keep him. You have a habit of not finding love. You need to let go of your sadness. Why are you always dressed in black?"

"I don't always dress in black," I said indignantly, but unfortunately, the point was moot, because I did only wear black. "Well, black is slimming."

"Someone with the letter J, a woman, is very harmful and bad for you. She has put a curse on you. It has lasted 19 years. You are just coming out of it."

"J. Oh, the only person I know with the letter J that holds negativity towards me is my mother. There is a lot of weirdness there."

"You take after your father, you look like him."

"I don't know my father; I was given up for adoption at a young age."

"You look like your biological father, but your character is like your adoptive father."

"That makes sense. I am very close to my father, even though he is deceased," I confirmed.

"You need to make yourself feel better so you can attract love into your life. Tonight, take a bath with seven red roses for your seven wishes, and light a candle," she instructed.

"I am staying at a hotel; I don't live in San Francisco, so this would be impossible for me to do."

"Do it before midnight tomorrow night," she insisted. "Call me 2–3 days afterwards."

I don't know what I was thinking, I even-handed a check over for more money. I never do that unless it's a pair of designer shoes. I am stunned that I handed money over without question. I guess I wanted to believe that I can help myself attract a good man into my life by following her simple advice. I felt that I was missing something more in my life. I was also surprised that although I knew better, I assumed my classmate reaching out to me meant more than what it was. I never was the girl dreaming of prince charming to come rescue her, but in the past year something inside me said it's time to look for a man—the one I will marry.

In a daze, I found Nordstrom, my Mecca. I bought the heavy, body-shaping armor I was looking for and returned to the hotel. My friend and I had planned to go see a movie. Throughout the movie, I replayed the events of the day in my head. Back at the hotel, I told Jules of my encounter, and she about smacked me.

"Why would you do that?" she asked. "You know that true spiritual help is always free. You don't pay for it."

"I don't know why I did a reading with a random gypsy woman. I was drawn to her," I confessed.

After a fun weekend of traipsing around San Francisco with my friend, I was ready to go home. My flight touched down Sunday night. As I unpacked my suitcase and got settled in, I found myself still thinking about what the stranger had said to me.

In a sudden surge of impulse, I went to the store to buy red roses.

At home, I poured a bath and lit a candle. I cut the stems off of seven red roses and placed the roses in the bath water. After settling into the hot, fragrant water, I picked up a rose and imbued it with intention. I wished that my true love finds me, that he recognizes me. I hoped that we would find love and get married and have children, that we would have a happy marriage and family life, that I would be a successful artist, and that we would be healthy. In short, I wished for everything I desire.

I relaxed and repeated my seven wishes to my seven roses.

I finally finished my bath, toss the roses, and throw the thoughts out of my head as I blew out the candle.

John, my old classmate from USC who had recently contacted me continued to flirt with me over email, and from time to time would tell me that he's coming to LA and asked me if I will be available for dinner. As history keeps repeating the same pattern of behavior with this friend, I knew that this small gesture meant nothing and would go nowhere. Upon closer examination of my feelings, I understood that we would not be a good fit. I realized that I projected my desire onto a situation and person who is not right for me, and that is not the right way to see the truth of the matter. Instead, if I focused on what I wanted to experience and how I wanted to feel, the truth would be revealed and reflected in the situation by the actions of the other. I understood that I can do this without a projection of desire if I stayed focused on the present and do not run ahead to the future, or version of the future, that I had imagined.

Chapter 34

Fantasy Finding:
A 9-5 Job that Pays Well

T HEY SAY THAT COOKING IS THE WAY TO A MAN'S HEART. I LOVE to cook. I used to not enjoy it because I associated cooking with being female and the socially constructed norm. Where women were not valued for their minds but for their beauty, reproductive ability, and housekeeping skills, which always seemed dull to me. When I was sixteen or younger, my girlfriends would pick out the names of their children and imagine their boyfriend as their husband. Many of those girls married early, in the end.

I, on the other hand, could not wait to go to college. I was interested in philosophy, art, history, and literature. I would dream of studying at Oxford or the Sorbonne. I dreamt of visiting the famous museums and travelling all over the world—and I *did* visit many famous museums, and travelled all over the world. Haven't made it to Oxford or the Sorbonne except as a visitor, but hey, that could still happen, if only I were more organized.

I turned my home into a heavenly sanctuary with beautiful things. I started wanting to cook delicious meals at home for my friends and myself, and to serve dinner on lovely china and crystal. So, I did. I started reading cookbooks and experimenting with different recipes in the kitchen. I forgot how fun it is to create a little masterpiece, a little slice of heaven that everyone can enjoy!

I laugh when people suggest that the way to a man's heart is through his stomach. I feel that there is not one path to a man's heart. Each man is different, and it is more about when they are ready to commit and timing than any one thing a woman can do. It is best as a woman not to betray your true self by pretending, manipulating or chasing a man. Or making him believe you truly love him or want him in a way that is not true to yourself. So, I do not chase or pretend to keep someone by my side anymore as I have learned that these actions are pointless and bear only temporary benefits. My true nature always gives me away, as I get bored, resentful and irritated. I have also learned that I do not want anything or anyone on false pretenses. Coercion is not a tactic that I will use in love, as love should be a free exchange.

I sometimes see cooking as a way to share your creativity and love of life with others. My many friends are often invited to an incredible dinner where I can always experiment with at least a dish or two, and it gives us all time to talk and catch up with each other.

Somehow, I surprised myself when I found the experience of cooking and entertaining to be deeply satisfying. However, without free time, cooking can be an endless and tiring chore. When I feel that way, I know that my life is off-kilter.

Still, I am a truly independent woman and need my alone time, and vacillate back and forth between being social and being by myself.

Chapter 35

Illusions of Love

BEING HELD BY A GOOD MAN IS NOT THE SAME AS THE IDEA OF one. I realize that I have so many times fallen in love with the idea of a man and not paid attention to the real man. I ignored his lack of actions. I observed the inconsistency of his words against the actions. That does not equate to a good relationship. It is time to say goodbye to myths, legends, and archetypes of prince charming.

Standing alone, I now have the visceral understanding that the only one who can save me is myself. I must transition gracefully from a place of desire to a real place of substance and love. Even if what I find is only the love of myself. The love I can give myself, the patience I can bestow on my soul and the healing I give to the wounded places will be a better gift than a diamond from an insincere place. I am the diamond that shines and sparkles. It is my laughter and inner beauty that is the jewel. I must recognize this first before he can see it in the dark and among other faces.

Unrequited love in the modern era is like being caught in a nightmarish Victorian love story. A story where the plain woman or man of no consequence does not marry well, in fact, does not marry at all. Jane Eyre walking the moors, looking for her love, was homely, and a governess with no family connections, and even she managed to marry. Why not I?

I have been single now for a year and four months. I have had a few passing flings, but for the most part go to bed alone. At first I was too busy in the middle of a career change to notice. Then I switched companies again. Now that I am fitting in and adjusting to my new, slower pace of life, I have looked around and noticed that I have not had a man around in ages.

I miss how they take up the bed and sleep loudly, whether snoring or breathing. I miss having someone hold me as they fall asleep. I have enjoyed my freedom. I listen to classical music. I am about to get my pointe shoes for ballet class. I have plenty of time for friends. I eat potato chips and chocolate in bed. I watch whatever I want on TV. I read a lot.

The other night, I gave myself a beautiful bath. After a chemistry experiment with bath salts, lotions and oils, I lit candles, played arias sung by an angelic chanteuse and turned off the lights. It was serene and peaceful, beautiful and calming. Each week, I should plan a nice date with myself, whether going to dinner, the movies, taking a bath or a beautiful walk, something just for me.

So, all of a sudden, I find myself in a fit of tears and wonder why the waterworks today? I was thinking about how the most difficult kind of love is unrequited love. The kind of love that is insinuated by both parties but not boldly claimed. It wreaks havoc on both souls. There is less pain in confronting or acknowledging a lover's lack of desire than both having desire and never acting upon it. You remove the vague hopes and intentions. You aimlessly wonder and daydream, and then catch yourself in the act. You think you move on or get lost in work and other activities, then by chance fall upon the person's gaze, memory or thoughts, and remember the beauty of that person's soul and start dreaming again. Then you get caught unawares since you alone hold the dream, and the other has walked off down a different path while you were too busy pretending not to notice. Perhaps they, too, waited for you by the tree, but forgot to tell you that they would be there, or did not see you come. They then became disheartened and walked off, thinking that you neglected them in some way. So, both of you walk off, thinking the other has forgotten them. Forsaken and forlorn, you both distract yourselves and move onto another quest, some impersonal challenge that consumes your attention. For that would be easier than claiming the love you desire, but are afraid to grasp. Today, that is why I cry. The eerie song of another haunts me, the dream of a love that will not be. I am a siren of the lost dreamer. I have to find my way out of this dark, enchanting forest for I fear that if I do not, I will be forever lost.

As they say, everything happens for a reason. As time passes, I will understand and appreciate why this love never grew.

Chapter 36

The Marine-Soldier On

NOTHING COULD BE WORSE THAN BEING WITH THE WRONG person. I knew Richard and I would not work, but thought we could have some fun together. As they say, while waiting for Mr. Right, have fun with Mr. Right Now.

Richard and I met at the San Francisco airport three and a half years ago. He was flirting with me, and I was reading Vogue magazine, flipping through the pages. I had time to kill before my flight, so I talked with him. He was an older Italian man, a marine living in Hawaii. On one hand, not my type at all, but my type is emotionally unavailable bad boys, so we exchanged emails and started a rapport.

He was always very sexual in his emails and instant messages. He was always insinuating that he wanted to visit me among other things. We would talk about our past relationships. We were friends who flirted. We were in and out of many relationships but would drop each other an email or instant message, or talk on the phone. Through the course of our conversations, I learned more about him and his interesting past. He told me that he's a divorcee with two children and that his ex-wife cheated. I should have started running.

I did not go home for Christmas this year and decided to throw a little dinner party on Christmas day for the other orphans. Richard decided to fly from Hawaii to meet me and spend some time together.

I honestly did not think he was coming. I thought he would change his mind at the last minute—maybe I was secretly hoping he would change his mind. He arrived at the United terminal on the night of Christmas Eve. He was wearing brown pants and shoes with a beige button-down shirt and heavy black leather jacket. He tilted his head to the side often and had a cocky walk. When he saw me, we gave each other a hug.

"Am I what you remembered?" he asked.

"Yes, for the most part. Am I the same as you remember?" I asked.

"You look better. Your hair is different, and you look slimmer."

"I was thinner when I met you, you big jerk! How was your flight? Are you tired?"

"No," he said. "I took a Xanax and fell asleep immediately. I woke up when they served food, ate and went back to sleep. I woke up as we were landing."

"Great. My car is over here."

I opened the trunk, and he put his two backpacks in the car. As I drove, he kept asking how far away we were from my place.

We arrived at my condo in Hollywood. I showed him my place and turned the Christmas tree lights on. I love looking at the lights on my beautiful tree. I invited Richard to sit down on the couch in the living room and made us some cosmopolitans. He told me how beautiful I look and that he likes my legs. I showed him my balcony.

"You have a lot of plants. I like your place, it's a nice set up," he said.

"Thanks, I like it too. Richard, are you hungry? I made some chili for dinner, would you like some?"

"Sure."

I set the table for him. I removed my table runner that I want to use for Christmas dinner, so that there was no chance of anything staining it. I set a place mat and napkin for him. I heated up the chili and put the garnishes on it, sour cream and cheddar cheese. I placed the food in front of him.

He inhaled the food and said he enjoyed it. He asked for more. I fed him some more and at that point he was stuffed, as well he should have been. It is a filling dish. We cleaned up the dishes and had another drink. It was getting late and we went to bed. I was distracted by the fact that a man was in my bed. We kissed and touched each other. His style was rough, which is not good for me.

He was commanding in bed and liked things his way.

After days of his whining and bossiness, I was fed up with him. He had given me backhanded compliments, trying to use his drill sergeant tactics on me. Break down my spirit and then build me up again. I am too smart for that. Disturbed by his cruelty and too smart to stay entangled, I planned ways to minimize contact with him and pictured how I would end this meaningless encounter.

By the last evening, I am practically in tears as I ask my neighbor, Mike, if he would like to join us for dinner. I tell Mike that I never want marriage, or children, and don't even think I want a relationship. Because if I had to marry Richard, a selfish lover, a selfish man, who is unromantic, demanding, and demeaning, there would be no point. It would be like slavery or jail with no chance of parole. I knew that my soul would die. I would never allow myself to be so mistreated. As kindly as I could, I told Richard I did not want a relationship with him. His silence was understandable. Maybe I should have waited, but I did not want to carry my anger around anymore.

I have vowed to myself to love and appreciate myself more. I should be thankful for all that I have, to know that I choose my fate each and every day. I will not marry someone to fulfill a biological or societal pressure. I can only marry for love. It may not happen in this lifetime, and that is OK. I'd rather be true to myself than live a life of misery and hopelessness. I may not actually be a pioneer or a revolutionary, but I feel as if I am, somehow. Telling friends, family, and colleagues how I feel is my battle cry.

Chapter 37

On Pointe

MIRACLES DO HAPPEN. I DREAMT OF BEING A BALLERINA AS A child. I used to stare at the older dancers while they were finishing class as I was waiting for my class as a little girl. I would look at all the pictures of dancers striking incredible poses, with their slim and lean legs that are straight next to their ear with pointed feet.

I have been dancing for the past several years. I have tried different ballet instructors and schools but always danced with Katya, an aspiring ballerina who teaches ballet class when not auditioning for ballet companies or performing. Katya and I became friends.

One day, I arrive at the studio for class. I am in my usual black sleeveless leotard with black tights that cut off before the ankle. I stretch and warm up before class.

"Hi, how are you?" asked Katya. "It will just be you today in class."

"Okay, I am fine," I said, stretching on the floor while we were speaking.

"Let's pull out the bar and begin class," she suggested.

Katya and I walked over to the mirrored wall where all the bars were. Katya stood on one end of the bar and I on the other end. We lifted the bar at the same time, walked toward the middle of the room, and placed the bar so class could begin.

As Katya walked away and toward the stereo and her chair, I stretched my calves on the bar.

Katya said, "Facing the barre, give me two tendu devant, 2 a la seconde, 2 in arabesque, en croix, demi and other foot, two times, releve and hold." As she said the choreography, she mimicked her request with her hands.

"Okay," I responded.

"Ready?"

"Yes."

Katya turned the music on and counted. I executed the choreography as requested. I was moving my legs and trying to stand extremely straight with pelvis tucked in, shoulders back and stomach in. I was dancing as if in a trance, and looking at my feet in the mirror.

Katya was also looking at my feet and body position, commenting as the dancing is occurring.

Katya yelled emphatically, "Shoulders, turn out more, feet-pointe those feet!"

As the combination was complete, and the music ended, Katya said "Good, your legs are looking good. Ok, now give me tendu from fifth, 1, 2, pause 1, 2, 3, devant, side, en croix, repeat with jeté, releve, hold passé."

We progressed through all of the standard barre exercises: fondu with rond de jambe en lair, rond de jambe with jette passe, adagio, and other staples. The music started, Katya counted in and I moved as directed. Katya had a pleasant smile on her face and says, "I think you are ready for your pointe shoes."

When I finished the combination, I excitedly asked, "Really? What happens next?"

Katya in an irritated voice said, "I tell you, you are ready, and we go shopping for shoes. It's that simple. You just buy them."

I asked because Katya has been promising these shoes for months now. It felt to me like an elusive dream. Every time my ballet instructor would tell me I am ready for the shoes, there would be a correction that required urgent attention and took weeks to remedy. The list was growing longer and longer, and months had passed since the last serious mention of pointe shoes.

I felt that I could study for the LSAT, pass and get a law degree faster than getting the approval from Katya for pointe shoes. So as happy as I was to hear Katya's approval for the beautiful ballet shoes, I understood that it was not the same thing as having the shoes on my feet. So, I kept dancing, listening to the choreography, taking the corrections and applying them without much serious thought to the constant comments about pointe shoes. I had heard these remarks many times in many classes before.

As I finished adagio, a slow, excruciating Développé leg extension in each direction one time on flat and then on relevé, with a passé hold. Katya said, "It's time. Congratulations, you are getting your pointe shoes!" She had a big, beaming smile, and looked so proud.

I was so overjoyed and could not wait to complete the combination. My legs were shaking from tiredness and strain, but I finished the combination with lightness and joy. I was so elated. I almost felt like this was a dream. Squealing with delight as my instructor repeated, "Congratulations! You are ready. Your legs look great. I will bring in some shoes on Tuesday's class. What you will need to buy are: some ribbons, a stitch kit, and ouch pads. Bring them to the next class, and we can begin working on pointe. Let's wrap up center work for the day."

In utter joy, I ran over to Katya and hugged her. "I am so excited! I can't believe it's finally happening. I will finally have my pointe shoes. I thought this day would never arrive. Okay, we will plan a time for dinner to celebrate this." After some combinations in center and some jumps, I was able to stretch and do my front and back splits.

"Okay give me reverence," said Katya.

As I did the ballet bow to the right and then left, I clapped my hands and said thank you for class.

After stretching out my sore muscles and putting on black sweat pants, a black tank top and a black sweatshirt on over leotard and tights, I gave Katya a big hug, thanked her, and walked out of the studio. I was ready for pointe shoes. I was so excited by my good fortune! I had to call my friend, Julie.

I had my first lesson on pointe. The shoes are beautiful, and I love that they are pink satin with pink satin ribbons. The beauty ends there. Trying to stand on your toes is so hard, and then standing on your toes onto one leg while the other leg lifts without falling over is excruciatingly difficult!

Chapter 38

Risky Business

ONE DAY I RECEIVED A PHONE CALL FROM A COLLEAGUE FROM one of the large consulting firms where I used to work. He had started an independent consulting company and was pitching a new client and wanted to know if I would work for him. It was a large pharmaceutical company, and the pay would be more than double what I was currently making. It was an irresistible offer.

I researched the company and prepared for the interviews. I accepted the job and started a new life one month later as an independent consultant. This job as an independent consultant would be my first time without a corporate identity. I left my office, title, and short commute to take this risk.

My daily commute was from Hollywood to Orange County—which is quite grueling, to be in a car for more than three 3 hours a day, depending on traffic. I realized that I did not ask enough questions. I did not ask about payment terms or my new boss's working style. Although we were on the same project before, we never actually worked closely together.

Once I joined his company for this project, my rate was significantly less than what we discussed. Also, the payment terms for an independent consultant or contractor is much longer than a full-time employee. If I had known this upfront, I might have changed my mind about taking such a bold step. Sometimes it is better not to know all the details or one will never make that change or take that step. The mantle of corporate security is hard to shake.

I did complete the project, but it was very difficult working for a controlling person. I did make more money and that was what I wanted, but it came at a big price.

My boss and I were no longer friends after this experience. I learned that one must investigate how something will affect you. That one does not always need to sell themselves. The potential employer needs to sell to *you* why their company is a good choice, why you should take a gamble on them and make them successful. I needed to remember that I am the talent, and my brain is a product. I needed to remember to not sell myself at a discount, to mark myself down as if I am last season's items that did not sell.

The personality conflict between my boss and I also made me realize that I was unhappy with the corporate career path that I had chosen by default. I did something respectable, but not something that I was passionate about. I was ignoring my true nature by repressing it to fit the model employee that I needed to be in order to excel in the corporate environment.

I was never ready to take the risk until now, never confident to venture off the well-marked path. The path I chose was not unlike the one I was on; the only difference was that now I was responsible for finding my work, for obtaining contracts and negotiating every detail for myself.

Later, I would learn that this risk would pay off in that it taught me to hunt for myself. I learned how to find and procure my work, a tool that I would need for the career goals that I have for myself, to be an independent and published author.

Chapter 39

On the Edge

A FTER THE PROJECT ENDED, MY FIRST ONE AS AN INDEPEN-
dent consultant, I did not realize that there would be a significant time lag before my next project, something I had never experienced before. Although I had savings and was diligently job searching,
I started to become stressed and fearful that I would not find another
project.

I wrote in my journal a private reverie, one of pain and sadness
with bursts of sunny memories. It had been four months now since my
last project and more since my last pay check. I was burning through
my savings. The transition to independent consultant was a lot harder than I had imagined. Now I was responsible for finding my next
project, my next client, which was not an automatic occurrence. I had
always easily had great jobs and excellent pay. I never imagined myself

in this current situation. I never thought that I would not have enough money for my next mortgage payment. No extra income for the rest of the month's bills. I was not booking the jobs. I did not know where to go. No one could help or even suggest help to me. Instead, they blamed me for my situation, except one or two dear friends. In this situation, my family was the worst critical and apathetic voice I had in my ear. I did not regret leaving the stable job because I was deeply unhappy, underpaid and unrecognized for all of my contributions. Also, the department I worked for was reorganized and dismantled, so really, there is a strong possibility that I would have been in an even worse predicament than I was now.

It is times like these that I find myself utterly alone in the physical plane. I do believe in God, angels, Ascended Masters; spirit guides are around me and helping me. They are trying to answer my frequent prayers for help. I was trying to remember how I got out of my last difficult situation. How did I manage? What did I do to land that job and be okay and have everything covered? I needed the inspiration and hope to continue.

I felt no hope or joy. I didn't know a solution other than death. Can one have a painless death? I didn't know where to go or what to do. I prayed, chanted, visualized, and said positive affirmations. I reached out to everyone I knew. I searched for jobs. I felt sad and alone.

I spoke with my friend Elise. She is smart, compassionate and down to earth. She has been a great friend and teacher to me, always sharing books, ideas, and suggestions. She kindly came to Hollywood and treated me to dinner.

At the restaurant, I confessed my fear of not finding a job and possibly having to leave my place. I told her how I sent résumés every day and had interviews, but nothing was sticking. This experience was my first time without a job.

"I was reading a great book, and there was an interesting suggestion that I think you should try," she suggests.

"Oh really? What is it called?" I ask.

"Well, I forget the name of the book, but in this book I just read, this woman was talking about how she was always experiencing negative things and lack…and one day she tired of feeling that way. So, she decided to write a gratitude journal every day for everything in her life that bothered her. She would write, I am grateful for my ugly house. I am grateful for the ugly walls. As she did this every day, all of these small miracles started happening. She went to the hardware store, and the paint was on sale so much that she was able to repaint all of the walls in her house. Or that money came to her. Things she said she was grateful for no longer bothered her."

"Hmm, that is interesting, so you journal for what you don't want, what's bothering you? I don't understand how it works."

"I think it works because you stop focusing on what you don't want. As you do that first thing every day, it no longer is a problem and gives way to something better. I think it's part of the Law of Attraction in that you no longer are giving power to what you don't want by being grateful for it and acknowledging it, so you let it go. The author said she did it nonstop for 40 days and saw miracles in her life."

"I am not sure about this," I replied with a skeptic's tone.

"Well think of it this way: you have nothing to lose. Try it and see."

As she said those words, I realized that she was right. I had nothing to lose. This activity would not interfere with all the things I had been doing to find a job. So, I set out the next day to do it.

159

I got a journal, and every morning wrote all the things that I feared and was unhappy about with gratitude. "I am grateful that I do not yet know when I will have my next job." A few days later I received an email requesting a face to face meeting with a VP at the company I left. Every day I continued to write in my gratitude journal. As things happened, it changed what I wrote about.

I decided to go to Irvine and meet the executive face to face. I wrote a formal thank you letter and recapped my experience and interest working for the company. The next day, I received a request to submit a proposal on a project. I went from desolation and despair to success and hope within a week.

I now know the power of the gratitude journal, to journal for all that bothers me and to say that I am grateful for it. My proposal was accepted by the director. This was exciting news. My start date was in three weeks.

I was and am deeply grateful for everyone involved: Elise for the suggestion, the VP and director who brought me on board, and for the vendor who processed my invoices and always paid me on time.

It's such a relief that the job worked out for me. I did not know what I would have done. I also now know that the gratitude journal is a powerful tool and share this with anyone who is in need of a little miracle to turn their luck around.

So much can change with just a thought. On Memorial Day weekend I was crying, feeling sorry for myself and contemplating suicide. Three weeks later, I had pitched for two projects, and had other potential opportunities to contemplate. I now know that I will be able to make money as an independent consultant and pay my mortgage. As a bonus, I have a date with someone who is exciting and successful, and have many interesting things to do. All is well. Sometimes, in the eleventh hour, everything works out fine. You do not appreciate it or believe it until the very end. After imagining all the horrible scenarios that can happen to you—being penniless, destitute, out on the street—you realize that everything came together for you, and the horrible imaginings of disaster are averted.

Now I realize that my mind should not automatically arrive at the conclusion of wreckage and chaos as the first option. My mind should not have disaster planning as an option at all. This new way of thinking is something that I would have to train myself to do. Panic and disaster scenario planning should not be an automatic response. There are many options in between, and the first option should be an assumption that all is well, and all will turn out exactly as it should, and in the best way possible for everyone involved.

Chapter 40

Dark Night of the Soul

THE FINANCIAL HICCUP AT THE WRONG TIME THAT PUT ME IN a situation where I was at the edge of the cliff, hanging on for dear life, still had repercussions throughout my life. The bank would continue to send me requests to apply for a new loan modification every six months for over two years, so it always felt unfinished and tenuous. My subconscious mind would inform me what was happening, what I was ignoring during waking hours. I would dream of falling off cliffs, of a policeman telling me I did something wrong. Our soul tells us the truth whether we are ready to hear it or not.

I was too prideful to discuss this issue with anyone but my closest friends. I managed to restructure my home loan again via a home loan modification and then slowly began refocusing on the basics. I prayed intensely and now understand the power of prayer. I prayed for the opportunity to make everything right. My prayers became answered as I was able to work on multiple projects and make more money. I was negotiating with my bank regularly. When my home loan got sold to another bank, the new bank did not recognize my loan modification and demanded the money in one payment and threatened the "F" word—foreclosure—if the balance was not at zero within six months.

By now my depression had lifted and my feet were firmly planted in reality. I knew what I needed to do. I worked non-stop, took on more projects, and created a payment plan with the bank to pay off the past due balance in six long hard, grueling months. All of my money went to my past due mortgage and it needed to be on time. I paid every cent of the balance. The personal mortgage debacle was confusing, because my loan modification should have incorporated the past due balance into the loan and the life of the loan extended. It was as if I lived the threat of foreclosure twice.

Unfortunately, I learned many valuable lessons the hard way, such as:

Make sure all the details of your business, whether pleasant or unpleasant, are complete and wrapped up. Follow up is essential to success.

Past issues will haunt you until acknowledged. I relived the abandonment I felt as a child, being without parents in an orphanage during the war. Now that I finally dealt with it face to face, I am free to move beyond this test, this experience, but that was not always the case.

Like a predator, my abandonment issues stalked and followed me every step I took. Attacking when I felt safe, always lurking in the shadows. Then my predator stalked me in broad daylight, charging with full force, demanding my attention and staring me in the eyes, wrestling me to the ground and knocking the wind out of me. My fear said, as its sharp paws tried to snap my windpipe and suffocate me with despair, "You must reckon with me. You must face the beast that is me." My fear wanted to subdue me. "I will not be dormant, living on the edge of your awareness. I am here, always."

After the crying and screaming, the denial and the shame passed, I realized that I am not a victim to this tragic event. I created this unfortunate series of events with my fearful thoughts and passive actions. I could un-create the situation and create a better one for me, an experience that is more pleasant. I summoned all of the knowledge that I had been reading or advised about to help me solve my problems. Like a gale wind, I channeled the spirit of positive thinking and remembered that nothing is real, there is no wrong way. I am here to learn, to be responsible, to love others and myself. I am here to understand emotions and past events and move forward. I recalled reading that anything can change in an instant, a thought, if powerful, forceful and genuine, can change my reality in a moment. I do not need to wait to die in the grip of fear. I can choose a different ending, but I must choose and commit to it. I must not waiver in my conviction of redemption.

Fear will dominate you and annihilate you if you let it. I almost did. In the end, I realized the worst that could happen was more about who I think I am, or what others think I am, than my true self. For one's true self does not need things or external affirmation. Your pure self has no need for designer labels or shoes or a swanky address. Your eternal self needs love and joy that cannot be bought with a credit card. Your eternal self knows that suffering is from desire, from discomfort with your true nature. All it desires is the embrace of kindness and acceptance. I had to master my fear, to conquer the insecurity and doubt by dealing with what it brought me, by facing the truth. As I did so, my fear weakened and ceased to torment me. By debunking the fear,

I took away its power, and it became no more than a thought, just like any other, with no residual emotion, requiring no more attention.

I realized then that Timothy the shaman was right, but not for the reasons he stated. It was my abandonment that was my biggest burden and limited me in ways I had not fathomed. As I became proactive, paying off the monthly payments to the bank, I had written every morning in my gratitude journal and prayed to make enough money to pay the past due and maintain my normal life. I was able to do all of this and more. As the balance grew smaller and smaller, I felt more confident and safer. I knew that I had stood at the edge of the cliff and looked down. I had contemplated the impact of the fall. I gathered my senses and summoned my strength and the strength of all I could pray to for deliverance for help. My prayers were answered.

I used the tools I learned about to help me through this crisis. The gratitude journal, sending everyone involved love, meditating, chanting, asking for help and visualizing a positive ending. I came to understand that these were the methods I would use to transition gracefully from lack to plenty.

I realize that there are angels here to help you, heavenly and earthly. You have to ask for their help, and you have to take responsibility for your actions. You must do your part, but if you do, you will be rewarded in ways beyond your imagination. I was advised to send love to everyone involved and imagine the best outcome possible. To be thankful for the help, I received and to be accountable for my actions. I had no one to blame but myself. I let the balls drop in the air, no one else. I made the bad decisions. No one forced them on me.

A series of problems and challenges that I dealt with proved a pivotal moment in my life. When I paid off the past due balance and everything went back to a calm state, I noticed that my energy had returned. I was able to handle a lot of scope and pressure and perform at a high level. The sadness of feeling alone and abandoned had dissipated. It was as if I were emerging from a long, dark underground tunnel and slowly saw a distant light approaching, signaling that the end of the dark is near.

The experience helped me to understand the dark night of the soul. The dark night of the soul was a time for my eternal self to face its fears. It was the time in my life where I was forced to fall off the edge of a precipice of illusion—that sharp, stony cliff—and to survive it, to illuminate it, to overcome it. When you have experienced the darkest night, you can recognize this event in others, you can tell by their eyes, the vibration they give off. Now you can try to encourage and enlighten others, but need to remember that this is a personal time for the sufferer. The troubled soul needs to learn how to end their suffering on their terms and in their way. Your kind words and gestures can be like a lifeboat to buoy their faith or hope and to help them pass through their treacherous journey. A kind word or gesture can help cast away the shadows for a brief moment.

When all seems lost, when you are forced to let go of material possessions, you are really at a crossroads to choose a higher path, a better way for yourself. When you feel most alone and vulnerable, just know that you are not alone. Beside you walk angels and Ascended Masters, besides you is the spirit of the divine entity you pray to. They will help lift your burden, pray and ask them out loud, on paper, or in your head, for help, ask them to help show you the way to the light. They will always give you a simple answer. They will always point you to the most loving direction. That is how you know it is them, it is your angels. If you doubt the advice, you will hear it in passing. It will be in an article, maybe, or someone will come up to you and tell you exactly what you need to hear. You are guided to the answer. That is how I slowly found my way back through the desert to the oasis. That is how I learned not to fear abandonment, because we are not alone.

I have seen others experience similar events and now know what it is and know how to comfort them. The biggest thing we can do to shift the sad and negative energy is to replace it with a happy memory at will until you start feeling good again. The mind doesn't know if it is happening or experiencing a memory. The body will respond to the more positive vibration just as easily as it will to the negative one, so why not try to select the positive thought or feeling?

Chapter 41

Rebuilding

PAYING OFF THE DEBT AND WORKING WERE SIGNS THAT MY LIFE was improving; however, just as a seed grows roots underground before it breaks through the earth, I was getting closer to the light, but not yet completely out of the dark tunnel.

I had witnessed manifestation in practice and started believing in my intuition more. I started connecting more with my spirit in quiet time, in prayer. I started to stay home more or walk in nature, in the woods or by the ocean. Each walk helped renew my soul and trust that all is well.

It's amazing how powerful music can be. It heals and touches the soul in a way more profound than any prescription drug can. I am sitting in my French Louis XVI style chairs at my Provençal style table listening to Sarah Brightman's angelic voice sing Rachmaninov's "How

Fair this Spot". This song is a piece of heaven. Her voice careens and caresses your soul and the notes are soothing like piece of silk against your skin. I see fields of green, undisturbed nature when I hear this song. The violins are like a gentle wind carrying this angel's voice to all of us. The song is peace itself.

I am in a new phase of life, that of rebuilding, as I learn to manifest what is good and to love myself.

I bought a piano and started playing music again. Music can transport your soul into other dimensions of awareness, to help you feel serenity and love. Music helps you feel inspired and keeps you in awe of the majesty of the universe. Beautiful, soulful music has an ethereal quality about it, making you wonder if it was channeled by more advanced beings, if the composer is connected in spirit and the angels gifted him or her with the ear of this heavenly, other worldly aria. The song is a gift for tuning into the muse. I only say that because it is so perfect and complete, it is angelic.

Chapter 42

Warrior

ONE NIGHT WHILE SLEEPING, I HAD A DREAM SEQUENCE ON the astral plane that was so real, so gripping that I must have been there.

My soul alights onto an astral plane and I arrive in a beautiful white kimono with an embroidered floral pattern on it, with light blue, orange, pink, green and purple chrysanthemums and vines. I arrive in a stone courtyard with cherry trees and wisteria blanketed by mist. As I walk through the cold and empty courtyard, faces and people appear until I arrive in a place where my spirit guide is, along with samurai and other warriors, both men and women.

Welcome Tristan, you have chosen to fulfill your destiny. We have been calling out to you, but only now are you strong enough to answer the call. I nod my head, mesmerized, as if it makes complete sense. A part of myself connects with this and knows what will happen before it unfolds before me.

"I am Sara, your spirit guide. I have come to show you the way of the warrior." Sara is a tall, lean Caucasian woman. She has blonde hair and blue eyes. Her face is narrow, and her fingers are long. She has a sense of strength and poise about her. She is elegant and strong at the same time. She has visited me before. She was my guide in Vietnam and reminds me of her presence once in a while.

"As a single woman, you will transition from girlish innocence to the heart of a warrior. You will not make this change through violence; however, you will die, kill and be killed. Just as a samurai, the soldier, the Spartan have learned the art of warfare, learned to forgo pleasure for freedom, so will you. Blood and tears flow in both instances; however, you will shed metaphorical blood and actual tears.

"You ask what is the heart of a warrior? Is it not only the strength to take a life to protect others? Is it to face your mortality with honor? The answer is yes. However, it can be through spirit and not through flesh. You are a warrior of spirit, because you will fight for your freedom to be who you are without constraint. In doing, so, you fight and defend all others who wish for the same freedom to be without persecution and judgment. You fight to help others to be their authentic self. You fight for the right to be unconventional and not conform, to imagine a better and more harmonious way to live for all.

"Know that when you are true to your authentic self, against ridicule, you fight a war for others who don't have the courage to do so, but can benefit from your example. The lessons you learn you must pass on and share with others. In turn pass on the code of the warrior and teach them to pass it on, like a torch to burn bright throughout eternity within each person's being. When you believe that you are worthy even though you are betrayed, undermined, belittled, you show the fierce heart of the warrior. You fight to protect your honor, your word, which is to show integrity, a lost value."

This dream exchange showed me that inspiration and understanding come in such mysterious and ironic ways. *Xena: The Warrior Princess,* showed us Taoism's central principle, The Way, in an episode. The episode explored the old notion that power is ruthless and to have will over another is to have power, but to have will over one's self is to know the way. You can only achieve that when you stop willing, stop desiring. I see what that means.

Impatience and action can be detrimental to your end objective. I saw that from my situation. All of the activity I pour into things doesn't mean that they will happen any sooner. I can bulldoze people into fulfilling my will, but that is an empty type of power. To know the way, I think, is to harness the power of creation. In the episode of *Xena,* it meant to harness the power of heaven and earth. Only when you can let go of anger, pain, resentment, and the negative can you have a positive energy available to use for good.

At the crossroads of life, we enter many times that intersection of the old ways, fear and new hope for a better life for yourself, for your dreams. You break or bend the rules by arriving to work late, expressing your unwanted opinion, suggesting alternative ideas. The tendency is to shrink back and allow others to influence you or to tell you that you are not enough, and that you are wrong. Be brave, be strong, and speak what is true and pure. Sometimes rules need to be adjusted and questioned, and new thoughts need to appear. Otherwise, we are dead fish swimming with the tide. Dare to be true to what you believe to be right.

Controlling your desire to lash out and run away is to control yourself, to have will over yourself. Instead of reacting, remind yourself of your greater purpose, your ultimate goal. Hold your course and steer your ship. Pray for the happiness of those who torment you and make you guess yourself. Pray for their happiness, for they are afraid. You will leave them behind as you move forward. Speak your truth with love for what you say about others will be said about you. Know that you are protected and loved. No one can hurt you unless you allow it to be so.

I refuse to allow people to hurt my feelings, to make me feel wrong anymore. Those are past experiences that I will keep behind me. I send love and happiness into the world and pray for my enemies. In the end, when we all turn to dust, these small battles will be memories. I want my memories to be beautiful and to be meaningful.

Sara reminds me that I will receive visits by different animal guides. Each animal guide will teach me a lesson, ushering in a new chapter of my life. Since all life is connected, these lessons are to be shared for all of humanity.

I see the panorama of the different faces of warriors of all kinds: beautiful, strong, delicate. The mist grows thick once more. The cherry trees and stone courtyard now fade in the mist.

I awoke with these fleeting thoughts that I wrote down.

Chapter 43

Introductions

I LEFT THE BUSY PACE OF MANAGEMENT CONSULTING AND worked for a large entertainment company near my home. I met a lot of great and interesting people during my short tenure there.

As part of the team at Warner Brothers, I quickly learned that the climate was chaotic and hectic, not at all the peaceful and cohesive picture presented during the interviews. There was a lot of political drama and tension, and most people in my department were unhappy and stressed…all, that is, but one person. I noticed how calm she was every day and asked her what her secret was.

She told me that she chants *nam myo ho renge kyo* and is a practicing Nichiren Shoshu Buddhist. She also explained that we have created our good and bad karma, so if you chant *nam myo ho renge kyo* daily, you are cleaning/eradicating your bad karma, which will help improve your life. She also stated that the practice is one of actual proof. This idea of chanting intrigued me, so I googled it and tried it for myself. At first I chanted just to be more calm and centered.

I noticed instantly that I felt happier and more at peace, and continued to chant.

One day, I was struggling with my new boss's erratic behavior. Sometimes my boss was kind but mostly irrational, accusatory, forgetful, and aggressive. So, I asked my friend what to do. She said to chant for his happiness.

After chanting for his happiness consistently his behavior toward me greatly improved, and we began getting along, although his behavior toward others remained the same. In addition, my friend brought me to the temple and taught me gongyo, which are the daily prayers recited every morning and evening in Japanese. I learned gongyo in front of a Gohonzon, the enshrinement of the essence of the Buddha and his life, the essence of enlightenment. So, my practice was developing. As a result of practicing and my natural skills, I obtained a solid performance review with compliments (that was a miracle in itself). Eventually, we all saw an improvement with our boss as he tried becoming more supportive to others. To the surprise of all, my boss was laid off.

Eventually, he found another job and was doing better than ever. The layoff gave him a break from work to reconnect with friends and family. I was an unofficial reference for him, and kept everything positive.

As I had stated earlier, my main reason for chanting was to feel more centered and calm, stop worrying and being anxious over everything and everyone.

As obstacles appeared there was no longer panic, just the realization that I have negative karma to work through and to increase chanting.

I no longer called everyone I know to ask for their opinion or to vent about issues (another miracle in itself).

I started experiencing a lot of car troubles. The mechanic told me to replace my engine, yet when I first came to them a year before, they said there was nothing wrong with the engine. So that alarmed me. As I chanted and told my Buddhist friends, another temple member told me about her incredible mechanic, that he was excellent, honest and inexpensive. She helped arrange an appointment, and he fixed my car, proving to me that I did not need a new engine and confirming my suspicion that the other mechanics did not do the job I paid them to do. He helped fix my problem for $800, a tiny fraction of what I had paid prior.

I applied chanting to my health. I have high blood pressure and mitral valve prolapse (my valve from the aorta to the left ventricle does not close all the way, so I believe that is why my heart has to pump harder). I think my high blood pressure is due to the mitral valve prolapse. However, sadly, my doctor doesn't agree with my analysis. My cardiologist told me that I would need to be on medication for the rest of my life. It seems crazy, since I have always been an athlete. In junior high and high school, I did cross country, track, winter track, and swim team. I lettered in Varsity by sophomore year. I continue to run, hike, swim, work out with a trainer, and take ballet classes weekly. I would get cramps and numbness in my feet and legs. I thought that was because of dancing on pointe, but after talking with a friend I realized that it was due to the medication that uses snake venom to thin your blood. I started researching more natural ways to reduce blood pressure and started meeting with an acupuncturist. When I met with the acupuncturist, she took my blood pressure for a benchmark. I had already reduced it to 140/88 on my own via herbal supplements. With acupuncture, I am now at 132/88 after two visits. I am in the normal/high range all on my own and of course with a little help from my friend, the Gohonzon.

My observation about this practice so far is that your experience with chanting will be personal and unique to your life. However, there are some benefits that we will all share. For example, everyone will experience a greater sense of peace and serenity in their life. So much so that people will notice and ask why you are glowing, are you in love or are you pregnant? In addition, obstacles in your life will not be as overwhelming, and the right solution will appear for you. And most importantly, you will experience increased compassion for everyone and yourself. Because Buddhists not only chant for world peace and peace for the deceased, but your heart grows and allows you to share more of yourself with others in a healthy way. You will be inspired to share the benefits of the practice with others so that they too can feel the peace and happiness that you feel when chanting, doing gongyo and connecting with the Gohonzon. In fact, I know that it was through the great compassion of our friends that all of us were drawn here to start our journey with this practice.

Chapter 44

Mio Solo

DRIVING AROUND THE CITY, I RECEIVED A CALL FROM MY FA-vorite ballerina, Katya.

"Hi, Tristan, how are you?" she asked.

"Hey, you! It's great to hear from you. I am fine, how are you?"

"I am well, thanks. Are you interested in seeing the Mark Morris Group perform Sunday at 2:00 at the Dorothy Chandler Pavilion? I would go, but will be out of town, and I immediately thought of you."

"It depends. How much are the tickets?"

"No cost…the tickets are free. My gift to you."

"Really? Wow, yes, sign me up."

"Okay I will confirm with you if it's two or four tickets and then help arrange for you to pick them up," she offered.

"Thank you so much for the tickets. I look forward to attending the event!"

I proceeded to call my friends to invite them to join me for a free event. All of my friends replied that they are busy. Their responses made me realize that many people do not appreciate the fine arts, which is ironic living in a city built on entertainment. I think that creativity in any form is noteworthy and an interesting way to study or draw inspiration from other forms of expression. So, with the lack of interest on the part of friends, I decided to attend the event by myself, not letting lack of companionship deprive me of a golden opportunity to watch a dance company perform, especially since the tickets were free.

Saturday quickly came, and after completing my workout with my trainer, I went to my hair salon in Beverly Hills. I sauntered into the salon excited and happy, and was greeted by my statuesque stylist with air kisses. My stylist noticed that I have a big shiny ring on my finger and proceeded to tease me about it.

"Girl, take that ring off that finger and place it on your other hand!" said my stylist, Naomi.

"Why? Don't you like it?" I questioned.

"I love it but then no man will want to buy you a ring if he sees that on your hand."

"That's ridiculous!" I responded.

"So where are we going tonight?" she asked.

"Nowhere, it's for tomorrow. I am going to see the Mark Morris Group perform tomorrow. Do you want to come? I have an extra ticket."

"Oh, I would love to but I can't. I am going to Vegas with my mother, but thank you for the invite."

"Okay, no worries," I responded.

Sunday finally arrived, and I am excited for my little adventure. I wear a beautiful fitted strapless silk black cocktail dress with a beaded sweater and Jimmy Choo black peep toe pumps. My hair, makeup, and jewelry were perfect and classic. I looked like I was ready for the show. I drove to the performance, praying that I would arrive on time and be able to find my seat before it started as there was so much traffic on the 101. I was anxiously pulling out my ticket which states clearly, NO LATE SEATING. I began pleading with the angels to help me reach my seat before the curtain. Please Archangel Michael…help me get there on time. Miraculously, I made it even though there were traffic delays and a blocked street before the parking garage. I was able to be seated as the performance is beginning and let out a sigh of relief as I found my place. I was pleasantly surprised that the free tickets were in the perfect location, in the orchestra section. I felt so sophisticated and glamorous, looking fabulous and rocking the faux eyelashes and attending a performance on my own. As I looked around the audience, I saw couples and pockets of women who, just like me, were sitting by themselves. Yes, it is okay to do what you love and be alone in public. The curtain closed; the orchestra pit illuminated, and the most beautiful baroque music by Handel played.

The violins were delicate yet strong. You felt lulled into a beautiful dream. The curtain opened and people dressed in bright colors pranced about the stage while opera singers sang a poem by John Milton, set to Handel's score. You can hear Mozart in this music and felt as if both Handel and Mozart were watching the performance proudly and shared a synergy of form through their music. I became so relaxed and content. I felt so much joy and happiness and was glad that I did not let a little thing like attending an event by myself prevent me from watching a visually exciting performance. While listening to the most incredible music, I felt as if I had angels watching over me while being fanned on the famous shell, as depicted in Botticelli's painting, *The Birth of Venus*. I was content and at peace, surrounded by beauty.

Chapter 45

Corporate Gypsy

I AM A CORPORATE GYPSY. I AM TALENTED AND RESPONSIBLE, BUT unable to stay in one place for too long. I get anxious, restless, and need to move on constantly. It is challenging to stay calm, centered and peaceful when everything at work is chaotic.

I am continually in a state of unhappiness at work. I am frustrated by people's shortsightedness, lack of responsibility, overwhelming expectations, and limited reasoning skills. I am always seeking a way for a more simple and cohesive experience, with others or without them. I am not a person who will stay for many years in a situation that I have outgrown, where I feel underappreciated or disrespected.

They say that everything you experience happens for a reason. Either you must learn something or you are a teacher. They also say that you need to appreciate all that you have; even the difficult people and hardships are a gift in order to release something or recognize an important lesson and move on.

I do believe that we are always learning in each situation, and we learn most from the difficult times. I am also observing that it is difficult to shift your mind, thoughts, speech and habits to reflect what you want and not dwell on the undesirable things you are hoping to escape. That is the challenge, to transition from the state of negativity to that of a positive position. It takes so much effort: You must carefully monitor your thoughts and speech. You must spend time in nature and do things that you enjoy. You must be in a state of joy to create what you truly want.

Sitting on my shabby chic overstuffed chair, with fabric swatches ranging from green and pink toile to beige damask, I sing myself out of my bad mood.

The breeze is gentle and the cool evening air feels crisp. I think of songs from my childhood that I enjoyed. *My Fair Lady* comes to mind. I sing part of "Loverly", channeling Eliza Doolittle, herself in her Victorian rags singing in the streets of London imagining a better life for herself.

My soul tricks itself into singing by gently humming, and then in a soft soprano voice sings, *"All I want is a room somewhere, far away from the cold night air, whoever takes good care of me, oh wouldn't it be loverly? Lots of chocolate for me to eat, someone's head resting on my knee, whoever takes good care of me, oh wouldn't it be loverly, loverly, loverly, loverly, loverly?"*

I smile as I fondly remember singing in the play of *My Fair Lady* as a child and watching Audrey Hepburn portray Eliza Doolittle many times on the silver screen.

Another great song from the musical *Camelot* pops into my head. The song where Guinevere asks King Arthur, king of Camelot, in that famous song, "What do simple people do when they are blue?" One of his answers is that they sing.

I am taking King Arthur's advice and singing to shake the negative and toxic energy that I have been feeling after talking with different people lately. I started singing, *"The hills are alive with the sound of music,"* and picturing myself dancing on the Alps like Julie Andrews as Maria in the *Sound of Music*.

I ask my father's spirit what was a song that we used to sing together when I was a child. The name of the song that popped into my head was from the play *Annie*:

The Sun will come out tomorrow
Bet your bottom dollar that tomorrow
There'll be sun

Just thinkin' about
Tomorrow
Clears away the cobwebs, and the sorrow,
'Til there's none.

When I am stuck with a day
That's gray, and lonely,
I just stick out my chin
And grin, and say

The sun'll come out tomorrow
So ya gotta hang on 'til tomorrow
Come what may

Tomorrow, tomorrow
I love ya
Tomorrow

You're always a day away!

Flashback of me performing this song while playing the piano during the fifth grade recital. I remember that singing at the time was scary, but now just seems a comical memory.

Singing these songs does make me feel better. Somehow, singing while folding laundry and putting things away makes your place seem brighter and sunnier, even though it may be dark outside. I recommend singing to everyone.

Chapter 46

Calls: I Will Call You Tomorrow

L IKE MOST WOMEN, THE FANTASY OF BEING RESCUED BY A knight in shining armor has been replaced in the modern age with the image of a man with a well-paying job and assets. His financial security allows you to have the freedom to do whatever you please. Eventually, if you decided to delay getting married, the criterion for your knight gets more precise. You become harder to please. You are forced to make your dreams come true, as waiting passively for someone else to facilitate your personal desires becomes less attractive. It is not an option, since you have learned to be the master of your fate. I learned to take myself on vacation, buy myself jewelry, appreciate myself, and be committed to my career and my goals. I did not forgo an experience to wait for someone to do it for me.

It is interesting how one can be so focused and determined about something that your objective reasoning skills disappear, discarded for that idea of something. Especially when involving a potential relationship aroused by the desire for someone. Then, as time passes and your focus turns to other activities or interests, the initial obsession, for lack of a better term, fades or disappears. How fickle it seems is our human heart. Not like the rocks and mountains or trees that stand the winds for hundreds of thousands of years. It seems our attention may be fleeting. I reflect on the faces of people I was interested in and wonder why was I interested and why am I not now? I guess passion, or even love itself, is a flame that interest and desire must fuel. Otherwise, even the hottest fire will eventually grow cold.

When this sudden disinterest happens, you can look at relationships as companions. You can accept the good and the bad, as you know that you cannot change the object of your affection, and they cannot change you. You have more to bargain with because you won't give yourself away so cheaply. You can take yourself to dinner or on a vacation. You can buy your jewelry and accessories. Although they are not the benchmark of self-worth, they are reminders to not lower your value so easily. You are not on sale. You do not need to mark down or discount who you are to make someone else happy or to settle for anything or anyone you do not truly want.

Chapter 47

The End of the Road

HAVE YOU EVER DATED THAT ATTRACTIVE PERSON THAT YOU knew was trouble from the moment you saw them? The person you would avoid. The person who always found excuses to talk to you and blatantly asked you out, or asks for personal details. I let my guard down and dated an emotional disaster masquerading as a single man in Los Angeles. The type of guy who tells you they don't want a girlfriend, but they adore you, and if they wanted a serious relationship you would be it, you would be that girl. I knew better than to get entangled, but eventually stopped listening to reason, a dangerous habit of mine which always gets me into trouble.

Against my better judgment, after months of him chasing me and his flirting, I said yes to dinner. He is handsome and attractive. As we start our affair, he appears more charming than I imagined. Gary surprised me in many ways.

But there is a drawback, which is that he does not want a relationship. So, we have a fun affair, but he disappears without explanation. Or the story he tells me is that he is working. I know better. I know that I am wasting my time, so why do I continue?

I finally accept the limitations of my affair and appreciate what he has to offer, which is physical fun with an attractive person who compliments me. We have an extremely casual, no strings attached, on-again-off-again type of affair.

One night he comes to my place and takes me for a drive in his BMW, a two-door coupe with a turbo engine. He drives his fast car along the winding Mulholland Drive. He pulls over to the side of the road and blasts a song and gets out of the car and dances and sings for me. He made me laugh. Cars flashed their lights in appreciation of his dance.

He was always fun and physical. However, he was also disappointing and inconsistent. He never kept a promise. He would disappear like a ghost, leaving me to wonder of his existence.

He got lazy, sloppy, or whatever the reasons are. I will never know. I couldn't rely on him for our casual affair. I had to demote him as my friend with benefits. That is quite funny, as friends with benefits is not a taxing situation to begin with.

He isn't even fuck buddy material, how sad is that? His commitment issues are so bad that he can't even manage casual sex. He can't perform and isn't available. I don't think it can get any worse than that. Like a drug, I had to stop cold turkey and detox from him. It was time to stop. The next time he called, I did not answer. Eventually, we both forget about each other as the distance continued to grow between us.

He was a great reminder for me. He reminded me that you must always look at people and their actions and stay focused on the present moment. There cannot be a projection or assumption that as time passes this person will want what you want or be what you need. If that occurs, then that is the exception, not the rule, and you will see signs of them changing of their own volition. However, the reality of life is that timing is important. If someone is not ready or does not want or value what you do, you must respectfully allow them to be who they are. If it does not coincide with where you are at, then gracefully hold onto your desires and focus on that, and remove yourself from their path, as it will only cause destruction and disappointment to both parties.

My affair with this unavailable friend was a lesson to focus on the present moment without making someone wrong for being who they are, and not changing what I want and accepting less than I deserve.

There was no externally dramatic phone call or fight. We just stopped answering each other's calls. We stopped the predictable pattern we had with each other. I did feel sad, but I felt more freedom and relief than regret. I always knew he meant what he said, and his behavior never improved. The writing was always on the wall and I outgrew him. He replaced me with someone or something, it does not matter what.

I feel like I could write a checklist on what an unavailable man looks like, and what you should do to stay far away since I have dated so many of them.

Chapter 48

Spiritual Warrior

T HERE IS A BEAUTIFUL SPANISH-STYLE FIVE-STAR RESORT OUT-
side of Santa Barbara in the mountains that I have always enjoyed.
Ojai Valley Inn and Spa is situated on an amazing property, a world-re-
nowned spa. It is a peaceful place. I stay there from time to time and
will read the newsletter that they send about upcoming activities and
events at the resort. In one newsletter, they had a feature article about a
spiritual counselor and intuitive who gives readings using Native American cards. It was the first time I heard of such a service offering, and
course mulled it over in my head. Per the article, her residency was ending the weekend before I would arrive at Ojai for my personal summer
vacation that I planned for myself. I scheduled a week out of the office
to go horseback riding and to the spa, and to relax.

Something about meeting this spiritual counselor seemed intriguing and kept popping up in my head. Her last day at Ojai Valley Inn

and Spa is on June 30th. I was resistant because of my planned vacation there the following week, and I did not want to make the long drive for a short appointment.

However, my spirit would not let go of the thought of meeting with her. I ended up cancelling all of my Saturday appointments and rescheduling them for another weekend. Interestingly enough, I was able to get my hair, a manicure, and a little shopping done. It seemed like icing on the cake. Of course, I was a few moments late, but considering all that I did, it was a miracle that I even made it to the appointment at all.

I dropped my car off at the valet and ask for directions to the Herb Garden. I was walking in high wedge espadrilles down a steep slope—the journey I must make to seek truth as a fashionista is treacherous indeed. I was accompanied part of the way by a beautiful, large orange monarch butterfly that hovered around me at waist level.

I arrived at the Herb Garden pool, but it is a gated door to which I did not have a key. As I waited, hoping that someone would open the door for me, I kept noticing that my appointment time was slipping away. Finally, the door opened, and I sneaked through the gate. I asked the staff where my appointment was, and then a few moments later a tall gentle woman with a kind face appeared. She was sweet and patient, and not at all upset with me for being late. She brought me to a lovely room with a table close to the wall. The table displayed beautiful crystals, organized by color, clear to pale pinks to the deepest blues, greens and purples, an enormous feather and small drum. In the middle of the room was another table with three decks of cards. She introduced herself as Nancy, a Native American Spiritual Healer.

She took me outside and had me close my eyes. She asked me to be present and think about all that I would like to release. She smudged burnt sage around my whole body and asked that I release all negative toxins, thoughts and experiences. She waves the feather over my head, face, and heart and, as I turn around, waved the feather over my shoulders and back. I breathed deeply and contemplated all I that I desire to be free of…all items to let go from my mind and heart.

"Now look at the table of crystals, select two or three that speak to you, bring them to the table, and have a seat." As she gave me her instructions, she placed the feather gently on the table and picked up the drum.

I squealed in delight, because as I walked into the room, I had immediately noticed this beautiful and large heart shaped pink stone. I picked up the pink stone and declared "I am attracted to pink right now." Well honestly, I have always loved pink, but have had to hide my love of it as classmates said it was too girly.

"True, that happens a lot; people get excited about the stones, especially the pink heart," laughs Nancy.

"I love blue too, though," I said. I picked up another beautiful pink marble stone and a pale yellow stone in the shape of a tear drop, and sat down at the table. I looked out of the window and saw a hummingbird fly and perch on a tree branch. I gazed from time to time, realizing that the hummingbird was watching over us.

"Now that you have your stones, hold two, one in each hand. We are going to do a centering exercise before we begin," she recommended.

I picked up a beautiful pink heart shape stone and the other pink marbled stone, and placed one in each hand as per her instructions.

"Okay, great. Please sit comfortably in the chair, hold each stone palm side up, and close your eyes and breathe deeply."

As I close my eyes and breathe deeply, she started drumming on her drum. The small Native American drum, which had a deep sound, reverberated throughout the room. In a beautiful, powerful yet serene voice, she sang a Native American prayer. She asked that I be protected and know that Angels are standing to the right of me, to the left of me, above me, below me, in front of me and behind me. As she continued singing this prayer, tears came streaming down my face as if my soul knew how true her prayer was. I know angels are all around me, yet I forget to know that they are here and always protecting me. It is my angels who brought me to her to confirm for me all that I know, all that they tell me and guide me to know.

After her last beat of the drum, she told me to open my eyes and asked me, why the tears?

"I guess I realize that I need to be here, and it's time to work on releasing old habits. To let go of thoughts and people who are no longer good for me, that do not serve my highest good. Also, I pray to my angels every day, so I connected deeply to your call to the angels."

"Tell me why you are here," she asked. "What are the questions that you have for me that you want to address?"

"Well, I would like to know if I will meet my husband, have a family and start my new career of being a writer/screenwriter?" I asked. "I focused on having a career and did things I want so that I would not be like my mother. I would not be stressed and bitter that I never had a chance to do all the things I wanted because I had children. I don't want my family to feel that burden. I wanted to get myself to a healthy place before having children and a husband."

"Great, well, pick one card from each deck," Nancy encourages.

I pull a card from each deck as instructed.

"Good," she says, beginning her reading. "The first card is the White Buffalo, which is the card of abundance, showing you that all of your needs will be met. The next card shows you that you should have gratitude for your wisdom. The last card, the beaver, shows that you will have a partner to make a life with, a family, and a person to build your dreams with. Yes, your wish for your husband and family will come, and it will be manifested from your higher self and God. The third card lets you know that it is time to let go of people in your life so new ones can enter, people who will be more like-minded."

"I have been letting go of people and asking for help in letting go of all that is toxic within me and my life," I revealed. "So, this is helping me. I decided that I would play the piano again as I know that I do not have any true friends right now, so piano is a healthy and beautiful way to spend time with myself. I have been journaling about this every morning the past few weeks."

"Do you know about eagle medicine?" Nancy asked.

"No, what do you mean?"

"It means that you are so far ahead and see over all things and that you have a different view of things. It may take time for others in your life to catch up or understand you," she explained.

"Let me tell you about the stones you have selected," she continued. "The heart is pink quartz and is about self-love. Be gentle with yourself. Do not force. Just allow things to be. The next stone is about assimilation and integration. You have entered a time where you need to integrate physical, spiritual and emotional experiences. The yellow calcite represents that you are manifesting from your higher mind."

"Wow that is incredible!" I burst in excitement. "I have started reading about the Akashic records and recognize that I need to tap into my higher mind to improve my manifestation skills. I think the cards implicitly tell me that the man I will marry is not already in my life, he is someone new. I know I need to let go of Gary and others, but for some reason it is hard to let go of Gary for me…he is another bad habit."

"Let's consult the cards. Cards, tell us about Gary and where he is at right now regarding Tristan. Select three cards from the pink deck."

As I select the three cards and turn them over, she asks me to choose another, and another, and another. "The cards are telling me a story, so keep selecting cards, and I will tell you when to stop."

"Does Gary see other women?" Nancy asks.

"I don't really know, but I assume so. He gets upset if I speak the truth. He freaks out and leaves. I know his mother was an alcoholic and committed suicide in front of him, and he married someone who cheated on him. So, I think when he disappears and gets upset, it's more about that."

"Yes, that behavior is about him, not you. You understand that, right?" she asked me.

"Yes," I confirmed.

"The cards say that he is attracted to your wisdom, your power and your light. The Grandmother card is present. That means that he sees you as a powerful woman, but you are too light for him now. He is dark, has deception, and cannot provide for anyone right now. He needs to transform the darkness within him. Whenever you point out the truth he feels bad, and it reminds him that he couldn't save his mother, and that is why he leaves and gets upset. He hasn't dealt with the darkness. He will not be able to provide you with what you need. The only way to be with him is to provide unconditional love. He will only heal and feel safe if he works on his issues, but if you help him, you will sacrifice your dreams. He is dangerous to you as you will not live the life you are meant to live."

"It confirms what I have been thinking about; I do recognize that the past baggage he carries around prevents us from being together. It is still hard for me to let go of him, when he's happy and good to me, we click so well! It's amazing."

"Let's pull a card for you that speaks to what you should do. Pull a green card," instructed Nancy. I pulled a card from the green card deck…the Hold to your Truth card. A warrior with an arrow appears on the card.

"Here's the answer, let go as you know you should. You need to be a spiritual warrior. Work with spirit to help you. He is dangerous for you and will delay your dreams. Pull another card."

I reached for another card and turned it over. This card is the Vision Quest card.

"Vision Quest," said Nancy. "How appropriate. This card speaks to creating a sacred space. Native Americans would go into the wilderness and find a place, mark their territory, and not move from that spot,—not eating, not sleeping, not speaking until they received a vision. Take your issues, fears, your questions and desires to God. Take a walk in nature—that will have the same effect. Mother Nature is your true mother. Ask her your questions and she will help you."

"Wow, how perfect. I started last week returning to Point Dume to walk, and I will do it tomorrow. I always go there when I need to clear my head. Also, I will spend next week here in Ojai…to relax, be alone, write and think."

"You are so wise, yes, you will have your vision quest here. Ojai is the perfect place. It is sacred and the energy here is magnified, like a portal. Also, Point Dume is another holy place. I go there as well. Your inner guidance is right on target. You need to honor the wisdom inside you. When you walk in nature, ask, pray for help about whatever, whoever is troubling you. Pray for help with Gary, to ask for wholeness, support, comfort, and truth."

"Okay, let's address your career desires. Pick three cards, one from each deck."

As I pick three cards, I said, "Yes, I feel that it is time for me to start looking for a new job. I also want have time to work on my book. I want to publish it and turn it into a screenplay. I am visual. I need time to be able to write and get this done."

"You pulled the Shaman card," Nancy confirmed. "It's death and rebirth. Yes, the time is coming up or ending where you currently are at in life. You will need to find something new and start your new life. The other card says your fear of lack is preventing you from manifesting your dreams. You need to work on releasing the fear. If you can, you will accomplish this dream. So, you have some homework that you need to do to manifest clearly what kind of job that you want."

Nancy took a piece of paper and drew a large circle on it. On the inside of the circle, she told me, "Write what you want in your next job. On the outside of the circle, describe what you are no longer willing to accept in a job, like commuting. You can do this for anything."

"Perfect, I will do this next week when I am here."

"Well, this is all I have time for with your session. This time has been a great reading. You are wise, and I ask you to honor this time."

"Yes," I confirmed, "this was an incredible experience, a perfect reminder of what type of phase I am going through and what I should be focused on."

I took my notes and my homework. We stood and hugged each other, saying our thank yous.

"Bye, precious, this has been a pleasure," said Nancy.

"Thank you! This was amazing. I can't thank you enough, and look forward to working with you again."

I strolled out of the room, happy, excited, refreshed, my mind buzzing with all the newly gained insights. I walked as if floating on a cloud through the herb garden. I felt as if I were visiting the south of France as I walked up the stone terraced pathway with beautiful pots of red geranium and wild lavender. The natural setting was framed by a mountain vista. It was dry, but green.

I walked to the pub near the center of the resort and had a late lunch. I was in my private world as I sat at the table. I reviewed my notes and replayed the insights in my head. In these moments, I was serene, joyful and at peace. It is such a nice feeling when you realize that you are in sync with what your soul has planned, and that you are on your right path. I ordered and ate. I indulged my appetite, trying many things. Finally, I paid my bill and was ready to leave and drive home.

As I strolled through the beautiful grounds of the Ojai Valley Inn and Spa, it was still hot and sunny outside, yet green and lush. People were everywhere, enjoying a variety of activities: eating, playing golf, walking, or going to the pool. I felt happy to be alone with my thoughts. I had had a relaxing and inspiring time within the grounds. I approached the valet desk and handed my ticket to the man at the desk.

As I get in my car, the valet told me that Abba is playing in my car and wished me a safe trip home to Los Angeles. I sat in the car and start to laugh. The song played, "*Knowing me, Knowing you, uh huh, there is nothing we can do. Knowing me, Knowing you, uh huh, we just have to face it this time we're through, breaking up is never easy I know, but I have to go, Knowing me, Knowing you, this is the best I can do.*" As I drove off down the long drive, away from the resort and toward my home in Los Angeles, this song was playing and I understood that everything happens as it should and nothing is a coincidence. As Abba sang, I knew that I was supposed to let go and move on from my past with love, it is the best that I can do, "*Knowing you, Knowing me.*" The irony and humor was not lost on me at that moment. There was no need to blame or be angry anymore, and it was time to accept the truth and move forward.

I am a spiritual warrior and my call to arms is an Abba song, as I know that I must fight against temptation, weakness, fear, desire, deception, insecurity and loneliness. I must find the strength to move on and break these negative habits. The dragon I slay is not someone's character, for we are all the best we can be at any moment. We all have our past and traumas that scar us and mark us in life, cripple us inside so we cannot love, laugh, accept and allow. I must kill my fear, look it in the eyes, this multi-headed serpent that wears many faces and has many guiles and guises. I must break all of them to find the prize of self-love, strength and the knowingness that we are all loved, always, and we are protected. We hold the key to our happiness. I do not yet know what my key looks like. I have a feeling that it is near. My journey takes me on a vision quest where I will wait for the vision of what my dragon looks like, where I will find it and how to slay it to get the key.

Chapter 49

I Do Believe in Fairies, I Do, I Do !

I AM AWARE NOW, NOT IN A MORBID WAY BUT IN A REAL CON-scious way, that our time on this earth is limited. Now, for this next part of my life, I want it to be focused on love, joy, and my dreams. I have focused on the material aspects of life, on success, on what others have expected or wanted from me. Now I must be brave and dare to have and be the person I dream of and feel compelled to be. I am a strong person who can give and receive. Who can share without losing herself in others, and who can help those around her receive the gifts they desire, which can be a kind word, acceptance, allowing, joy. I want to write and share with the world all of the beautiful and hard lessons that I have learned, all the bits of wisdom that I have gleaned from all who have entered my path and shared.

One Saturday evening, instead of going to dinner, I decided to stay home and watch TV. I caught myself watching *Peter Pan*. After the scene where Peter Pan brings Tinker Bell back to life through his belief and chanting, "I do believe in fairies, I do, I do." It reminded me that we can alter the course of any event at any time by our belief and feelings.

Belief and feelings are the magnets that draw to us or repel from us what we desire. I notice that when times get hard, we sometimes stay stuck in the disbelief, the shock and the anger of what is happening, which acts as the glue keeping us bonded to the catastrophes. With that awareness reinforced by Peter Pan, I realize that it is time for me to think of what I want, not what I don't want. However, as time reveals, it is a challenging road to be able to constantly focus on the good and remain in a positive, energetic state. We are complexly wired and influenced by so much that we need to constantly monitor and reassess our conscious and subconscious thoughts and feelings. The best barometer of how you are thinking and feeling is to observe what is appearing in our lives and how smoothly things are happening.

For some people, life progresses in a straightforward and linear direction. Transition from phases or chapters happens as they do in the stories, easily, simply and happily. For some people, that is not how things happen. It seems more as if life is cyclical with peaks and valleys, highs and lows. Sometimes many experiences are repeated and get worse before any improvement is experienced. Sometimes events spiral down and into darker, deeper areas of chaos, and sometimes events spiral up and out, and spill beyond our imagination where happiness and good things are experienced.

There is an endless repetition of events and experiences, sometimes with the same cast of characters. The same type of people and situations repeat. Maybe your new boss has the same personality or attitude towards you that you were hoping to escape. The gender or background may change, yet the same critical and unappreciative person, albeit like a parent appears. Or a friend who marries someone exactly like their dominant parent.

As we get off track, we have the power to improve our situation by changing our thoughts and feelings, just like Peter Pan did. He chanted his belief in fairies, turned his tears into joy, and brought Tinker Bell back to life. We have that same power, that same magic inside of us to turn the downward spiral in the opposite direction. To chase the rain clouds away, have the sun appear and to have magic in our lives.

I do believe in fairies; I do; I do!

Chapter 50

Visitor

Sometimes in my dream I am in a lovely place. Then in front of me is a beautiful baby boy with dark curls and violet eyes. I exclaim how beautiful the child is and ask the people around me, "Whose child is this?" Everyone just looks at me in silence. There are no words and the child is quiet. The child takes my breath away.

When I have that dream or a version of it, I like to think that I am being visited by the soul of the child I lost that I wasn't ready to have. I get to feel the joy and the wonder of beholding such a beautiful, perfect and innocent soul. I wake up in peace and smile thinking of my visitor.

I may meet him in this lifetime or another. I am grateful that he gave me the time I needed to sort myself out. I know that we are chosen as parents to help teach lessons, but that we too will learn many lessons as a result of our children.

It is also a great reminder that we are here to help one another and that everything is an agreement between souls. I am as ready as I will ever be with parenthood. I now know that I do not need the help of a man, but will greatly appreciate the support from the right person for me.

Every setback in our lives helps to fill in the details a little more clearly about what is important, what we want, and what we need to prioritize. The child I did not have taught me so much already. I can only pray that I can do as much for children who cross my path as I have already experienced.

Chapter 51

Chords and Discord

I BOUGHT MYSELF A USED UPRIGHT PIANO THAT IS IN DECENT condition. The piano is dark brown and from Hallet & Davis & Co, Boston. Being from Boston myself, I felt like this was the right piano for me. Also, it has slightly curved front legs and an ornately carved music desk. It has been sheer joy to play music again and re-learn old classics that I played as a child. Of course, the goal-oriented side of me needed to learn a new piece to challenge myself, and for that challenge I selected *Adagio in G Minor*.

Listening to *Adagio in G Minor* by Albinoni, I realize that the bass harmony is as beautiful as the melody. I think I was not able to appreciate it until now, to slow down and hear the echo the bass provides to the melody of the strings. It sounds like a waltz of two souls, the feminine and the masculine embodied in this music. It appears as if the melody, the beauty, the nymph, leads the way and is being chased by the stag, but could it be the other way? Was the composer showing the man, the strength supporting the grace and delicate nature of his flower? As we age we recognize that it is not always the beauty, a bright flower, but also the earth that holds our attention and serves as the perfect complement, creating the beautifully haunting and enchanting piece.

Is that what partnership is? Allowing both to give and receive within the octaves they can vibrate at and understanding the nature of both is to mirror in different ways the same tune, the same love. Sometimes F clef leads and G clef chases, and sometimes G clef dances in the wind while F clef billows behind. The song to me feels like I am a star in the night sky breathing love into my soul and blowing a kiss to all to sleep well and dream well and be well.

This lovely feeling is how I want to feel in a love relationship with another: supported, complemented, protected and free to be all that I am, and able to mirror that for my partner. I now know that without a true love match that you desire, it is better to be alone, or you will always be disappointed.

Chapter 52

The Guide

I DREAM THAT I AM WALKING IN THE FOREST AT NIGHT. THE canopy of trees covers the path. The forest is serene, and sounds of animals rustling through the brush echoes in the stillness of the night. The moonlight casts patches of light where it can escape the thickness of the trees. Looking straight ahead, I see a low figure coming toward me. As we both approach each other, I see the figure clearly. It is a wolf. A white wolf with streaks of gray and dark fur stops before me and looks into my eyes. I also stop and look into its eyes. As we lock cycs with one another, my mind is racing. Is this really a wolf? Will the wolf harm me? Am I in danger?

The Wolf then changes direction and walks by my side. As we walk in silence together down the moonlight path, I know that the wolf is not here to harm me. I know that the wolf is my guide. I am walking in the presence of wolf medicine. I will have many lessons that the wolf spirit will show me. I relax and feel the strength of his silent solidarity. The wolf activates a heightened sense of awareness as I am bonded to the wolf spirit. I know that it is time to observe, to listen to what the wolf wants to say, to show me and that these are hallowed days, as the wolf spirit has come to teach me. I, too, cannot be afraid to walk my path, whether I will be with others or alone. I must now learn to do what feels right, I must stand up for myself and I must forge ahead to find my bliss.

"Wolf medicine teaches us how to live by our inner guidance and not get stuck in the safety of a well-worn trail. She/he asks us to remember how we once communicated with our animal relatives and how we once made room for all forms of life regardless of differences. Wolf shows us how to become teachers so that our experiences of learning can help others as they seek their answers. The way of the Wolf is the way of listening to the silent self, and following the scent within to find one's unique way through life. The Wolf advises us when to strike out on our own and when to stay safe in the protection of the pack as explained by Wolf Medicine: Pathfinder."[3]

For now, I understand that he is my teacher. I have things that I need to learn and to be aware of, all of which will reveal itself in time. In retrospect, I see the wolf foreshadowing the time to change my path. Your soul knows these things long before your mind does.

---

3   "Otter on a Rock" (2012). ""Wolf Medicine: Pathfinder" [Online]. Available" http://otteronaro-ck.com/may-totem-wolf-pathfinder [2012, May]

Chapter 53

Magical Moments

ON A WHIM, ELISE AND I DECIDED TO SEE THE JOFFREY BALLET perform *Cinderella* at the Dorothy Chandler Pavilion. We did not buy tickets in advance and arrived about 40 minutes before the curtain time. There were long lines and masses of people at the front door and courtyard. We waited patiently for our turn to purchase tickets. When we arrived at the box office window and asked if there were tickets left, we were presented with the option to buy two orchestra seats which were next to each other.

Elise is more frugal than I, so I paid for the tickets as a gift. We walked through the doors and showed our tickets to the usher, who pointed out where we should go. Lady Luck found us in the exact center of the orchestra, only a few rows back.

The ballet was beautiful. The music, the set, the dancing and costumes all conspire to make everyone forget about your troubles and problems and become enthralled in the performance.

At the end of the ballet, there is a beautiful scene where all the fairies line up on the sides of columns in the classically designed courtyard. Cinderella and Prince Charming do a beautiful pas de deux. As they dance to confirm their love and happily ever after, the midnight blue backdrop comes alive. Glitter in bold jewel tones of red, blue, gold, green, purple and pink showers the stage while dancers do their final poses. The scene is magical, and I felt transported out of myself, out of my mind and thoughts.

The audience was still in awe of the beauty and magic we just experienced through the ballet, and there was a hushed buzz of energy as the house lights turned on and everyone exited the hall. Elise and I went to the French brasserie nearby for dinner and to relive the incredible performance for a moment longer by sharing our favorite parts with each other.

Art, fine arts, different forms of expression are so powerful and can transform your experience of life, if only for a moment. The artistry that I was honored to witness has left the most enchanting and beautiful impression on my soul and has reminded me that the essence of magic is within us and around us all.

Chapter 54

Believe Yourself

I REALIZE THAT MY MOTHER NEVER TOLD ME I WAS BEAUTIFUL. Instead, she always belittled or criticized me. So, as an adult, I made poor choices with men. I needed to hear their praise and adoration of me to obtain what I missed in childhood. I would continually call until I became bored. I wanted a man to help me fulfill the need to have the confirmation of my beauty because I was unable to see it for myself. No mirror could ever make me feel secure and no embrace could erase the past damage.

I understand that there are rare times when a man will tell you that you are unattractive. In that case, he is trying to control you. He puts you in a place where you will be dependent upon his attention and will cling to whatever scraps of attention he feels like showering you with at any given time. Reverse psychology, when used by an insecure man, signifies that he has no real power or card to play in the game of love.

When a man recognizes that you have your sense of power and are independent, he will use this tactic trying to tear you down and then rebuild you in a way that makes you dependent on his love. He will tell you that you are unlovable, and that only he is brave enough to love you out of charity. But tell me, does a charitable heart mercilessly tell you your flaws? We all know the answer is no. The kind, generous and gracious heart helps you see the beauty in you, can only see the beauty in you. That is charity to give what is not there.

Do not accept that. Believe you are beautiful. Have a strong chin and hold your head up high.

It is painful to review my memories of childhood and realize that my mother always tried to make me feel small. However, it would not be until I was much older that I would come to know that she did that because she did not love herself. She was not able to love me or teach me how to love myself in a positive, proactive way. It would be much later before I would come to understand that she has deep wounds from her childhood. That she learned to love the way she received love; she could only share what she inherited, what she observed. Therefore, one must ultimately understand, learn and have compassion as the imperfect teacher learned from an imperfect teacher, and I too, will be imperfect.

When you are young and hear and experience harsh and critical words and unloving behavior, you internalize it. You blame yourself and agree, maybe I am not intelligent, maybe I am not savvy or quick on my feet. Maybe I am not tall or thin enough, or...fill in the blank. You begin to feel cursed, like something is wrong with you. Your mother or father, or whoever is belittling you is older, wiser, more experienced, so they must know the truth. You give in and agree with the assessment of your character.

Eventually, you stop fighting and struggling because it is exhausting to always be wrong, to feel someone else's strength. Somehow, some part of you, that little voice inside says, they are wrong, something is wrong with them and not you. The voice inside you says do not give up so easily. Who cares what they think. They are not right. They do not have to be right. You must override what you have been told to think about yourself and the world, and you must decide how you want to be and how valuable you feel.

Slowly, the balance of power will shift as you make your decisions and take back control of your self-worth. It is difficult to do this, and it is easy to be manipulated. It is easy to fall into the familiar patterns of childhood, those familiar subservient roles, where you defer to the opinion of the parent or elder you need to please. For me, I had to understand that I would never please my mother. It was impossible. I would never get praise and something would always be lacking or wrong with me in her eyes. I had to learn to listen to her opinions and not accept them, not feel obligated to follow that advice or believe in that judgment. I had to learn to say no and say yes to me more.

I started taking back control by not going home for Christmas, and by putting myself first. The establishment of boundaries continued with not sending gifts on Mother's Day, or calling out of obligation, but only when I felt appreciated and when the sentiment felt sincere. Eventually, I could appreciate all that my mother did for me and return to being thoughtful, but sometimes we need to take a break and reevaluate why we are doing something, and decide if it resonates with us. Initially, it was difficult for my family to accept my increasing distance. When you change your behavior, people feel uncomfortable and are not ready for you to change. And even after the barrage of phone calls from different siblings trying to appeal to my senses, to guilt me, incent me, bribe me to not change my behavior, I still did not budge. I had to stick to my guns and make the change. In the end, the break was good and healthy for everyone.

I have to let go of the abandonment from my biological mother and my adoptive mother and realize that I am always loved, always safe and protected by God and the angels. I have nothing to fear. Mother Earth is the mother/nurturer of all, and all you need to do to feel her embrace is to connect through your heart or take a walk in nature.

Chapter 55

The Dragon

ONE DAY AFTER A BUSY PERIOD AT WORK, FEELING A SENSE OF accomplishment as we completed the initial milestone of requirements and process mapping, I decided to go shopping. Strolling through the jewelry section of Bloomingdales at South Coast Plaza, looking at the shiny baubles in the glass cases, the jewelry sales assistant suggested that I look at the John Hardy line. I reluctantly agreed to her suggestion and followed her to his display section. I was never drawn to his designs before.

"I see that you have a lot of David Yurman jewelry. You should consider John Hardy. He is having a promotion next week so if you see anything you like, you can pre-sale the item with me," Ana, the saleslady suggested.

"Okay, sounds good," I responded.

"John Hardy draws inspiration from Indonesian culture, and all of his pieces are created by local craftsmen," she said as she opened the glass display cases housing many different shiny items. "Is there any-thing that interests you in the collection?"

I seriously studied the items in the display cases and to my surprise saw some things that interested me.

"Yes, what is that?" I asked, pointing to a bracelet with some kind of head on it. "Is that a snake?"

"Oh no...that is a dragon," she said. "The snake design is over there."

"Oh…" I responded. "I am not fond of the snake design, but if that is a dragon I will look at it."

"That is part of the Naga collection. Let me take it out so that you can try it on."

"Great." I tried it on and looked at it more closely. "Oh, it is nice, I like this design."

"Yes, the bracelet is white gold, crafted in a single piece with white topaz."

"Beautiful," I confirmed.

"There are other items in the Naga collection over here." She point-ed to the other side of the L shaped case where there was a grouping of items, necklaces, bracelets and rings in gold and white gold, with gems and without.

"Oh, wow, that is so cool. What is that?" Can I please try on that ring?" I pointed to a double-headed dragon ring that coils around the finger.

"Of course you can," She took the ring out and let me try it on.

"Wow, this is cool and stylish."

"Yes, this is hand crafted, and white gold. Naga in Indonesian means dragon. Legend says that the dragon is the protector, during the day the dragon protects the jewels and at night it returns and protects the village. Apparently, legend says if you wear the dragon it will bring you love, prosperity and protection."

"That works for me, all the things that I want. Ring me up, I will take it."

"If you want to save money pre-sell with me now, you can take 15% off but you cannot pick it up for another week."

"That's okay, I will take the ring now. True or not, I like the myth that goes with the ring. I could use a little love and protection and who doesn't want more prosperity. Sold!"

We both laughed and agreed. "Well," said the saleslady, "other people have bought this ring or other pieces in the Naga collection and swore that it has brought them love and prosperity."

"Wrap it up," I chuckled while laughing.

As Ana wrapped up the item, another sales assistant, Catherine, came over to help complete the transaction. As I paid, Catherine told me how she loves the Naga collection and has bought a few pieces which have brought her luck and wealth. She told me that this piece would bring me good things. I happily paid for the beautiful double dragon ring and walk out of Bloomingdales as if walking in my private runway show.

During meetings, the shiny ring caught the eye of my meeting participants. As I walked around I started to notice dragonflies everywhere. I felt like they are a good omen, keeping watch over me as the ring promises. Later that week, I dreamt of a dragon. When the dragon appeared in my dream, I knew that I had somehow connected with dragon energy. Even though the dragon is a mythical creature, it is a powerful symbolic entity.

In my dream, I was flying over the ocean by holding the hand of a fairy who was holding a golden chalice and saw a dragon appear out of the sea. The rising body saw me and the fairy. The dragon saw us and captured the fairy by swallowing it. Not to eat it, but to imprison the fairy in a separate chamber in its belly. I asked the dragon why it did that and it replied, "I want to harness the energy of all things, the fairy is a magical creature, with it I will have all power." Of course, I was distraught and tried to find a way to free the fairy.

After waking up from this dream, I could not help but wonder why I had a dream about magical and mythical creatures. The only conclusion I have so far is that all things, even ideas have power, have an energy vibration that you can access. The idea or symbol has its wisdom that it shares with those who tap into the energy. The dragon energy is powerful and was informing me that we are powerful beings if we choose to be aware of that and connect to things beyond our realm of understanding, of logic. That we can harness the power of all living things, in that we can summon creation, we can imagine things greater than our small individualist perspective. It triggered for me an episode of *Xena*, one where the notion of power, to harness the power of all things beyond yielding individual power, was the theme. The dream reminded me of the ability to be limitless, that heaven and earth and all forces can conspire to help you create an incredible existence.

Chapter 56

Within So It Shall be Outside

I T IS INTERESTING HOW THE SOUL IS ALL-KNOWING IF YOU TAKE the time to stop, listen, and follow your intuition. You will always be guided to your highest good and right action for that moment. You may not even realize or understand how the pieces fit, why the sudden interest in Kundalini yoga and breathing deeply and yoga overall.

To find that, you are being guided to open you heart. As I sit there I ask, how does one open their heart to love? The answer I hear in my mind is to choose love, not fear. I read an angel card that I pulled from the deck of angel cards. The card says to do chakra work to open your heart, do energy work, forgive those who have hurt you, be kind and loving to yourself and heal any fears about giving and receiving. How uncanny that I have been doing acupuncture and started yoga and Kundalini yoga in which certain poses, especially cobra, are designed to open your heart. Kundalini yoga is all about opening your heart and balancing your chakras.

The soul is divine, if only we would spend time listening to its guidance and not the guidance of others we would be okay. However, it is a comparison between the external and internal that enables you to have faith and trust in yourself. When you see your inner thoughts reflected in external events it confirms that you have the right guidance that you are on the right path.

I am reflecting on how I have held myself back. How I have tied myself and entangled myself into expectations, fears and bad decisions. It is funny how saying goodbye to Gary has left me with peace because I know he was never there for me. I realize that no one will be there for me until I learn to be there for myself. I have been pondering what that means. I believe that it means when I stop letting myself down, stop judging myself, enjoy the moment, appreciate my accomplishments. To remind myself, I am loved no matter what I do, how much I weigh, what I look like. Gary and other dalliances made me aware of a new mathematical equation: two half-empty shells of a man does not equal one whole man.

I realize now that I wanted a man who is wealthy, thinking that his wealth would protect me and make me feel secure. I also thought that money would buy me freedom and happiness. However, as I have closed the door on many so-called rich men, I realized that their wealth is an illusion. They dangle their love and trappings of success like a fish in the deepest, darkest parts of the ocean, with lights and lures far ahead of their jaws and predatory intentions. These men use their money and your desire for marriage as bait to hook you in, all the while never intending to be sincere, masking their true intentions and limitations with talk, empty promises of what might be, never showing you or speaking what is. For they know the truth would have you running or swimming so fast their head would spin.

However, as time goes by and nothing materializes, you know something is not right and that you are a victim to one of the worst kinds of fate, that of deception. Once you make a stand for yourself and let go and realize that your quest for security and happiness has nothing to do with others, and everything to do with you, once you realize that you are strong enough to carry on and reach for the stars in your eyes and bring that twinkle to your life, you can let go and will never need to look back.

I had always heard it said that a moment can change a past hurt or wound, can heal in a single moment. I never understood that saying, possibly because I process everything in my head first. Having coffee and a conversation with my friend's friend, an artist, made me realize that what I am truly seeking is the wealth of someone's heart, not their pocketbook. A wealthy heart is open, generous, kind, thoughtful, and is a sweetness that gives, yet still has boundaries and remains intact. I had that excited feeling when speaking with him, a nervousness that had me talking quickly.

I enjoyed his calm and serene demeanor, how freely and easily he spoke. Most of all I appreciated that he honors his word and follows through on what he says he will do, not leaving me to question his words. Actions speak far greater than any empty, hollow promise. His thoughtfulness has made me smile again. I experienced uncontrollable curvatures of the lips and openness of the eyes, as I realized that my heart had found another who is true. It is enough that we met. Nothing further needs to happen. I know that I was supposed to feel light and trust again in the idea of love with another.

Chapter 57

Déjà vu

CRYING IS THE RELEASE OF THE ACCUMULATION OF PAST TRAU-
mas, from this and other lifetimes that you grieve. Unless it is a
result of current physical pain, it is about so much more. When you
cry, you are acknowledging the pain, the event, and then you slowly
heal yourself by allowing yourself to express and connect to the emotions and therefore cry. Yet, we always feel as if we should not cry and
that it is a sign of weakness.

It is funny how fate twists and turns. When you are young, you
show love by doing things or buying gifts, the nicer, the bigger, the more
exclusive, the better. Then as you mature, you focus on what that person
truly wants, maybe it is an experience or a moment that you try to help
them have. As we get older we also realize that it is not the gifts of things
that people want. We may no longer show up for the birthdays because
we are showing up for the passings, the last moments, the deaths.

We show our solidarity to our fellow loved ones, no matter how
estranged we are to them by being there for them in their final mo-

ments. We support those who are witnessing their loved one's final days and breaths. That is a sign of love to comfort one and let them know that they are loved and cherished in any state of being, physical or non-physical. To remind someone that they are safe to let go of their pain and move to a better place, a place of peace. To reassure them that they will not be forgotten once they cease to exist physically, and that they will be remembered fondly in our hearts and memories for eternity. So, it was time that I must break the ice and call home to comfort those in need, putting aside my ego to help console others.

I had received a series of messages from my sister over several months that a dear family friend was terminally ill. I called my mother, knowing that this person meant a great deal to her, to all of us. Sadly, months later, I was informed of his passing. I immediately booked my flight to return home and attend his funeral, to give my condolences in person to his family, whom I love very much.

As I stood in line to speak words of comfort to my friends regarding their father's passing, I wondered why I was unable to recall the funeral parlor. After all, it is the same exact place where my father's body laid resting before his memorial service, almost thirty years before.

I have always had such an incredible memory. I can remember colors, the smell in the air, the look on someone's face and the exact words they said. However, I walked into this building and did not recognize anything. What I do recall, though, is the sadness and surprise of losing someone, even when you know it is their time to go. That is an unmistakably eerie feeling. It is a feeling that you see and feel with all of your senses, in dream time and awake. The passing of my father's friend is similar to my father's passing, just 25–30 years later. They both had an unexpected stroke, followed by much testing which resulted in the diagnosis of a brain tumor, leading to aggressive chemotherapy, surgery, radiation, and medication. The proactive medical treatments are followed by no hope and eventual physical demise. Home care is where the patient is made to feel comfortable, but it is acknowledged by all involved that no more can be done. The tired faces, the understanding that this is his time to go, is the same.

I am glad I was there to help my friends grieve and honor their father and mine at the same time. I am also witnessing yet again that everything happens for a reason. I am able to grieve with real emotion as an adult, not the child that I was, who suppressed all my feelings and pretended it was a bad dream. I am listening to the memorial service, the memories and funny stories tinged with grief from broken but grateful hearts. I am observing the faces sitting in the same congregational church that sat there and listened to my father's memorial service. The paint on the walls may be different, the age of the congregation may be different, but the sentiment remains the same.

I am grateful to see people and how they show their concern, love and support for their fellow friend, husband, father, uncle, neighbor, community member, or coach. They show up with silent strength and knowing concern. They watched you play and grow up as they watched their children play and grow up. Even if they only knew you from a distance, a polite nod of acknowledgement, I know that there is a deep reserve of emotion and compassion that resides in their heart. The light mauve, champagne pink walls that accent tall arched windows have enclosed many gatherings. The off-white simple pews have seen many good and sad times in the lives of those who have sat inside this simple, austere yet elegant building for centuries. It takes us all in as silent observers, witnesses. There is peace in the halls and walls of this old New England congregational church with a black spire jutting from its roof. The organ plays beautiful music as it has always done.

The choir sings. I feel the presence of the deceased walking around, watching, listening as his life is being recounted by those he loves. I know it was the same for my father.

After the funeral and the reception, I walked to my mother's house from church, as I had many times before. I passed by the James Library, the Victorian building where I used to have piano lessons as a little girl. I walked to the front doors and saw that they were open, so I walk in. I saw books and tables and chairs where you can sit and read. In the main hallway is the staircase that leads to the second floor. As I climbed the staircase, I imagined my father walking beside me with his newspaper and pipe as I held my piano books. When I reached the top of the stairs, the landing part with its slight alcove is intact. I turned my head as if expecting to see my father sitting on the couch while waiting for my lesson to be done, as he always did. The double doors to the main room were open, and I saw a beautiful black grand piano.

People were arranging seating for a concert and reception that will be held there later that afternoon. The wide windows were clear, and bright sunlight filtered into the room. I reminisced and sat at the piano, trying to recall the notes of the adagio I was working on. I felt happy. I felt as if I were having a moment with my father, as if time in his world and my world coincided and he was there with me, on the landing, reading the paper and listening to me play the piano while smoking his pipe. I am sure that it was his soul that whispered to me, that guided me into the library and up the stairs to remind me that he is not gone, that I have not lost him, that he is always here for me in any moment that I choose.

Chapter 58

Search for Love

LEARNING TO LOVE YOURSELF IS THE HARDEST THING WE CAN achieve. Riddled with obstacles, loss, defeat, humiliation, neglect—the pathway for some of us is challenging. For some, love is easy and natural, and for others it is a painful reminder of what does not exist, what is lacking. For mistakes and flaws you perceived as a reason for the difficulty haunts your mind. We mistakenly assume that the color of our skin, our gender, economic scarcity, handicaps, weight, are the reasons, all of these potential barriers for some, to the path of love and self-acceptance.

The other most difficult task as a human that I have observed is to love others unconditionally, especially when your foundation is cracking and crumbling. The ability to extend to another that perfect love despite your issues and limitations is what prevents us from achieving happiness. The challenge to love another when you don't see it returned or reflected in their eyes and heart. But that is what we are asked to do to reach the Kingdom of Heaven, Enlightenment or wherever you choose to believe your creator/guides resides. In short, we are tasked to share the existence and practice of love for yourself and others.

I sit at my desk in a dull corporate office in a beige pencil skirt and light purple ruffle shirt accented by cream accessories. I have crossed a major threshold of life. I have learned to be utterly happy and grateful for myself, my life with the flaws and beautiful moments. I sit proudly, walk proudly into any room. I have learned to defend my honor and protect those around me. I am the benefactor in my life. I share my gifts with others and I know that it is through the grace of God/Spirit that I have the riches that I am temporarily in possession of. I see that materiality is temporary waves of energy that appear to be solid at this moment in this dimension. I can take a risk and know that I am not losing anything, but gaining clarity whether the risk results in my favor or not. I understand that it is not what I have, but how I act that will be the true benchmark of a life well lived.

The Dragon is teaching me love, as promised, as I am learning to love myself.

Chapter 59

"Carma"

I WAS DRIVING HOME FROM ORANGE COUNTRY IN RUSH HOUR TRAF-fic. My car, which I had just picked up from the mechanic, was starting to feel funny. The transmission light appeared. The very item that had been fixed/replaced the last three visits to the mechanic (and three rental cars later) was not working properly. The car started to shake, so I nervously used my turn signal and pulled over to the side of the road, near downtown Los Angeles. I called AAA and requested a tow from my location. The strangest things happened from that point onwards. AAA generally arrives at your location in 30 minutes or less. On this day, they did not. So, I called again to ask for the status of the tow truck.

"What is your AAA number? Where is your location?"

After providing my AAA membership number, I state "I called in my request a while ago. I am near the 9th street exit off of the 101."

AAA Operator: "Oh, yes, Miss Webster…we sent someone to you."

"It's been almost an hour, and no one is here," I reply.

"You did say the 9th street exit off of the 101?"

"Yes, near the Staples Center."

"…Which is *not* what the location says. You must be near the 110 freeway then."

"Oh yes, I haven't merged onto the 101 yet. My bad."

"Okay…we will send someone to you right away."

"Great! Thank you for your help."

The time passed quickly, and I was getting anxious. It had been an hour and a half since I made the first call, which I feel is a bad omen as AAA is usually much more prompt. A police officer pulled over to the side of the road where I was sitting patiently in my car with my hazard lights blinking. He asked me what the problem was, and I explained the AAA mix up and that I was waiting for a tow.

He seemed satisfied with the answer and drove off. Soon after he left I saw the tow truck driver finally approaching my location. I felt such relief seeing the AAA tow truck arrival. I could imagine how a soldier must feel while exhausted and fearing that his strength will give out. The soldier would be relieved and re-energized when seeing extra cavalry in the middle of a battle. The tow truck driver was a kind and polite man. He seemed eager to help. He introduced himself as Lewis and told me to wait in his truck as he managed to set up my car in preparation for the tow. He told me that he felt awful for me and would hate to think of his wife waiting here at night, in the dark on the side of the road by herself. I thought to myself, what a sweetheart.

Lewis, the tow truck driver, finished hooking my car to the flat bed tow truck and hopped in the truck once his task was complete. After he situated himself, he handed me a clipboard with a form and asked me to fill out the information.

"Ma'am…it will be $18 for a tow to Hollywood."

"Can I pay by credit card?"

"Cash only, sorry," he confirmed.

"I need to stop at a gas station and get change for a large bill."

"OK, just tell me where and when," he said.

He pulled off the side of the road and merged with traffic on the way to Hollywood. Finally—it had now been two hours since I placed the initial call to AAA. I was tired and hungry, and just wanted to be home.

Since we still had a bit of a drive left, I asked him how his day is going.

"It's slow, and I need the money. I have a wife and newborn baby at home. My wife isn't working. She is taking care of the baby. I work until 7 AM, so business should pick up by then."

"Oh wow, what a long day for you. Do you live nearby?" I asked.

"No, I live far away."

"That must be hard to live so far away from your job after completing your shift." I spotted the gas station at the exit. "Oh, pull over here so I can get change."

"Oh, you get used to it. Sure thing, will do."

He maneuvered the tow truck with my precious cargo on it. I got the money I needed and then directed him to the street where I live, on a small hill. When we arrived, I completed the paperwork and gave him the cash, plus a little extra as a tip for him and his family. His face lit up and he was genuinely appreciative of the extra money. I had my purse, laptop bag and belongings and was waiting as he unhooked my car from the tow truck. I waited outside on the sidewalk as the car was lowered to the ground. He unfastened the straps holding the car.

All of a sudden, in a flash of a second, my car was rolling down the hill. As the car began rolling, I was in complete and utter shock. All I could say is "Oh my God," repeatedly. He quickly realized what was happening and ran after the car. He tried to open the passenger door to put the emergency brake on and shift it out of neutral. As he reached for the car door, the car continued to pick up speed as it rolled down the hill. He somersaulted on the ground as he missed the door and dove in a brave attempt to grab that door handle.

As I watched this happen, I felt as if the world was in slow motion. I felt like a person in a horror movie who suddenly forgets how to run or start a car. I never thought possible until this moment that one could freeze and lose all motor skills. I saw people walking on the sidewalk, I saw all the parked cars, I saw the guard in the guard shack. I wondered if my car will injure anyone, what the liability of damages total would be by the time the car stopped moving.

As if the situation could not get worse, there is a curvature on the road, where the car hit the curb and went bounding backwards through trees. As I heard crashes and the sound of oncoming traffic, all I could do was picture the car barreling into the busy street and killing someone. I braced myself for the crash. I stood there breathless, thinking, *This is it. My life will be over in an instant, all my hard work for nothing, as I will have to pay for damages to any party injured due to this fiasco.*

What feels like an eternity passed. I heard a crash and an enormous thud. We peered through the trees down the hill and with relief noticed that although the car was surely a total loss, it did not hit the main street and did not appear to have injured anyone. The crashing noises we heard were due to a car crashing into a large tree stump and other cars that crashed into each other on the road which had nothing to do with my car.

"Oh, my God, I am so sorry, I am so sorry, I do not know what to say. I will call my company. I know they will take care of this for you, do not worry." As the tow driver said this to me with genuine remorse in his eyes, he stretched out his arm, and tried to return the tip that I gave him.

"No, keep the money. I know it was not your intention to do this; it was a fluke incident, and luckily no one got hurt and no other cars or property received damage during this accident." As I said these words, I pondered the significance of these events. Only the hand of the divine, of angels, could ensure that this incident did not impact others, so I could only surmise that this was meant to be. The karma between my car and I was over. My car had committed suicide. It decided that it could not drive to Orange County anymore. It was now in car heaven, and it was time to replace my lovely car. My car's suicide may also have been telling me that I should not be driving to Orange County every day anymore, as well.

Lewis arranged for another, more senior person from his company to meet us and help tow the car to their shop. Lewis handed me his company's business card.

"Here is our card. We will call you to make arrangements and determine if the car is fixable or if it is a total loss," he said. "We will make sure that you are taken care of, so we accept liability. You should go to bed now. There is nothing else you can do here tonight."

"I am still in shock. This was my baby. I can't imagine being without this car, or at least not yet." Holding back the tears, I said good night and thanked them as I took the business card.

I understand somehow that this was a pivotal moment in my karmic life. That I was forced to let go of and say goodbye to something dear to me, something I relied on, but something that also cost me dearly in many ways. I would have to face the ordeal of the insurance claim process and buy a new car and, in a way, deal with my self-esteem and sense of self-worth in the process. Your car is part of you, especially in a city like Los Angeles. I walked up the steep hill to my building, still in shock.

I called my best friend to share my story. As always, she patiently listened and consoled me. Then I called my insurance company and filed my claim. I went to bed weary and sad. I knew things are changing in my life. The familiar was now gone.

The next day, I shared the pictures via text with friends and family and told them my unbelievable story. My brother said, "Your experience sounds like an Allstate insurance commercial."

Laughing, I couldn't help but to agree with him.

Chapter 60

Sports Package

THE INSURANCE PROCESS WAS SMOOTH, FAST, EFFICIENT, AND easy, despite my fear of the inconvenience of the car debacle.

I flew back from Boston, from my brother's wedding, which was quiet, small, intimate but lovely. I had received the money I wanted for my car, and had all the bank information that I needed to go car shopping. Looking at cars at the dealership, I ironically fell in love with a sportier version of my previous car, a BMW and in the same color. This car is fun, sporty, sexy. I tried to look at other types of cars before deciding. However, for me it is no use: I guess once I started driving a BMW, no other car felt the road the same way, and I was drawn to another one, although I told myself I would never buy another BMW. As I left the dealership I felt like a million dollars. I did not know that the end of the prior car would lead me to a new love. I felt powerful, happy, and blissful, because I managed the purchase and financed my new baby on my own, which is how I have always bought my cars, but still, sometimes I sit in wonder as everything unfolds easily. I truly am a woman who can take care of herself and am learning to go with my instinct.

Chapter 61

Attraction is Distraction

I AM A CREATURE OF HABIT. ON SUNDAY NIGHTS, I USUALLY FILL my car with gas at this one gas station because they have a fair price and all of the men who work there are friendly.

I am in black sweatpants with a gray tank top and flip flops, my hair blow dried. I had it pulled back and had no makeup on, which for me means eyebrows are perfect and neutral lipstick. I pull up to the gas station in front of pump number 1. I get out of my car with my Louis Vuitton Speedy bag and go into the station to pay with cash. As I walk back to my car, someone is trying to get my attention.

I look over, and it is this cute, youngish looking guy walking toward me. "Hi, I love your car."

"Thanks, it's a smooth ride. I love it."

"What is the model?" He walks behind the car and then asks, "What does the IS stand for?"

"335is, sports package with a turbo engine. Powerful engine," I say proudly.

"Nice. Say, you are really cute. Do you want to hang out/go out some time?"

I feel so sexy and fun. I surprise myself and in an uncharacteristic and carefree moment, I say yes. I decided to say yes to fun.

"Cool, my name is Nick. Here is my number."

"Okay, great," I respond, accepting his number.

"Can you go out now?"

"No, I have things to do now," I say. "Let's do the weekend. Week-ends work better for me."

"Okay…cool! I'm a good guy. I am a gentleman. Make sure you call me. Text me back."

We smiled at each other and exchange small talk. Eventually, I leave the gas station with a big smile. I felt great and knew that it was all because of my car.

I laughed with my girlfriends about this event the next day. As I drive, I see men checking out the car and then me, which makes me chuckle to myself. I realize a big secret: *Buy a man's car if you want a man.*

Nick called immediately and made plans to see me. We went out on a few dates and everything moved quickly. He was quick to say that his mother would like me that I am the perfect girl. He confessed that he wanted all the things he imagined that I would want…marriage, commitment, love, and family. He said how beautiful I am. He said he loved me too quickly, which made me question his true intentions. I am no expert, but I do not believe you can fall in love in a week or two. I think it takes a little more time to get to know someone and trust them and even spend time with them to consider those feelings. A red flag raised in my mind.

After Nick had dropped the bomb of *I love you*, it was followed by another startling piece of information. "Babe, my car isn't working and I am short on money...can you please (in a pleading tone) lend me $700? I promise to pay you back in two weeks." His eyes darted everywhere as he spoke.

Thinking how to answer this request, thinking of how it would have been nice to have support when going through car troubles, reluctantly and against better judgment, I said yes.

"Really?" he asked, excited and hugging me.

"Yeah, sure. I know it's stressful as your business isn't doing well. You are not filling the orders with your fashion label and are looking for a new job. But you need to pay me back."

"Yeah, yeah, yeah. I promise I will pay you back. I love you! You are the best," he said.

I excused myself and go into my bedroom and get the money from my stash of emergency cash at home. I returned to the couch in the living room where he was sitting and give him the $700.

"Thanks for this. I got to get going. It's late."

"Sure, but remember that you need to pay me back." I regretted it as I said it. I knew I would never get that money back. I knew he was utterly insincere.

"Oh, by the way, don't judge me, but I have to go to court and will be talking with my lawyer."

"Oh, why do you need to see a lawyer? What are the charges?"

"Well, I was seeing this girl and she didn't have a car, so we were partying...it was late, like 3 AM. She needed me to drive her home, but I didn't want to. Well, we got pulled over because I had a busted headlight. The cop found a lot of pot in my car."

"Oh, well, do you have a medical license? I hope you weren't smoking it when the police officer saw you."

"No, it wasn't like that and yes, I have a medical license but it was hers. She wouldn't own up to it and since it was my car, and I already have a DUI, I had to spend the night in jail."

"Oh, wow, sorry to hear that. But what kind of people are you hanging out with who would do that?" I asked.

"Don't judge me. Don't be closed-minded. Sometimes shit happens. It doesn't mean anything more than that. I was at the wrong place at the wrong time."

I felt a little overwhelmed at this point with this news. What had I gotten myself entangled with here? Usually, it takes months for information like this to be revealed, not two weeks.

He stood up and gathered his things. I took that as my cue to escort him to the front door. As I stood at the door, he turned to me and kisses my cheek while saying thank you and goodnight.

I closed the door and then tried to reconstruct the conversation that just occurred. *Am I imagining things? Is he a drug dealer? Is he way too into drugs and out of control?* This sort of problem was out of my league. I was not prepared to deal with anything more serious than the typical selfish, self-centered man. Addiction issues take a strong and experienced person to handle that kind of chaos and instability. What was strange was that he appeared so normal and capable. He seemed presentable, which makes one realize that the stereotype of the type of person addicted to or involved in drugs needed to be expanded to include the boy next door.

Impatiently, I called his phone. He didn't answer, so I did a horribly neurotic thing and left a brutal voicemail. "Nick, hi, it's me. Look,

I can't do this. You are sweet and everything, but you have too much going on. Let's just be friends."

Ten minutes later, my phone rings with Nick's number flashing on the screen. I should not have picked it up, but I guess I felt that it was only fair, so I answered.

"Really? Seriously? I can't believe this! I told you not to judge me. You need to calm down. This drug possession charge is not a big deal. I am a good person. How can you do this to me, I need you. Let me get through this, and then we can figure out about us."

I felt ashamed for my behavior and understood his point. I decided to retract my earlier statement and apologized for being so quick to run away.

"Oh Nick, I am sorry, I just panicked," I explain. "I am just a simple girl. I have never met someone with your situation and did not know what to do. I am sorry."

"Okay, just calm down. I need someone on my side right now."

"I understand. Okay, goodnight."

"Goodnight babe. Calm down."

"Goodnight, sorry." I hung up the phone and tossed and turned in bed. My imagination propelled me from where we were, getting to know each other, to married to a man with the stigma of drugs and jail time, and how can I explain that to friends and family? What would that mean to me and my life? Thankfully, sleep allows you to put some distance between you and the problems you face.

Chapter 62

Redux

I WOKE UP WITH A FRESH PERSPECTIVE ON NICK'S DRAMA. I AM A problem solver for my career and thought about how I could improve this situation. I decided to pray on his behalf and give a donation at temple for the priests to pray on his behalf, to pray for the best outcome possible. As the prayers happened, the situation seemed to improve. However, Nick started acting strange. He stopped calling, stopped visiting or wanting to go out. His calls were for money, for a tow, for help or to talk about his situation.

When I would see him, he would not look me in the eye. He was vague and started to disappear. I felt silly being so involved to help someone and to wish them well when they were aloof and distant and not willing to help themselves, instead just pawning their problems onto others to solve.

I recognized a strange pattern of behavior or habit that I have, and wonder to myself why I hold on to the past. What am I afraid to let go of, what does this situation reveal about me? I pondered this while seeing the irony in the situation, as what I am afraid to release has evolved into the thing I feared most. As I watched another interaction do the awkward dance of abandonment, secrecy and betrayal, a combination that I know all too well, I realized this time that I perpetually re-experience the same abandonment and disappointment. The pattern repeats over and again, just with a different cast of characters, situations, and trigger points. It always leads to the same experiences and feelings. I felt out of control with my emotions. I felt let down and chased after Nick to explain, to show me, to respond, as if I expected logic to pull me out of the emotional trance of fear. I wanted to be able to stop the feeling part of myself from feeling anything bad. When someone lets go of a connection to you, you feel devastated. It forces you to reckon with and realize the karma for when you let go of the connection with others, and how the other person must have felt as you callously disappeared or did not respond. This experience reinforced for me the notion of compassion, that it is possible to kindly say no without hurting someone. It shows the importance of honesty and genuine action not just for the other person, but for you as well. Being an authentic person enables you to live a life with clarity, non-deceit, and non-entanglement.

This dance has shown me much about myself. It reminds me of the things I have known about myself and reveals shortcomings that I am trying to improve. It shows me how much work I have yet to do. I need to stop focusing on what the other person is not doing and focus on my thoughts, actions, and feelings that have brought me back to this place. I hope that one of these days, I can stand in the courtyard of abandonment without falling apart. That I will be able to view these actions as if watching a movie, a sequence of images strung together that you have no particular feeling or attachment toward.

I did feel that this time, in this dance, I was not a victim, as I was fully aware what each action or non-action meant. It was like watching an existential play, where you contemplate and see how no action has as much significance as action does, reminding you that the actor chooses each action or absence of action. Thus, by not choosing you, he is choosing. It is fatalistic and real.

I did not ignore the clearly marked non-relationship disguised as an attempt at one with this person. All of the physical signs of disinterest were present: the empty promises, the unresponsiveness and lack of consideration. The actions juxtaposed against the words that come so freely when needing something like money, attention, or empathy. The see-saw of available and interested to unavailable and disappearing, demonstrated when they stopped responding to you or reaching out. When they let days go by without acknowledgement that soon is chased by weeks passing without seeing you. Then out of the blue they need you, and they call you babe, sweetie, pretty girl, all to fade into black when whatever crisis has been solved by you. I find it interesting to observe that all of those so-called friends that he spent all his time with were apparently not around when he needed help. When you start hearing the voice of another woman in the background, you know that you have lost his heart. Better you know that no heart exists in his body. You ponder, how can I desire someone so unworthy of my love, so incapable of fairness and respect? How can that kind of person even have a heart to give? You question why you are still here waiting, what is wrong with you that you have not moved on or removed this nuisance from your life?

The answer is that their heart is just a mechanical device. It has never grown to experience true genuine love, only self-serving love directed to themselves. They recruit their lovers by seducing them and turn that lover into a victim with false words. Their acts of devotion and interest can only be maintained for short periods of time. For to them, giving is draining, taking is what empowers them. "Vampire" best describes the type of love and relationships they will provide. I will always try to treat people with respect. I will never insult someone again or leave them hanging. I do not want the karmic debt on my soul. I apologize for the mistakes of my youth, for my carelessness and thoughtlessness, and pray for your happiness and ask for your forgiveness, all of you.

I sit on my down overstuffed pink and white chair and pull angel cards. I keep getting the card, "Decide to be Happy Now." It has constantly appeared, and I feel that it is an unfair card, as I am grateful for my life, my place, my job, my car, my friends. I have learned to have gratitude.

However, I am tossing and turning in bed. I could not fall asleep. I had been imagining what he was doing and who he spent his nights with when I did not see him. All of a sudden, my brain flashes a picture of a beautiful ballerina, in her tutu on pointe shoes and thought, one day that will be me. I am a beautiful dancer inside. I am a beautiful person. I am happy now and think how amazing it will be to have my happy thought meet me in reality. So maybe I will dream of pirouettes and fouetté turns, graceful poses and grace, and know that I am beautiful and happy no matter what someone is or isn't doing.

Just allow the sadness to come, beckon those tears. It is not a sign of weakness. It is releasing, letting go of the past, which you need to do in order to embrace and move toward your future. When you cry, what do you think of? What do you feel? Alone? Tired? Unattractive? Misunderstood? Unloved? Undervalued? That is okay, because these are all false. Your soul knows greatness beyond comprehension. It is more than you can imagine. It is limitless if you could only believe it to be so.

Sit there, daydream, and imagine for a moment your life without limitations. What would it feel like? What would it look like? What does the perfect love look and feel like? Fall asleep to those thoughts and feelings instead of the memories of the horror show you are living or have lived.

Chapter 63

Taking Flight

"RIGHT BEFORE THE FINAL DEMONSTRATION, THERE IS A BIG demonstration,"[4] says Florence Scovel Shinn, the author of a great book titled *The Game of Life*. I pondered this thought as I was about to leave another pseudo-relationship of empty promises behind. Like a spider's web, he entangled me and ensnared me with words and charming promises. But my heart knew these were false and kept warning me to run as fast as I could away from him. However, hope kept me spellbound and motionless in his trap of lies.

At least this time I was grateful that I figured out his real intentions rather quickly. I stated the obvious. I declared my reasons for departure, all in vain, as he tried to pin me in a helpless position, with those beautiful eyes and pleas of staying by his side. However, I knew that I

---

4   Florence Scovel Shinn, *The Game of Life* (1925).

needed to break free now. I did not need to call, or have a face-to-face meeting over my feelings. We had already done that. I knew that all I could do is to walk away with the love in my heart intact, and wish him happiness and send him blessings, but from afar. I imagined that he may not even notice that I will be gone. As he seemed caught up in himself, his problems and issues, I knew that he did not think about me except when he needed something from me. My mistake, I would come to realize, was to take his actions as a personal affront or to hold any meaning to them. To value him and his opinion was a meaningless endeavor.

I decided that when my plane left LAX and is in the air, en route to Japan, so would my attachment to him take off and disappear. I planned to metaphorically cast my sadness over the ocean and mountains that I passed on my trip. Maybe the winds and torrential rains would sweep through my heart and mind, clearing me of the debris of unreturned love and disappointment; for what wreckage they leave behind to a common mortal heart is too heavy to bear at times. The heart is both frail and strong at the same time. The human heart and experience of love is such a strange thing. The attempt to achieve love can be painful, yet we keep striving for it. We see the signs that all is not right in our partner, our relationship, but we keep hoping it will magically turn around. We hope that it will become one of those few moments of wonderful that we remember and treasure, like a special keepsake or heirloom from a deceased loved one.

I want this experience to be beautiful for everyone. I want this experience to be accompanied by peace and joy. Are emotions a duality because we constructed the concept of duality like good and bad, life and death? Or do we just not believe things can always be good and limit ourselves and curse ourselves with experiencing less, by not holding onto the belief of more for oneself? Maybe the notion of heaven or enlightenment is merely the state where no duality exists, things just are and it is peaceful. You always just choose a better thought and feeling.

Why can I not master the creation of a better life now? Why am I so flawed that I can only bring myself negative and painful experiences? Why am I always disappointed? Am I just more comfortable that way? Why am I having trouble letting go of what I do not want to experience? I need to focus on what I want, visualize what I want and believe that I deserve it and can have it.

As I sat in my dining room, in my tasteful wingback host chair with an elegant pheasant pattern on it, I pondered the state of my heart. How could I follow such a device that has steered me wrong in relationships? Was it lonely? Was it truly sad from past lives that were impacting me now?

This trip would do me a world of good. I would be able to pray and chant at a holy place. I would see the world through the eyes of another culture. I would pray for the peace and happiness of everyone I know and do not know, and for the world. I would ask for peace for my own heart.

The way of the warrior calls upon you to walk in silence at times, to walk by yourself. These past years I have had many guides. The wolf, dragon, snake, deer all have walked beside me both in a dream and waking life. As I assimilate the many lessons they have shown me, I hope to keep the courage in my heart. I want to be strong and vulnerable, loving and independent and hope to call to me all the goodness I seek. I will not be afraid of the dark, of the loneliness, of the creatures in men's hearts that bare their anger at me. I am protected as I make my journey and let go of the past and the limitations of fear to find the rising sun of my heart.

I boarded my plane and settle in for a long flight to Tokyo.

Chapter 64

Serenity

I HAD THE HONOR OF VISITING A BUDDHIST TEMPLE IN JAPAN AS a pilgrim. I was able to pray and chant the Lotus Sutra with other devoted practitioners. Once you step onto the temple grounds, the modern world is placed on hold as you live and pray on the temple grounds. The temple is a place of peace. It is built, maintained, and designed by and for priests, for people of peace. All around you is the blanket of true calmness, the purity of serenity. It is in the air and the water that meanders through the property. It is also in the trees and the rocks. You know that in this special place, there is no hatred. There's only love. This feeling that permeates the temple is what love feels like. It's non-judging, simple, pure, open and strong.

I felt so alive and awake, even though I barely slept. I prayed for world peace and for all those I care about. Being with friends who share their practice opened my compassion and reminded me that there is so much to life beyond my job, material things, and petty concerns.

Being in the presence of such pure people also showed me how important authenticity is. I saw and felt that a genuine and pure heart is priceless. People give their time to teach you the practice and share the knowledge that they have learned. They welcome people of different races and faiths who find themselves here at this Buddhist temple, as a bodhisattva, a person striving to reach enlightenment. I felt free, not because I took the time away from the office, but because I was around people who do not judge. I was among people who put humanity's needs above their own, who sincerely pray for the peace and happiness of all souls and envision an enlightened and peaceful world. They say that the Buddhist practice reveals your true nature and the true nature of all beings and entities around you. Therefore, my practice reveals the true nature of all beings around me.

After leaving the holy grounds, I went to my home away from home, The Westin Hotel in the Meguru area. While walking around Tokyo, I still felt a sense of deep peace that I was not clear was from my stay on temple grounds or from being amongst this calm and gracious society. I was impressed with how polite everyone is, even to foreigners. The concierge at the hotel made it clear after answering a million questions that tipping is not necessary in their culture, which was a piece of refreshing news to hear as a tourist.

After shopping in the Harajuku area and walking around the city and its many parks, I was ready to return home to Los Angeles. I was ready for my soft and plush bed, and my French fries.

Chapter 65

Smoking Gun

UPON MY ARRIVAL BACK TO LOS ANGELES, THE CHAUFFEUR dropped me off at my house. I carried all of my items to my place. Walking through the door of my beautiful, sparkling clean apartment, I felt happy and relieved to be home and back in familiar territory. The best part of travel is returning home, to appreciate all that you have through renewed eyes.

I was exhausted and wanted to go right to sleep. However, jet lagged, my body was unsure if it should be asleep or awake. So, I opted instead to call Nick.

"Hi, how are you?" I asked.

"Hey, I am fine," he said before blurting, "Oh, so, the deal is, I will have to go to jail for two weeks."

"Oh, well, it could have been eight months. I thought there was more time before a decision would be made."

"I am carrying something. Can I call you back in fifteen minutes?" he asked.

"Sure."

As I waited for his return phone call, I was concerned for him, replaying the last conversation we had in my head. I impatiently texted him questions. "What happened how did the decision get made already? Why don't you have more time?"

"I have a headache. can we talk about this tomorrow?" he texts back.

I called his phone number. The call went unanswered. Instead, an angry text message appeared on my phone. "Did you not get my text? I am tired and don't want to talk with you now."

"Oh, ok wow…" I text back.

I unpacked and went to bed. I was puzzled by his cold behavior and felt like the facts did not seem to add up. I also noticed that he had not asked about my trip. He just launched into his life. In fact, we always just talked about his problems. He never acknowledged anything great going on in my life. I thought to myself, what a strange person who never says thank you or asks another person how they are.

The next day I did receive phone calls and text messages from him apologizing, asking how I was, and if he could see me, and what kind of gift did I bring him from Japan?

Hours later, he arrived at my house. He seemed different, cold and aloof. His gray jacket reflected his eyes that appeared as steel. He was not the warm and handsome, charming man that he generally presented himself to bc. He was a complete stranger at this moment.

He sat down on the couch, and I greeted him with gifts, chocolate, and the $800 he requested via text right before he came over. I brought him a drink and sat facing him.

"How are you today? How are you feeling?"

"Not so great, I don't want to go to jail, but my lawyer thinks that I will be there less than a week, especially if it is around the holidays."

"That is good. I am sure it will work out for you."

"Yes, we were discussing today if we should go to trial, but you never know, so I think it is best to get this over with as quickly as possible."

"I agree with you."

"Thank you for the cologne," he said. "You have great taste. I like this one, Gucci Envy."

"You are welcome. So, I have a question. Why do you not respond to me when I text or call you?"

"I'm busy," he defended.

"That is not true. When I am with you, you are constantly texting and talking to other people. I do not believe that for an instant. I know this is not the right time to talk about it, but where do you see us going?"

"We are friends. I appreciate your friendship, but I am not physically or sexually attracted to you, and you are too old for me. You don't like to do the same things I do."

I struggled to hold back the tears, but they started coming all the same. "I do not want to be your friend, as I feel that you do not treat me with respect or consideration. You do not call or respond to me, so how are we friends?"

"I am your friend," he said. "You know I would be there for you if you needed anything."

"How can you be there for someone if you do not respond to them? To me, your actions are not one of a friend, and since you do not want me as your girlfriend, I do not want to be around you anymore."

"What? That is ridiculous. You are saying you don't want to be friends with me because I am not romantically interested in you? You must have known that I am not attracted to you. I did not introduce you as my girlfriend. We haven't had sex in a long time because I don't want you. I am not attracted to you. Have you had plastic surgery? Twelve years, that is a big age difference. I do not feel that we are compatible for the long term, but I want you as my friend."

I was trying to hold back the tears, so shocked by his words. I thought to myself, how can you know someone's character when you don't spend time with them? "No, thank you. You only call me when you need something or money. You need to pay me back by my birthday. You owe me $1,500." I know he will never pay me back.

"I love you in a different way. I want to be your friend," he insists.

"Stop. Why would you hold onto something that you claim you do not want? Why would you waste your time? If you do not want me, why would you spend time with me? I will not waste my time on what I do not want. I want to find the right person for me, to be married and in love. If you do not want that with me, that is fine, but I cannot and will not be your friend."

"Our interests are different, and I think that you would want to spend all your time with me. Oh, and, by the way, I have a six-year-old son in Riverside."

"Wow, how often do you see him?"

"Every weekend, or every other Saturday," he said.

"Well he should be your priority. That is fine, what you think. You don't know me because we have not spent enough time together, but I accept what you are saying."

"Well, are we still going to dinner tonight? I don't want a girlfriend right now. Maybe it will change later. Be opened minded."

"No, I cannot go to dinner now. Thank you, you have set me free. If you take anything from me, take this: that your thoughts create your reality, you are responsible for everything that happens in your life, call on God and the angels, pray for help and focus on your career and your responsibilities." As I got up and walked Nick to the door, the tears stopped. I opened the door, and as he walked through it, I told him, "Best of luck with everything. These next ten years are critical for your career. You need to focus on it and make it happen. Good luck."

He stared at me coldly and paused as if waiting for something to happen. But nothing happened…except that the door closed. I knew I'd never see him again. I wept as I replayed the conversation in my head. I replayed the cruel words from someone who had only taken from me, had never given anything but empty promises.

As your tears come, know that you are not crying over the loss of this person. Rather, you are feeling how you felt as a child when you were unloved, belittled, ignored, ruthlessly criticized, or even beaten. Whatever the childhood experiences, the crimes against your soul, those are the reasons for your tears. You are made to feel helpless and defenseless once again by someone's callous remarks or actions. You are not crying over the loss of a person. The person triggers those feelings and reactions in you. The person is inconsequential to the learning you are dealing with by facing those emotions.

Be strong, take heart. Accept their words and actions as a gift, for that is what they are. The gift is in showing/revealing to you the true cause of your pain and to forgive and let go of all of it. Let go and forgive the original source of the pain and all the various reincarnations, and forgive yourself and let go of any blame you hold onto for bringing it into your existence. Understand that every person and experience is a lesson, if you choose to look closely enough. Be gracious and wish the accuser love and happiness and never look back. Close the door on the past hurts as well. As you do, you will slowly feel lighter and freer as the chains of past hurts are loosened by your newfound understanding.

Everyone has had someone tell them that they are not beautiful, not special, and not worthy of love at some point. For a moment, the insecure and fragile ego allows the hurtful words to sink in and decimate your sense of self-worth, your strength. However, do not let that happen to you, because what they are saying is that they believe that they, the accuser, are ugly inside, deeply wounded and afraid that they are unlovable.

As I walked along the reservoir after completing a run, I came upon a corner that allowed me to see the reservoir. This dark corner shaded by trees was a great outpost to view the picturesque scenery in the middle of the city. The view of the dark green, almost emerald water was beautiful and serene as ducks swam in the distance. The wind whipped around me as if removing the sting of the words Nick said to me, which were playing over again in my head. My mind underwent a familiar pattern of ceaseless repetition of the negative, reliving the hurt from every angle, dying a thousand deaths on the same sword.

I knew that he is damaged and incapable of loving anyone, not even himself, which is the only person he cared about. I knew that his leaving me before I left him was a favor. The biggest gift he could ever give me was his cruelty, as he had set me free, not just from himself but from the pattern of narcissistic love that I keep repeating and re-experiencing. The belief that somehow, I am not good enough, and that my talents do not need to be recognized or acknowledged. And that I should give endlessly to others and not to myself.

I walked alone, as I have many times after a break up or loss, but I felt different this time, and the voice inside me said: *"Dear One, you are never alone, angels walk beside you. We are with you every step of your journey whether you realize it or not. We walk beside you, in front of you and behind you, above you and below you. We are everywhere."*

Tears are streaming down my cheeks as I walk with this awareness. I feel a chill or rush of energy that is deep and powerful that is connecting me to something greater than myself. As I tune into what I feel, I continue to hear the voice. *"Dear One, all you need to do is ask, ask us to protect you, to uplift you, to help you with your burden. Remember, you are loveable and dearly loved. Remember that we are here. If you are quiet and listen, in the stillness you can feel the unconditional love we have for you. If you look around you, you will hear us in the wind; see us in the birds or butterflies that come across your path. Make no mistake: we are here."*

I contemplated this and knew that this time, the pain would not be here long, for now I saw an oasis in the desert. Many times, at this juncture of pain and unreturned love, I had only seen and felt the vast stretches of empty sand. I only saw the vastness of emptiness and loneliness and felt the unrelenting barrage of the sandstorm of disaster. This time was different. As I walked toward my car, I thought that the pain can only damage you if you let it, if you think it can. It has no more power than what you give it, what you allow it to have. You can change your thoughts to something better. You can choose to feel better and then nothing can bring you down, unless you allow it to. This understanding is when you know that you are leaving the winter of your life. That the desert has an oasis, that you can find paradise wherever you are. Salvation can be found in the middle of the cubicle, a barren field, in the middle of a dead-end job or a marriage. You have the power to choose more for yourself, whether someone wants you to or not. You have the ability to be in a state of Grace for yourself, not just for others. When you can do that, love and nurture yourself, you can truly love, and heal, and be happy.

Chapter 66

The Heroine Within

M Y MIND IS RESTLESS, AND I AM UNABLE TO FOCUS ON ANY one thing. I feel as if I have a sickness, like I am tossed about a rough sea without a direction, without a compass to find due north. Maybe the desire to be married is for the illusion of stability, and to feel grounded when one knows their soul is untethered. Maybe the lack of a serious companion is the result of the soul's inner wisdom and guidance protecting you from the illusion that the restlessness will disappear or quelled by another's love. Love is wonderful but does not solve your issues; that is our unique job to do. Connection to others does not change your inner demons. It only intensifies and magnifies whatever spirit work needs to be done. How strange that I can begin to read the heavy and melancholy chords of Beethoven's 8th Sonata, *Pathétique.* Maybe my soul is at the same frequency Beethoven's was when he composed this piece. I can play it as I am resonating the sense of anguish, peace, and chaos, of constant movement; my feelings traverse the octaves as his piece does.

I have experienced a Jane Eyre moment. I am a heroine in my own life. I stand up for myself at work and in personal relationships. I do not let people's harsh words and actions define me, yet I still believe in love and hope for it. I will not be with another to stop loneliness. Instead, I relish my time alone to contemplate and be.

On the moor, the vast unending landscapes, the heroine walks alone in the rain and the sun, just as in Charlotte Bronte's *Jane Eyre* it is Jane who rescues and saves Mr. Rochester. He always knew that her love was too good for him, although at first it appeared that she was not good enough for him. Her plain looks and lack of fortune labelled her as unworthy of love. However, her true and genuine nature is more beautiful and lovely than all the jewels one can find, and Mr. Rochester is captivated by her.

I have discovered that it is not beauty or wealth that makes someone love you. It is your heart that is true and that you share with another. Jane was able to do this with Mr. Rochester, and he fell in love with her. Although, she ran away and felt undeserving of his love, and there was the matter of his wife. In the end, after reflection, she returns to him, and she is the real heroine of the story, for she saves her prince charming. He is freed of the past that was haunting and tormenting them both. With his physical and material state in decline, he is humbled and can only offer his heart. She returns to him and gives him her love, which one can imagine then saves him. For now, he is loved for himself, and is not shackled to a lie. He is redeemed by love.

I have released past lovers and the idea that I can only be with a particular type of person, such as one who is financially well off. This old idea of a worthy partner has been a limiting criterion in the search for love, as money and success may not equate to generosity or sincerity.

Instead, I will be my own heroine and create my fortune that I will share with the one I love. That way I can focus on finding only the qualities that matter most to me, the qualities of a person's character, not the external trappings, the line items on a résumé or bank account.

Chapter 67

Cheetah

A CHEETAH ENTERED MY DREAM LAST NIGHT. THIS ANIMAL guide represents that it is time to work on my goals, to be active toward my dreams. That it is time to finish my creative project no matter what the cost, no matter how tired I may feel. The cheetah was in my bed next to me. I pulled the covers back and got out of bed. The cheetah followed me and jumped on me. Its two front paws pinned me to the wall as it stood on its hind legs. Strangely, I was not afraid. The cheetah then kissed me and turned into a beautiful man with green eyes, and in his embrace there was passion. The transformation of the cheetah into a man was slow. Every part of the cheetah morphed into masculinity, and I noticed that I was then with a lover. A lover who was kissing me passionately. I looked into his green eyes and saw a gentle expression.

Cheetah medicine can help us focus on our goals with speed and focus. The cheetah period is one of extreme action followed by rest.

The cheetah is showing me how I will attack my goals, and that it is time to focus. The cheetah shows me that this is not a period of just waiting or thinking, but a time for action. When animals appear in my dreams, it is time to listen and watch what insights they are bringing to me. Sometimes it is a message of warning from the snake, or it is the elephant telling me there is nothing to fear, or the wolf walking the path with me in my solitude.

Each animal totem is a guide, a messenger imparting its essence, which is a key ingredient that you need at the moment, in the upcoming phase of your life's journey.

Chapter 68

Reckless Abandon and Abandonment

I AM HOPEFUL FOR LOVE. I WANT TO SHARE ALL THAT I FEEL with someone who is a good match for me. I adore the rush of energy one feels when excited about someone new. You feel like you are on a high. You smile constantly, wonder how they are, are curious if they pause during the day and think of you and smile. You cannot wait to hear from them. You want to make them happy. I want to feel wanted, needed, adored by another.

I had seen these shoes on sale at Saks Fifth Avenue, a sleek gray ankle boot by Jimmy Choo, perfect for winter. I walked over to them and this tall, slender, handsome man with salt and pepper hair, looking like an Italian model, smiled and said hello.

"Is there something I can help you with?" the salesman asked.

"Yes, is Christopher here?" I asked, requesting a familiar salesman.

"No, he is not here. Can I help you?"

"Oh, yes. Can I please try these on in a size 8?"

"Yes," he said with a big smile.

He walked away and returned with one of the shoes in the size I want. I was seated on a chair and tried the ankle boot on.

"I can't find the other shoe right now. I will keep looking."

I tried on the right shoe, and it fit. I decided that I love them. When he returned, I told him that I was ready to buy the shoes.

"I love them, I will take them."

"Great," he said. "But I can't find the left shoe. So, you will have to give me your number, and I will let you know when I find it."

"Okay, well, should I just pay for them now and then pick them up later?" I asked.

"No, just in case I can't find the other shoe. Let me look and get back to you," he suggested.

"Okay, thanks."

"My name is Jim, what is your name and number?"

"My name is Tristan, and my number is 555-8877."

"Great, I will keep in touch."

"Thank you, Jim!" I smiled and walked away.

I found him very handsome. I had noticed him before but never spoken to him. He seemed sophisticated and polite, very charming. I went to my hair salon across the street with a big secret smile.

Later that week, I was sitting in a small room with other people, excited parents, sisters, aunts, uncles, and grandparents, all anxiously awaiting a dance performance of the Nutcracker. My ballet instructor had choreographed a little performance with many of her students. The music plays and beautiful young girls pirouetted, leapt and gracefully moved in ornate tutus and delicate pointe shoes. The smiles on their faces showed their true hearts' desire was to perform as beautiful, elegant prima ballerinas. You could tell that these dancers would strive to dance in professional ballet companies, and may well become the next prima ballerinas that you must see perform *Swan Lake* or *Giselle*. Their happiness came from their love of the art, their mastery of technique, and exudes this incredible excitement this energy that was both enthralling and captivating.

After the dancers gave their final révérence and the performance was over, I walked to my car. I felt magical, as if fairy dust was sprinkled all over me, and I was floating to my car as I remembered the delicate butterflies who graced the stage just now. As I got into my car, I saw the license plate in front of me read BEMAGIC. I thought, how fitting, to see this now after such an ethereal performance.

I felt the rush of energy, the anything-was-possible energy. I felt as beautiful as the dancers and the music I just heard. I suddenly felt bold and couldn't stop thinking of the handsome new stranger in my life. Against better judgment, I decided to break the rules, to make the first move. The worst that can happen is he says *no*, that he's gay or in a relationship, and that puts me in the same situation I was right now, alone.

I grabbed my phone and texted him.

"Sorry to bother you, hope you are well and hope you had a very merry Christmas."

He responded: "No bother. Christmas was good. Hope you had a nice one as well. Happy New Year, wishing you all the best."

I replied back with my own form of flirting: "Same to you! I am going to the salon tomorrow and would like to know if you will be around? I appreciate your politeness and think you are very funny and kind."

"Yes! I will be there," he responded. "Look forward to seeing you and you are too sweet."

I responded with more flirting. "I look forward to seeing you too. You are so handsome! Thank you for indulging my text, sorry for the intrusion. Sweet dreams! I am sorry for being so silly."

"Sogni d'oro," he texted.

"Ciao Bella," said I.

"No you are Bella," he responded.

"I apologize, I am not like this," I offered.

"No need to apologize," he says.

"You just made me laugh so much the other day, and you are such a gentleman."

"Call me," he texts.

"Now?"

"Yes. Bisou."

I was so excited by his invitation. I called him. He answered the phone and told me what a pleasant surprise it was.

"Hi, handsome," I said, "I am sorry for being so forward, but I just think you are such an interesting and attractive person. I am not sure if you like women or men and thought, it would be nice to get to know you if you are open to that."

"I like strong, sexy, sophisticated and intelligent women," he confirmed. "I am not attracted to men. I have always thought you are adorable."

"How sweet!" I responded in great delight. "Would you like to meet for a drink one day after work?"

"Yes, that is a great idea. How about tomorrow? I will be done with work at five, if you have time to meet then," he suggested.

"Great! That is perfect. I have to get my hair done, and I always buy new underwear for myself for New Year's Eve."

"You should let me pick it out for you," he offered.

I quietly agreed. "I will buy something pink, because my friend said in her culture you wear pink on New Year's Eve to usher in good luck."

"Great. I will see you at five tomorrow, then. I have parties to go to after, but it would be great to meet you for a drink."

"Great, how about the restaurant across the street?" I suggested.

"Great, I will see you there, beautiful."

 "Great, good night," I said.

"Good night. Bisou," he says.

I could not fall asleep though, because I was giddy with excitement. I felt so happy, so dreamy, and anticipated looking into his beautiful eyes and hearing his charming voice.

I floated through the next day. I got my hair done at the salon. I bought my New Year's Eve undergarments and a beautiful new night-gown. I walked over to the restaurant and got a table. I ordered a drink since I was early, and waited for him to arrive. Part of me feared that he would forget somehow and not show up.

My fears were unfounded. He appeared. My heart raced as I saw him approach my table. He was tall and lean, with salt and pepper hair and blue eyes. He wore a dark pinstripe suit and looked chic. I was trying to appear calm, but inside I wanted to scream and hide. I was fearful and excited. He leaned over and kissed me on both cheeks. He told me he finds me beautiful and adorable and brought me a small gift showing me that he listens to me: something pink to give me good luck for the New Year. As he sat next to me, I could smell his cologne, a sophisticated and subtle fragrance that was unique and suited him well. I had never noticed it before.

He arranged for our next date while we were on our first date. I found him irresistible. He smelled subtly masculine. He looked at me with desire in his eyes. His hands were racing up and down my leg, my back and waist. I just wanted to be enveloped by his deep blue eyes.

Every woman should ask a man out once in her life. To make the choice to go for what you want, and that is what I did with Jim.

But I have gotten ahead of myself. The new man I was attracted to was suave, sophisticated, tall, lean, handsome, and was just charming to everyone. When I met him, I was hopeful that he was interested in me. This interaction helped me to recognize that I was still single and needed to accept that fact, and that I had obstacles in my way to love that I had to identify and remove before I could pass freely.

I received a text message from Jim telling me that he was free Friday night if I want to do something, and of course his signature closing remark, "bisou." I was excited, and jumped at another date with him.

I got my hair and makeup done and drove over to Venice beach. I was thinking we would go out for drinks, but once I arrived he seemed tired, and his homebody side kicked into gear.

"Let's just have drinks here. I have to work tomorrow and don't feel like going out," he said.

"Really? I want to go out. It's my treat, let's just go to a low-key bar."

"I am sorry, but that's not what I want to do," he said. I realized that he had a will of steel and that it would be a night at home. We sat on the couch on a Friday night. The beautiful sand-colored fireplace ablaze gave off a bright and warm glow. Sitting close to each other, watching TV, I was unable to enjoy the moment. I felt like he put no effort into spending time together. He was relaxed and comfortable, almost in a trance—or should I say coma.

He showed me pictures of his ex-girlfriends who married well and left him behind. I felt there was still lingering bitterness about the fact that he was without each of them. These ghosts he was dancing with prevented him from living in the present. He would rather have had his past loves haunt him then woken up to a new love in front of his eyes. Or is it that he did not know how to get over it, move on from the disappointment? The love was returned but somehow, love was not enough and these women, although they adored him, chose another way, another man. I was sure that the feeling of inadequacy, insecurity was internalized, which is a natural response to rejection. Many times, we do not know how to deflect the shortcomings of others, and we suffer because we believe that we were not enough somehow.

I felt a sadness, a chill, not from the winter's night air, but from his heart as the deep freeze was still there. I could not warm his heart, not with gifts, laughter, compliments, or kisses, because we knew that he was lost in the wilderness of sadness, betrayal, and the disappointment of unreturned love. Yes, the love was there. It existed, but it did not stay, and it felt the same as if it were never there.

As I sat next to the shell of a man who once was great, who I saw glimpses of when he felt strong, I realized that this love will never be, will never take off. He would rather be alone with his memories. He would protect his heart at all costs and fill his nights with busyness and friends, or retreat to the couch where he could feel the peaceful state of numbness. I know this because I have been there. Different reasons kept me spellbound, but I have been frozen, stuck in the past and the darkness of doubt and insecurity, where hope does not shine through, and all is dismal.

The TV finally powered off. All lights were turned off, and we walked to the bedroom. I tried to arouse him with seductive kisses, caresses and roaming hands. I received little to no reaction.

"Babe, I am not a young buck anymore. I am tired," he said.

"Really? You just want to sleep?"

"Babe, yes, I am so tired. I need to sleep now."

He shut down. I rolled off of him. I could not arouse the dead. He gave up. His resignation to a loveless night was too strong. He didn't desire me.

"I guess you are not attracted to me," I said.

"I am just not young any more. If I weren't attracted to you, you wouldn't be here."

"That is not necessarily true. We spend time with people for many complex reasons: boredom, loneliness."

"I am not lonely," he said emphatically.

"OK, good night."

"Good night, baby," he responded. He immediately started to fall asleep and was snoring. I was wide awake, contemplating his response. Was I projecting, since my last fling said he wasn't attracted to me? Was he genuinely tired? Was this what happens to older men, they lose their sex drive and cannot function sexually? No one had ever spoken of this side effect of age.

I lay there for 30 minutes in the dark, my mind racing. I could not fathom sleeping here or waiting for hours to pass by until I was ready to sleep. I slide out of bed while he was snoring. I quickly dressed myself and grabbed my shoes. I walked over to the edge of the bed and said, "Sweetheart, are you asleep? I am not tired, and I know you want to get your rest and be left alone. I am going home. Sleep well and have a good day tomorrow."

"Oh okay, do you want me to walk you downstairs?" he asked.

"No, get your rest. I can find my way to the car."

"Okay just go to the garage, and the door will automatically open."

"Okay, good night."

The snoring returns. I walked out of the bedroom and grabbed my purse. I walked out of the beach condo with stunning views, took the elevator to my car, and let myself out.

On my drive home, I contemplated. What was I thinking? Wow, he doesn't want a fling? Hormones had been coursing and rushing through my body. It was almost unbearable. I felt as if I was buzzing, but my passion was not matched. What was I doing? Why couldn't I just lay there and fall asleep and appreciate his warmth, and how he likes to hold my hand? Why couldn't I stay? What does he mean he is not lonely? Am I the only woman he cannot get turned on by? I drove home. None of my friends were available to talk. Alone with my thoughts, I climbed into my lovely palatial bed and asked for clarity.

Sleep is a great thing, as it tries to help you wash away the sting of unpleasant moments.

The next day, I woke up and slid out of my luxurious bed. I made coffee, sat on the couch, and looked outside the window to my balcony. I hear the birds singing and bees buzzing around me. The sun was getting brighter and brighter with each passing hour.

I had an epiphany that did not occur to me the night before. If I stayed in the present moment and did not judge his plans and the evening, I could have enjoyed just being there, his energy and experienced him at peace while sleeping. But because I was impatient and had already fast forwarded my interactions into a relationship and potential marriage, I judged the night, and I judged him, and my verdict was that he was guilty of not planning a satisfactory evening—therefore, not planning our future together and not interested in me, and it was time for me to leave him.

I could not see that while it was happening because I was not paying attention. Sadly, my mistake had made him rethink me and what I am about. He perceived me as flighty and not sure that he could trust me. He pulled away and did not reach back out.

I sent him a text message to reassure him that I adore him and wished him a good day. He thanked me in his response. Later, I realized that I have been pushy, forcing him to go where he is not ready to go, into a sexual relationship with me. I apologized for that. Now my hormones have returned to their normal state of balance, and I am calm and centered.

I understand that I triggered a sadness in him and that he triggered insecurity in me. I also see that my actions and words of what I really want are out of sync. There is discord, and that is why my relationships are not going smoothly. I had attracted someone with the same emotional discord.

As I worked and tried to focus on meetings and expectations, I tried not to dwell on the lack of messages or calls. I tried not to feel abandoned and left alone. I always want to tell the person, "I DON'T NEED YOU! I WILL LEAVE YOU ASAP." As I started going down that path, I stopped myself. Why can I not wait to hear from him? Why can I not give him space to think and process all that we have said and done, consciously and unconsciously, to each other?

I took a step back. I thought of all that I appreciated about him and sent him a message reminding him of my interest and appreciation for him, just him. As I fell asleep I imagined his face and smiled. I saw him and all I like about him. I forgave him for what I felt he had done to me. I asked the angels to send him love and happiness. I pictured love, told myself that I was loved and safe no matter what. I told myself that my being loved is not dependent or contingent on a person, on him. Because we are all loved unconditionally, the perfect state of being is that of unconditional love. It is amazing the energetic shift you feel when you think and focus on love. You feel lighter, brighter, and safer.

When I woke up the next morning, he sent me a sweet message and a kiss as his response. I understood now that he responds to love and appreciation. I sent a kiss back and smiled. I would honor the time he needed to himself. I knew that I am not diminished as a person by his disappearing act. I knew that love exists within you first. It is something you share with another and draw out of each other. If you cannot love yourself, it will be hard to love another. If you cannot trust your feelings, it will be hard to trust another's feelings.

Now I feel serenity. I feel like I see an oasis in the desert and know that my journey will not be rough, and that hardship will end. As I meet my subconscious, this stranger that has been there all my life, I can look this entity in the eyes and see how it has come to be. As I do that, I can decide to choose other thoughts and feelings and let go of the stranger in my life. For it is not unknown, it is all the parts of me I do not acknowledge, that I ignored, that I coped with and pushed and repressed. Now I need to respect it, face it, so I can let go and move on.

I will do this so that the ghosts in the closets of my heart and mind no longer haunt me and interfere with all the good I desire for myself and others.

Thank you to my teacher, my new friend who has shown me this. I sent him love and asked the angels to help him and bless him with all that he desires. I wondered at night if he was with friends or alone, if he could feel the kisses on his cheek that I sent him. If he heard the blessings whispered in his ear that I sent him, if he knew that the love he seeks was here if he opened the door to his heart.

Chapter 69

Reasons

A S I WALKED THROUGH THE HALLWAY OF THE OFFICE BUILD-ing in search of my client, I carried a small white bag filled with Godiva chocolates. I wanted to drop off the chocolate to two of my clients to wish them belated happy holidays and thank them for all their help during our long and demanding project.

I went to his office and saw it empty and locked. In fact, no one in the department was around at all. As I continued walking, I saw an open door and see my colleague and friend, Lauren. She was on the phone and saw me as she looked up. I waved, and she waved and motions me to enter her office. She concluded her phone call quickly, got up from her desk and walked over to me. We greeted each other hello and give a quick hug. "Happy Holidays. How are you? I am so happy to see you!" says Lauren.

Same to you," I offered. "I am fine. How are you? It's been forever since I have seen you."

"I am okay," she responded. "I am stressed with work. As you know, my boss has left to a different department, and now I have to do his job and my job. I was barely keeping it together, and now I am completely overwhelmed."

"I am sorry to hear that. What will you do about it? Are they in the process of filling the position? Would you take that position and replace yours?"

"Well I can't take that position as they have a different strategy for that role, and based on the criteria I would not be a fit," she confirmed. "In the meantime, I cannot sleep. I gained 10 pounds. I am overwhelmed."

"Well, you still look great. But I understand, with your commute it is already a big job, and now with this extra pressure, it is too much to handle. That is why I am now working with a new client and only here minimally."

"I am interviewing and starting to look elsewhere. The interview I just had has shown me that this is a tough market. It wasn't the right fit," confessed Lauren.

"Well, don't be discouraged. Don't give up," I advise her. "You will find the right fit. Tell yourself every night before bed that you will find the right job that is closer to home and provides more work-life balance."

"It is just so hard to know what you will walk into," she moaned.

She told me that she was at a meeting where the speaker said everyone has expressed or unexpressed vision statements about life. She realized that she had one that she used to evaluate decisions.

I asked her what her vision statement was.

"Challenge everything," she quickly responded.

"How perfect, because now you need to follow your personal vision statement and challenge why you are still here and miserable."

"Yes, I realize that," she replied.

"You will need to restate your goal every night and challenge your belief that you cannot find a better job for you close to home that allows you to have time with your family," I explained. "Try to write down all the qualities you are looking for, what your days will be like, how you will feel while at work. Get a piece of paper and draw a circle. In the middle of the circle, write down all the things you want in your next job. Outside of the circle, write all the things you are no longer willing to experience, that you no longer want." I gave this advice which Nancy, my shaman friend, had given me.

As I told her this, she contemplated the validity of this experiment, and her eyes grew wide. She realized that this might be a useful exercise, and she wrote down the instructions.

"I will try this. This sounds interesting. I always think of you when I wish someone I do not like or who bothers me happiness. Somehow, I feel better when I do that. So, I think this will work. I have nothing to lose," she said.

"Yes, you have nothing to lose, and you need to work with your subconscious to attract the right role. Wishing someone happiness makes you feel better because you are choosing a loving thought, and love is the most powerful energy there is."

"Yes. You are right. I love your earrings, by the way. They are fabulous!" said Lauren.

"Yes, they were my Christmas present to myself. Since I am single, I buy myself Christmas, Valentine's, and birthday presents, and I will reward myself when I complete a project at work. I take care of me."

"Yes, I do the rewards for work too. But I have been so busy these past several months that I can't even arrange to treat myself to a candy bar," Lauren said. As she spoke, her fair skin turned red. She was clearly upset and feeling how unfair life is.

"I am sorry to hear that. With all the extra work, this is a stressful time for you and you also need to look for your next job. Life is short, I know. You moved into your new house and your children are growing up. One has started college. I say, focus on your job search and tell yourself every day that what you wish for is possible." As I watched her think about what I was saying, I sensed her unhappiness and saw that she was desperate for change.

At that moment I thought, how funny that I am carrying chocolate, and she mentioned candy as a reward. If anyone needed a gift of chocolate, it was her. Although I had not factored that I would be giving a box of chocolate to someone who is not my client, I felt compelled. I felt that I must do this act of kindness. It was as if her angels drew me into her office to be the earth angel for her that she needed. Angels cannot express or show acts as they are but through others they express their majesty and grace as they direct and guide us to answer the prayers that they hear. Like a channel, I was there at the right time, with the right thing, for the right person. As I contemplated this situation. I knew that I would give her the beautiful gold box of Godiva chocolate to remind her to have hope, and that she was not alone in her struggle, and that although life is hard, we whose paths cross are here to light the way for each other.

As I reached into my bag and gave her that exquisite box of chocolate, her eyes lit up. She was grateful and thanked me. I knew that her sentiment was sincere. I wished her luck and told her to have faith. I told her to state her desire every day to herself that she will find the perfect and right opportunity close to home that will enable her to spend time with her family and enjoy her life. I stood up, and she did as well. We hugged each other goodbye and sent well wishes to each other.

I exited the office and knew that this encounter was meant to be. As I walked down the hallway and to my desk, I thought about how much of our job isn't really about documents, activities, meetings, and the busy lives we have. Rather, it is about how we relate to each other. Can we demonstrate collaboration? Is there an opportunity to speak up for yourself, or on the behalf of another? Do we see beyond a job title and make friends with everyone, from the janitor to the vice president? Do we show up for each other, and how do we show up? Do we drag ourselves into the office, or do we belittle and berate people? Are we fair and kind? Do we take responsibility for our mistakes and try to find a solution that suits all impacted? Most of all, I feel that our job can show us our humanity and the humanity of others. As we share our stories about our weekends, are we listening to what the other person is saying? Do we lend a shoulder to cry on? Are we cheerleaders for each other? Do we encourage each other to cross that finish line, to make better choices, to show up/stand up for ourselves in life?

I think about synchronicity and how nothing is an accident. How glad I was to share what I learned to help another, because I have received help in so many ways. I am glad that I can share, light the path that I see, the path to empowerment. That is a gift that is shared with us, and we are not always listening.

Hours later, I was at a sushi restaurant for my friend's birthday. I had already taken her to dinner the night before, but showed up with her favorite pie and a birthday card. She and her friends had finished dinner and were laughing and drinking. I gave her a hug, wished her happy birthday, and give the pie and candles to the server. Moments later, the lights were dimmed, and our server walked out with the pie and candles. We all sang "Happy Birthday," and she happily blew out the candles. As we were sitting, laughing and having pie, this young, handsome man approached our table with a big grin. "Hi, I am sorry to interrupt you, but I must tell you that you are the most beautiful woman I have ever seen." He was directly in front of me as he said this.

"Oh, you are so sweet, thank you so much, that is so kind of you," I said as I flashed a big smile at him.

"I can't stop staring at you. You are breathtakingly beautiful…" he said.

"You are so sweet," I responded. "Would you like a piece of pie or cake?"

The young man said no, turned around, and returned to the bar where he was sitting. The table of friends said, "Girl, that's not the kind of cake he wants." The table burst out laughing.

The young man returned to the table. "I will probably never see you again, but I am in love with you."

"What is your name?" I asked.

"Michael."

I stood up and said, "My name is Tristan. Let me give you a hug for your kindness."

"Hi, Tristan, it is nice to meet you."

We hugged each other, and he was beaming from ear to ear.

"I am in love with you. You are so beautiful. Have a good night."

"Michael, thank you. You, too."

My friends were laughing, and he walked out of the restaurant. I knew that he was my gift from the angels. That Archangel Michael and my guardian angels sent me a reminder of my beauty. To remind me of something my father used always to say: *Tristan, it is really not about your outer beauty, but your inner beauty that makes you unique.* Michael was my earth angel sent to tell me to love myself. To know that I receive love unconditionally, and that can never change, no matter what someone is or isn't doing or saying, or what the scale says. Whether Jim ever called me again, if I never had another date with him, I am still beautiful, and I am loved. What a powerful message. The elegance of the angels' work and grace is not lost on me. Inside I smile and thank them for their love and blessing. I know that angels walk beside me, in front of me and behind me, to the right and the left of me, above me and below me. I know that if I can just be aware of their love more often, my life will be enriched. I will be protected and reminded of that protection and guidance always.

There are reasons for everything, but sometimes they are not apparent until after the fact. I am grateful for my angelic message from Michael. When I fall asleep, I repeat to myself, *I am loved.* I feel such a sense of calm and peace that stays with me during the day. I know that Jim saw my beauty, the inner and outer beauty, and his choice to not talk to or see me was not about me, but about his fears. One day, I will find someone who says they are in love with me. I will be with someone who finds me beautiful and can stay with me, to walk with me on my path, and we will share our journey together. For now, I am learning to be patient and wait for Jim to share with me his thoughts as he gathers his strength in silence, or for me to happen upon the next person.

Now I will focus on balancing work with taking care of myself. I will work on the items in my life that are a priority, like my manuscript. I will place my health first and spend more time in nature. I feel like life can show us how magical the universe is, our existence is. Let our hearts be the guide to our lives, and we will see how easily things will unfold. The experience of pure love is what we are here for, our ultimate goal. It is a strong instinct and can override any dysfunctional and destructive programming or experiences that have shaped our lives.

I fell asleep alone in my bed, and I dreamed to know my love and the love inside myself. I asked the angels to guide me and tell me what to do regarding Jim. For now, they said, no more contact. Give him space without you. Let him reach out to you and then when he does, after listening to what he says, you will know what to do. You may suggest positive things for you both to do. In person, you may share with him all that you have discovered about yourself and how you appreciate him. As the famous existential writer Albert Camus says, "No action is an action." I always equated that to death of a relationship if your lover does not ask to see you or does not respond promptly to your message, that it was a sign about their true feelings. However, now I see that no action can be just a pause. A time to reflect before moving in a direction. Not a fatalistic sign that all was lost—at least, it is too early to say.

Reflection is essential to the soul. It is that space where the ego is quiet, and you can be inspired to consider another way. I was now heartened, open to this time of no physical connection to Jim. I saw that it was a time for emotional bonding between myself and the angels. I felt that I need to stay centered in the knowledge that I am loved and that there is nothing to fear. That the right man will be there one day and what is more important is that I learn to love myself and be there for myself. Stay positive, stay focused, and trust that all is well.

I keep hearing in my head, *nurture yourself.* Not sure what that means. I thought taking care of yourself or buying yourself a treat, like a cupcake or something you truly desired, was the same as nurturing yourself. However, I am beginning to doubt my answer. I think the difference is, to nurture is to shield and protect. It means that I should be kind to myself. It means that I should say nice things to myself, especially when I feel alone, insecure, or disappointed. To nurture myself means that I should speak and think kind thoughts about myself as I would speak to another to comfort them. I should allow myself to rest and be gentle with myself. It is a reminder that I do not need to achieve and push to make things happen all the time. It is a reminder just to be in the moment without judging myself or it.

There may or may not be a romantic love partner in my life, but there will always be love if I choose it. My relationship with myself will reflect in everything I experience, so I must forgive myself my mistakes and the mistakes I perceive others have made against me. I must learn to trust my heart and follow it, for it will show me the way to my path of happiness, that elusive Holy Grail that I am searching for through the desert of my life.

Chapter 70

Assuming is Consuming

A
S I WAIT PATIENTLY FOR ANOTHER'S ATTENTION, I PLAY THE
piano. The piano forces you to concentrate, demanding all your
focus. You have to follow the composer's direction of speed and tone.
Everything on the sheet is information: there are notations for where
your fingers should be placed on the keys, the tempo, the strength or
force of your fingers. As I play various pieces, that part of me that
wants perfection repeats each phrasing until I get it right. I play the
phrase over and over again until it is without flaws. Hours pass. I feel
as if I poured all of my emotions into my piece of music and I have
none left over. I am exhausted. All of the blood went to my fingers. I
feel weak. However, I also feel mentally free and at a sort of peace. I
cannot say that I am in a place of complete quiet, because music stirs
your soul. You feel all the emotions, but most of all you are freed for a
moment from the tyranny of your mind. You are liberated from that
constant chatter and anxiety that can run rampant in your head. It is

as if nothing but the music exists for that moment in time. You enter a trance from which you ponder your life, or all life, and the emotional undertone of all things. Music, especially the intricate classical compositions, seems to me to prove the existence of angels, that a force larger than ourselves exists, as the complex sounds blend so perfectly that it appears divine.

I wonder if someone sends you kisses and proclaims love in another language, is it sincere or is it somehow not as serious, since it is not in your language? Can it be dismissed as a joke, as a greeting, as not the same equivalent? I wonder why Jim says "bisou" so casually. Is it the same as "ciao" in his eyes? The same as air kisses—not the same intention of a romantic kiss, but instead a light-hearted, flirty kiss? So, should I know that there is no depth of emotion behind his bisou?

Time reveals the truth of all natures, people and things. I did discover that Mr. Bisou is just a pretense. An image without substance, lacking sincerity. Kisses in French were all that he was willing to give to me. No doubt it was due to exhaustion, fear, and over-giving in past relationships, the usual suspects of self-protectionism.

Like most people, when something doesn't happen for you, at first you blame yourself, and then you blame the other and then you let it go. Once you do let go of the person, or rather the ideas of love that person represents for you, you are free, and you can relax and have fun. The other person, idea, dream, or archetype is a distant thought, just like a shadow you think you see in the dark, nothing more than shapes that form and un-form in the darkness before falling asleep.

Now that I have met another—a foreigner, no less—his words of love are in many languages. But more importantly his words are from the language of the heart, of his heart.

I thank my Angels, my past unsuccessful relationships, and his family for bringing this beautiful soul to me. It is true what they say that love is simple, kind, and flows easily. When it does not, then it is not there, and we need to pay attention to the reasons why. Sometimes, it is because we have lessons to learn, or they have lessons to learn, which reaffirms an understanding that you have just achieved, sort of like a re-test. Most importantly, both people have to believe they deserve love before it can happen.

Chapter 71

Lots of Love

CUPID, THE CHUBBY CHERUB, LED ME TO LOVE. MY GIRLFRIEND Tracy and I went for a drink after work.

"How are you? What's new with you? I haven't seen you in the office in forever! I stop by your desk every once in a while. Did you get my note?" Tracy asked enthusiastically.

"Yes, I did. That is why I asked you to meet me for a drink. I know, it's been months."

"So what's going on with you these days?" she inquired.

"Not much," I confirmed. "I started working for a new client that is closer to my home, so I am not here that much anymore. Not seeing anyone special...what about you?"

"I am great. I am dating. I am enjoying life. I joined OK Cupid. It's a free app. It's fun to flirt and go out. I am tired of work and not getting promoted."

"Wow, that's great. Yes...you seem much happier now."

"Yes, it's great because if something doesn't work out, you just move on to the next guy, and there is always someone," she chuckled. "No need to sit around wondering if he likes you or not. If the guy annoys you, just say NEXT! Here, let me show you the list of hotties I am flirting with." She whips out her iPad and logs on. She scrolls through a lot of pictures.

"See this guy? He took me out last week, had an amazing time. This one, we are going out to dinner tomorrow night. I am flirting with this one." She laughed and showed me more pictures.

"Wow, those guys are cute! This is exactly what I need, a fun distraction."

"Yes! Do it! I totally recommend it. I have had so much fun because of this app. I am totally over Steve now. Steve and I are finally just friends. Also, now that you are closer to home, it's time to have more fun and have a life outside of work. I don't know how you were so focused for so long."

"Wow that's great that you are over Steve," I responded in awe. "I always thought that you two would get back together. I completely agree with you. Thanks for sharing."

"Well, let me know if you want help with your profile. It should be simple and fun and guy friendly."

I started laughing. "I get it, simple, fun and not clingy, haha."

After we finished catching up and left the restaurant, many cocktails later, I drove home and thought about what she said. I decided that night when I got home to give it a try. I had nothing to lose. I searched for the app and downloaded it to my iPhone. It seemed very easy to use. I kept the information simple. I did not think of it as a serious way to meet someone, but more as a way to get my mind off the last unsuccessful encounter and cheer up. I uploaded some pictures, kept my profile brief and simple. I had no expectations.

I was pleasantly surprised by all of the messages I received and many cute pictures of handsome guys. I started flirting and responding. It was fun. Then I saw a message from a cute guy that read, "I think you are super cute."

As with all messages, I read the profile of the person and then decided if I should respond. The profile was for a young guy who was just looking for friends.

I had to think about this one. I waited until the next day to respond. After my morning meetings, I was still thinking about the cute guy. I decided, what the hell, a girl can have friends, right? He likes pancakes, and I love pancakes. Just say hi; it's not a marriage proposal.

I texted back and said: "Thanks for the compliment. You are cute too. Hope you are well. So, what kind of pancakes do you make?

"I am well. I make pancakes with Nutella on them"

"Wow! That sounds delicious, I love pancakes!"

"That's great, I make them almost every day."

Before I knew it, I was enjoying my banter with my new friend, so much so that I stopped messaging everyone else. We would message every night for hours. Flirting, joking, sharing pictures and personal details. The interaction was so much fun. I forgot how fun it can be when you click with someone's personality. I forgot how fun it is to flirt. How nice it is when they tell you that you are cute. It's a thrill, a rush, like a drug, and you just want more.

For some couples, there are many differences such as age or race, as well as economic, social, and cultural status, and other details where one may not think common ground can be found. However, there can also be a soul match. A comfort, an understanding, a resonance that two people share that can stretch far beyond conventional matters. It can be as if you share the same ideas, feelings, behaviors, and vision of love that brings you into synchronicity. That is how we were together. Although we had many differences, we shared many essential qualities that felt safe and comforting.

I had found someone that I enjoyed for more than a moment or activity itself. It was his company and presence that I desired, not a gift or the experience of a new restaurant or vacation. I found someone whose outer beauty was surpassed by his inner beauty, with an incredibly pure, generous, and open heart, with whom I no longer wondered or questioned his interest. He told me everything he felt and thought. I knew where I stood with him. Men are always telling us where we stand with them, either directly or indirectly. However, as women, we do not listen, or we think he will change his behavior.

I finally understand that love is a pure and genuine emotion, without strings attached. There is no motive except to give and to receive. That one must give unselfishly and from a place of limitless happiness. Someone who loves you will always remind you of their love for you; will always desire to protect you, and is happy with just you. Love does not need jewels, cars or money. Love is happy just to be. You do not doubt yourself or question their intentions. You see it and feel it as if it were a pillar to rest against. You desire the happiness and good fortune of the one you love regardless of the benefit. You realize this when in front of this person. You no longer think there is someone better. You have finally learned that love is enough. Love is all you need. Love can move mountains. Love can bring you the riches you desire because it can make you feel like gold, and the feeling can help you attract that gold. If you feel rich in love, then you are indeed rich and blessed. However, one must feel this way about one's self first before it can be truly shared with another.

I thank my angels for bringing me my sweetheart, whom I love and who loves me. He sees me as perfect, which helps me to feel perfect, and stop worrying about the last 20 pounds.

Last night, as I was lying in bed about to fall asleep, I felt a deep sense of satisfaction.

My thoughts drifted to how love and sharing can set your heart free to be daring and bold. How that when you feel like your authentic self, you feel free to take risks and to know someone is there to catch you, or that you are supported and can catch yourself. Love is easy, effortless, healing, and nothing more is required of you than who you are, because you now understand that you must love yourself first, that no one can save you but you. You are your own Prince Charming in the fairy tale of your life. You rescue yourself from the clutches of the evil witch (or work environment). You are also the one who showers the princess in you with love and adoration. Therefore, you can decide what love looks like to you and to care for someone and share yourself with them. Because to do so and to fail will not weaken you, as you are strong.

Sometimes the journey to love is treacherous, with many turns and twists and cliffs.

Looking out onto my balcony, I wonder if the state of my garden is a reflection of the state of my life, of my soul. As I water plants that I have neglected due to stress from work, and as I clip the dead leaves and branches, I cannot help but see the parallels these plants have to my life as it is now. I have kept dead plants around for too long as I have kept outgrown friends, lovers, and jobs. Is there a fear to move beyond and to let go?

Pure love is like a healing poultice, a mixture of natural elements with healing properties that you apply to wounds. It can revive even the most bitter shut-down heart.

Selfishness disguised as love is a toxin, an untraceable venom that causes nerve damage, but cannot pinpoint the source, as it is masked by deceit and false words.

The Law of Attraction states that our thoughts create an energy vibration, which draws to us situations and people at a similar vibration. Therefore, is changing the thought and a belief about the thought that powerful, that I can will myself into a loving relationship, a great fulfilling and flexible career and the house of my dreams? Do I need to believe and trust that I am worthy and capable of all that I desire?

Chapter 72

Manifesto for Manifestations

A S I REFLECT ON MY PAST RELATIONSHIPS AND ENCOUNTERS, I
see how my actions and choices reflect the insecurity, the lack
of self-worth in myself and in the other. Now that I had attracted
love from a good man, my attention turned to the hiccups in life
that kept repeating. I wondered what thoughts and beliefs I had been
holding onto that kept me in this unhealthy pattern of debt and under-
appreciation at work?

I think that watching our parents and how they dealt with money,
work, and challenges becomes the foundation of how we will approach
the same. I grew up watching my mother feel overwhelmed, over-bur-
dened, and generally stressed out. Her belief was that money doesn't
grow on trees. Hard work and education can give you money, enough
to have a respectable lifestyle, but not much more.

I realize now that I adopted those same beliefs. Beliefs that have
limited me and that I now challenge. I am beginning to experience

similar things, no matter how high my income is. This sense of inse-curity, overburden, not having enough, while making an excellent in-come, raises the question, "What are my thoughts that keep surfacing as negative experiences in my life?" How do I change these thoughts to expect more and enjoy life more? They always say that the answer to your problem lies within—within *YOU*. I am now beginning to grasp the meaning of this concept. My thoughts and fears that I repeat, and do not accept and let go of, are my constant companions.

I feel now that I have outgrown fear, insecurity, and poverty mental-ity. Instead, I prefer to make friends with abundance, prosperity, free-dom: limitless beings. I now want to focus on my true inner desires and stop making excuses for why I cannot be happy doing work I love. Why don't I have time to work on my dreams, and why do I put everything and everyone else before me, and why I am always the last item on the to-do list? It is time to choose me, and prioritize *my* needs. It does not mean that I will just stop working and stop talking to everyone I know. I realize now that what it means to prioritize yourself is to set time aside each day to do activities that you enjoy and that give you pleasure. Whether it is playing music, gardening, cooking, singing, writing, or reading, it has to be an activity that is solely for your happiness and regenerates you.

So, I will make friends with my new beliefs by thinking of what I want more frequently than what I do not desire. If a negative thought appears, I will acknowledge it and then choose a happier thought. I will dream, think, ponder the beautiful things and experiences that I want and just imagine them without needing to know the logical details like how, when, and how can I afford that?

I will ask the angels to help me release my fear and keep me centered in faith, to help me keep the faith that all is well, and that through faith anything is possible. I will ask the angels to help me remember that each and every one of us is loved and deserving of love and good things.

These thoughts are not new. These ideas are in *The Law of Attraction*, the discussion from Jerry and Esther Hicks about the universal laws that we constantly invoke without acknowledging. The channeled messages that they share with us from Abraham, the entities that want to help us improve our experience as creators, are signposts to living the life you truly want. I have had their books for years, and have read most of them. It is ironic how sometimes we are not ready for the knowledge we will receive from a book, teacher, friend, lover, boss, family member, or stranger that we encounter.

The more I review my life now, when I have a moment to stop the constant chatter in my head, to stop thinking of all the things I have to do, the more I see that I have created every experience in my life, good, bad, or indifferent. Therefore, if I am creating these experiences, why not consciously create? Why not create a manifesto to manifest what my heart desires?

Engels and Marx expounded their critique on the capitalist system and devised a plan for a communal state, and *The Communist Manifesto* was born. Whether you agree or not, appreciate or not their efforts, they did outline a theoretical plan to accomplish their form of utopia.

Now I understand that we as human beings must consciously do the same for our lives. State the type of life we want to live, describe what our personal utopia is, and outline a course of action. We are not just "a poor player, That struts and frets his hour upon the stage, And then is heard no more,"[5] as Shakespeare tells us through Macbeth's so-

---

5   William Shakespeare, *MacBeth* (Dover Publications, 1993), p.77

liloquy lamenting Lady Macbeth's death. We are the willing creators of our lives. We are the existentialists who choose by not choosing. No action is a response, just as living through the eyes of our subconscious fears and thoughts or blaming others for our predicament in life forces us to make choices, whether we consciously acknowledge the choices or not. We are shaped by our environment, which provides us an opportunity to then assess and choose our path.

I challenge myself to forgive and let go of the past. To choose happier thoughts, to believe and know that all things are possible and that I deserve happiness, love, and success. I challenge myself to be happy for other people's success, to know that their success does not diminish mine. I will continue to pray for peace and happiness for all on this planet. I refuse to play the victim in my life anymore. I will not be terrorized by debt, by my job, by previous rejections and disappointments. I will appreciate all that I have and ask that I have what is mine by divine right and comes to me in a perfect way, as Florence Scovel Shinn instructs in her book *The Game of Life*. I do not need another's house or riches or love. I want what is mine and know that there is plenty for all.

I give praise and thank God for my blessings and know that it will be so. I am learning that appreciation is vitally important to obtaining and maintaining success. When we believe that we alone hold the power, we are reminded that we are wrong. We may have success for a while, but as we continue to not appreciate and see the incredible synchronicities that make everything possible, we will lose it all. We will be forced to reckon with the creator within. We will face a dark night of the soul. This can last a minute or a lifetime. All of our wrong thinking is reflected back to us in our world. Things fall apart, friendships fall away. You are left alone with your fears and insecurities. Your task is to let go, ask for help, and to be thankful for everything that appears, the good and the bad. As your faith returns, so too will your fortune.

That downward spiral is a dark and difficult place. When you begin to see the light, to have hope and to smile, you know that your dark phase is ending. We are not meant to struggle, but we will if we give into the inner demons and of the mind. We create our lack, and therefore we can create our supply, through the help of spirit, the invisible hand. It would be interesting to ask Adam Smith, who is attributed with outlining the mechanism and need for a *laissez-faire*, free market system. If, now that he has passed, he still believes the invisible hand to be that of the market or that of God/Universe/Spirit.

Who would have thought that I, after being so upset with God for the loss of my father and for all that I have gone through, would come to realize that we are not alone? And that there is a presence of something much bigger than ourselves that creates with and for us?

But, after all that I have gone through, the good and the bad, I can see how things unfolded perfectly when I was in sync, and horribly when I was not appreciative. I understand that there is so much more to life, to us, than our minds and our achievements. I have come to realize that we are the perfect expression of something greater than ourselves. You may label this as you wish, for it does not take away its power.

It is unfortunate in the modern era that we have put so much emphasis on empiricism, on only what we can observe in concrete terms. Now I lament how we have placed all the power in the scientific explanation, that we have limited ourselves to experience the totality of all things. Our modern training has taught us that we cannot rationalize the existence of the unexplainable, although we know it to exist. I remember falling in love with Kant's categorical imperative and how his writing explained that mankind de-godded nature through the scientific method. I see that his theory is true and helpful to understand the values of our time. However, now I feel that the scientific method is not the whole story. The unexplainable is to be revealed in faith over time, when our consciousness has evolved beyond the five senses and can grasp what we cannot understand or explain with logic.

Chapter 73

Crossing Over

I AM GOOD AT WHAT I DO. I AM DETAIL ORIENTED. I FOLLOW through and am a clear communicator. I approach people with respect and ask for everyone's input. However, even with strong performance and excellent pay, work can feel tedious. I know that my soul cries for freedom and self-expression. My spirit desires the ability to create, to share, and to relate.

The cubicle in the sterile corporate environment, which provides little appreciation but many expectations, is getting weary. I no longer look to my job as my sense of identity and accomplishment. I now see it as a prison that blocks my freedom and creativity; however, I know that I still must appreciate the job and the opportunities, and bless everyone I come in contact with. Only through loving and appreciating what I have will I be able to transition somewhere else.

I need to ask for signs toward what my divine purpose is. I need to devote time each day toward it. Even if all I can manage is to imagine a better way, a better life filled with meaningful activities, one must think and believe it before it can be achieved. Belief and trust are the elixirs that true alchemists use to manifest their dreams. The alchemist can turn brass into gold or coal into a diamond in an instant. The belief is as strong as the element itself.

To turn the water into wine, we must believe in the power to do so, that it can be done, and not falter. We must give thanks that it has happened in advance. We must ask for it to be done in a perfect way. We must release our fear and our rational mind, let go and let God, or whatever you refer to God as into your heart. Only then can we be the alchemist, and turn fear into faith and brass into gold.

As I see how I left my last job, and subsequently manifested another job in a location I desired, I realize the power of my words. I told myself that I would no longer return to the old client, and that I would be done by year's end. That is exactly what happened.

Now I wish for success and love and know that it is done, and I expect to see it. The days of feeling like a helpless victim are gone. The days of asking others for help have passed—for I can resolve and fix it now with the help from spirit.

When I feel stuck and sad, I know now to listen, or play music, or go for walks in nature. Music and nature have a way of healing the soul and releasing the mind from fear. It is where I feel inspired, at peace, wondrous, and grateful for the butterfly that comes across my path, for the hummingbirds that buzz, and for the dragonflies that dart and reveal themselves.

It is also where I feel forgiveness for others and myself. Resentment, anger, fear, and lack of appreciation block our good. Holding onto situations and people who are not good for us delay the forward movement that we desire. We must bless them, wish them happiness, and step away. We can also wish for our happiness and know that all is well, regardless of what you see or feel in the present moment.

Chapter 74

Resolutions

NEW YEAR'S EVE IS A GREAT TIME TO CELEBRATE AND REFLECT on your life. At a small cozy gathering with a few girlfriends amongst Chinese takeout, cupcakes, and many bottles of champagne, we sat down while sipping bubbly and talked about our holiday, what we were grateful for, and what we were looking for in the New Year. Our hostess had markers and star-embossed paper for us to write our New Year's goals.

We all had something related to improving conditions at work, love, and maybe some new accessories—or at least that was on my list.

My list contained:
- Complete my manuscript
- Find love with my perfect match
- Take a first class trip to Paris
- Lose 30 pounds
- Spend more time in nature
- Diamonds

That year, I bought a new pair of diamond stud earrings, spent more time in nature, lost 10 pounds, and wrote but did not complete my manuscript. So, by the end of the year, I needed to meet my goals. Unfortunately, since food is a reward to me, and I am a stress eater, I have since regained those 10 pounds. So, either I had to increase the overall amount that I needed to lose to 40 pounds or decrease the goal weight so that the calculation could still equal 30 pounds to lose. If only math problems were worded in this way when I was in school, I would have related better and received higher grades in class. Maybe more gender balanced examples for math in our elementary school days is needed. At least, that is what the magically creative part of my brain is telling me. After all, I am magical.

I love being a magical creature. We are all magical because we are all creators. We create the good and the bad by thinking and feeling what we believe we deserve. Some of us are better at imagining beautiful things and experiences than others. No doubt, how we are raised greatly influences our capacity to believe in ourselves, in our own power, and in our own greatness without taking away from another's. I know that I was constantly criticized and belittled. I had to reach into myself and tell myself that I am intelligent, that I am beautiful. I think that is why many people appreciate the scientific method, empiricism. It is because with proof you can undo the bindings of discouragement that keep you trapped in a limited existence when all you can see are limitations and reasons why not. If you obtain good grades or praise at work, you can reprogram yourself to be a winner. However, during the dark night of the soul, observation and proof will not be enough to help you overcome your demons as they reappear and wreak havoc on your life. Only faith can restore you; however, that means you must let go or give up control to forces you cannot observe physically as a three-dimensional entity or object. You will see a trail of hope as you surrender your ego to God-force/Spirit/Source/the Universe/whatever name you label it. As you connect to that source, you then learn that you have always been the creator, and that sometimes we forget our power. We let others cajole and bully us. We ignore the truth of our power and play the victim to circumstance.

I have always been able to create excellent jobs for excellent pay, as if out of thin air. I have always felt successful in that arena. Lately, I have been contemplating a new job, as the one I created is not what I had imagined. Or rather, I did not imagine the details, only the destination, so I was dissatisfied.

Now, I wanted more freedom and creativity. I no longer thought I needed to run the entire show and all the pieces, so I could let go of control. My desire was to free my mind from the tedious details of work so that I could focus on activities that I enjoyed and that needed my attention. I was trying to rally my will to create more than I ever had before. To allow for expansion, freedom, and limitless expression of all I felt was good.

It is challenging to hold true to a belief in something that has not yet happened, a belief that is betrayed by every unkind word from others that threatens the embryonic state of this fragile new thought or wish of yours. I easily got distracted by what others said and did. I focused my attention on their limitations and not on my desire to be limitless. I looked at my current job as a jail sentence. The people were kind enough outside of the context of work, but the combination of expectations and competition created a negative, toxic experience, making me dread arriving to work every day.

Every day I read positive affirmations, I prayed to the angels and Ascended Masters for help. I meditated and went for walks outside. I chanted and visualized my already having what it was that I desired. I returned to my manifesto for manifestation, and I kept re-reading the knowledge that others had provided about these topics, hoping for it all to click. Without practice, I could not accomplish my goals.

Chapter 75

Be Careful with What You Wish for

SOMETIMES WE FEEL THAT AN EXTERNAL EVENT, SITUATION, thing or person is what we need to make us happy, to help us move to the next phase of our existence. If things flow easily and quickly then I agree. However, sometimes things do not move easily, and with our will and persistence we force something to happen that should not have happened. We use our will to create that which is out of synch with what we need.

I have finally come to understand that if you push against the natural course of something, then you may bring to yourself what you want, but it might not be what is best for you. In time, you will realize why that person, event, situation, or company was not the right choice for you. This process teaches me patience and to trust my instincts more.

It also reminds me how important it is to not bargain ourselves away for a watch or trinket. We need to ask more questions and ponder if the choice works for us, not just for others. We need to include ourselves more in the process, not just to sell our skills but also to buy a relationship, job, new environment.

Like a compass, you must keep resetting your soul against the markings you consider to be due north. You must listen and allow your higher self to point you in the direction of your dreams. To accomplish this, you must learn to quiet your mind and detach from the daily dramas and egos that surround you. Rest and peace are essential ingredients for clarity. Keep asking yourself to reveal your true desires and nature and allow yourself to believe in what is revealed, no matter what your insecurities or talents are at that moment. Belief is like a seed: once planted, it will grow beyond the tiny speck that is in your hand. It can grow into a flower, a shrub, or a tree that is hundreds of feet tall.

Ideas can only grow in fertile ground. Your mind must be able to hear the wisdom of your eternal self, whether it is communicated directly from your soul, or by others you meet, or through books and other channels. You must also grant yourself permission to accept the higher idea, belief, or thought. You must empower yourself to dream bigger and better. Only when you feel deserving can you move on to your next chapter. We are all deserving of better, of love, so the only permission needed is yours.

Allow yourself to imagine more for yourself. It takes practice to do this and to be comfortable with the new thoughts that you deserve more and can have more, but it is an investment in time that is critical for achieving your dreams.

I try to remember my understandings of manifestation, as the stormy seas of my world toss me about and even crush me at times.

It is the judgment, criticism, unnecessary comments we receive from co-workers, and the trivial daily events, like being cut off in traffic, that send us over the edge, to the dark side of our nature. When this happens, I try not to get engulfed by my human reactions, my own pettiness and anger. I try instead to focus my thoughts on what I want and where I would like to be, breathe deeply and smile as the images display in my head like a movie. Or, if I cannot think of the dream state, I must replace the negative thoughts and feelings with something I enjoy. This is where food or shopping comes in handy. A simple cupcake or dessert can turn my attention from the awful to the delightful in seconds. Sweets can draw us in and bring us back to the magical place, that place of joyful anticipation, the sweet spot.

Chapter 76

Finding the Muse

S OMETIMES OUR LOVE AND ARTISTRY LIES DORMANT, PUSHED aside by stress, too much work, too little time, responsibility, material needs, desire, office politics, and our petty dramas. When you find your muse, you must get to know her, understand her, listen to her, heed her call, or she will find another to inspire.

My enchantress has returned to me. She is beautiful and magnificent, drawing out the loveliness of the earth and our own human nature. I feel as if I am a water nymph chasing a unicorn with pure innocence. I feel the fluttering wings of a butterfly, the buzzing of the hummingbird. I am the scent of a rose wafting through the wind, or the ocean breeze brushing up against the rocks. I only see how beautiful you are and how kind you are. I see the best in you, in all of us, and I love myself at this moment. I feel as if anything is possible.

As I walk outside in the mini nature preserve in the middle of the city, surrounded by trees and near water, a hummingbird flies around and above me. Its humming is steady, loud and clear, its tiny wings flapping furiously as it hovers around me. I see its beautiful ruby red body. I feel as if this little angel is showing me the power of joy, reminding me to stop and be joyful and soar above it all, soar high to the clouds and stars with joy, not negativity or drama from our everyday mishaps with others.

I have learned now to seize the moments of clarity and inspiration and write, or call a friend and tell them they are missed and appreciated. When we are inspired to act, we are true to ourselves. We allow good things to happen for ourselves and others in those moments when we don't wait, and don't question, and do what we know and feel is right.

The notion that reality is temporary makes me think that if that is true, then life is not about what we are doing, but how we are doing it. The measure of "how" is not based on logic or linear thinking, but on love and authenticity, I think. Are we treating each other with respect and kindness? Are we expressing our authentic selves, not a fake self for others or our perception of what others want or think, but are we living the truths we believe? Do we find ways to resolve conflict without making the other person a villain, resulting in violence or character assassination? Are we able to state honestly that someone has done something wrong and still greet them each day with a smile and respect them?

Chapter 77

777

I KEPT SEEING THE NUMBER 777, EITHER ON LICENSE PLATES AS I drove around the city or on receipts. The repeated number appearing out of nowhere made me consider that there was a significance to them. As I saw number sequences repeated, I realized that it was a sign, a clue that I am on the right path. I believe it is true that numbers are a universal language. Doreen Virtue, author of *Angel Numbers 101* has translated for us the meanings behind numbers as provided by angels.

As I look up the meaning of the number 777 in *Angel Numbers 101*, I know that it is a positive message.

The meaning of the number 777 is: "You are definitely on the right path in every area of your life. Stay balanced and spiritually aware so that you can continue moving forward on this illuminated path."[6]

6   Doreen Virtue, *Angel Numbers 101* (Hay House, 2008), p. 183

This is exactly the message I need at this moment, as I have made a lot of changes and started focusing on my new goals. Sometimes I feel brave and confident about my actions, and sometimes I feel anxious and crazy for moving forward. Sometimes doubt still lingers in my head, and an ounce of doubt can destroy all that I am working for, all that I believe in. Therefore, I am grateful for the message of 777.

It is interesting how much reassurance one may need, or subconsciously seek, especially as you change the way you think or reach for that stretch goal. What has changed for me is that the encouragement I used to look for was external and from other people such as family, friends, boyfriends, or bosses, in the form of compliments and recognition. Now I know that I will find affirmation all around me. I will be reassured when I meditate and when I go for a walk outdoors. By paying attention to what is happening around me, I can see the clues. It is as if the universe conspires to make your wishes come true, so we must be careful what we wish for and what we focus on. If we focus on the wish happening versus not happening, then we are more likely to accomplish that wish. I no longer need the consolation of friends and acquaintances, because no matter what another person says, if you do not believe it, it will not help you. Therefore, believing in your dream or vision is necessary before you can recognize the signs that you are fine and that everything is okay. It is easy for us to recognize when things are out of sync. You cannot connect with someone, the job is not available, the terms of the contract do not fit you. You know and feel when something does not match your needs, and although you may be disappointed, you know that something better is supposed to happen.

The statement is true: "When the student is ready, the teacher will appear." It is said that sometimes we are a student and sometimes we are the teacher. Therefore, in each situation it is interesting to observe what role you are playing, and observing how you feel and what insights you are gaining or sharing.

Have you ever tried running away from your present situation? Have you ever had thoughts of, my life will be better when I leave my current job, leave my current relationship, or buy that pair of shoes? I regularly have those thoughts. Each time I do leave a job, I realize that I cannot run away or leave a situation until I have completed everything. "Everything" does not just entail the actual work, but also how we deal with the different and challenging characters and road blocks. This realization occurs as I repeat the experience of the same personalities or issues in the new environment.

True to form, I started searching for a new job after landing one at a chaotic and disorganized company. As I slowly acclimated to the drama of my new workplace, I started interviewing and networking. As I researched my potential new companies, I realized that I was meant to be where I was. I would not be released from there until I came to terms with the chaos and challenges. In short, there was no escape from the now that had presented itself to me. The challenges I faced were there to tell me to hold onto my vision for myself and not be distracted by other people's drama. They were to remind me that no one is really evil or good. We choose to assign a value to someone's actions. If you detach emotionally from your surroundings, then you can view everyone involved with compassion. It is a reminder that others help us reach our next chapter in life by showing us how much we have grown and where we still need to be careful of our thoughts. I created my current situation and I did have the power to change it, but not by escaping to another island, but by creating my dream. That was the situation I created and hoped for. That was the situation I needed to complete.

We are indeed the soldiers in our lives. We battle daily with negative thoughts, with limitations set by ourselves and others, which at times can feel like enemy encroachment in your base camp. We have demons that we must banish so that we can end the torture of our minds and souls. We also have insights and kindness to share and uplift others with. We have the ability to light the path for others by sharing our joy and love, and sharing the understandings that we have gained.

Chapter 78

Lessons

N O MATTER WHAT I SAY ABOUT MY MOTHER, SHE HAS BEEN MY greatest teacher. She has taught me many painful lessons, the most difficult of which was learning to love myself despite what others say or do, including her.

The easiest lessons for her to teach were: independence, the importance of family and community, etiquette, the art of hosting, and good housekeeping. She is an incredible hostess and keeps a beautiful house. It is those closest to us that teach us life's most challenging lessons, because only people who know us are so invested in our success and have the courage to tell us the truth. We need honesty with each other and ourselves. It is the only way we can grow.

I had to learn to accept my mother's personality and recognize that her critical statements come from a place of love. I am the one who decides if there is truth in what is said and only I give life to those words. I can easily disregard them, too.

As her voice gets smaller and my inner voice gets larger, I understand that she has accomplished her goals as a mother. She has taught me to take care of myself, to thrive, and to mother myself before I choose to mother others. She has taught me to know myself by forcing me to solve the problems of my own life. Everyone gets there on different paths. Some people have extremely supportive and nurturing parents and still feel begrudged by life. We are not cutouts of each other or easily replicated, but we share in common human experiences. The shared experience of love and connection, of belonging while standing tall on your own, is the foundation grounding all of us to each other.

I am strong and brave enough to now pursue my dreams. How fortunate for those who feel that strength at a young age and live their dreams, and ask for support and help in creating their dreams. Life is not a race. I do not need to beat or compete with someone else, only my own limited views of myself. If only I understood this point earlier.

I am, however, grateful for the insight and understanding now. It truly is never too late to try to reach for your dreams, or to be more loving toward yourself and others. It's never too late to be kinder to yourself and put yourself and your needs on the top of your to-do list.

Chapter 79

The White Wolf

THE WHITE WOLF APPEARED TO ME, BECKONING ME TO FOL-
low my instincts and complete my manuscript. The way of the
wolf is one of lessons. The wolf is a teacher, sharing the secrets of how
to hunt, and urges you to follow your own inner guide, whether in a
crowd or alone in silence.

The white wolf appeared at the edge of the table which was set in
the garden. She appeared when no one but me was looking. I am
now familiar with the wolf, and felt fearless. She caught my eye, held
my gaze, and then turned around toward the woods, signaling that it
is time for me to forge my own path. She looked back at me again to
make sure I was following and understanding the intent of her visit. I
do not need to take others with me for this part of my journey. I must
leave behind the drama and the opinions of others, so that I can gain
the clarity needed to move toward what I know is right for me. She
tells me that the answers I seek can be found in silence, and reminds
me to turn to and tune into nature.

With her visit, I go to one of my new favorite walks at a reservoir where I see deer, hummingbirds, bluebirds, turtles, and other creatures bustling about. It is a wonderful feeling to be at peace in nature. I always feel calmer and more centered when walking among the trees and near water. It is as if your worries can be wiped away, diminished by the peace and energy of nature. Nature has stillness and movement at the same time. You see beautiful flowers growing in the thick underbrush facing toward dense trees, being blocked by its neighbors. It makes one wonder if there are similar metaphors for people, who are beautiful, yet blocked by their surroundings, by the limitations we placed on ourselves and others have put on us due to fear.

As I walk through the reservoir, I wonder if I am I like that beautiful, bold red bloom that is growing strong yet facing nowhere, the flower that is not curated in someone's garden, not facing prime real estate or direct sunlight. And although in a non-optimal location, I still have been able to blossom and grow in my life, taking the negative lessons and thriving versus being defeated.

A hummingbird dances in the wind, telling me to bring joy, be joyous, and to have joy. Life is about joy and it is all around us. We just need to observe and listen. Its tiny green body shimmers like glitter in the sun, its wings beating so quickly they cause a buzzing sound, that distinctive sound that gives its presence away. The hummingbird's nature is not about stealth. It is not trying to sneak around; rather it is a vivacious, dynamic harbinger of pure joy, and you can hear its buzzing long before you catch a glimpse of it. The hummingbird is a messenger, reminding us that joy is everywhere, to stop and reflect, look within and around nature, for joy is simple and accessible in every moment. We need to choose it.

Chapter 80

Follow Your Bliss

O NE CONSTANTLY HEARS THAT WE SHOULD IDENTIFY AND follow our bliss, do what makes us happy. We know that we are the ones who put limits on ourselves and provide reasons why that cannot be so, and why we remain where we are stuck and stagnant. We put pressure on ourselves to make money, to pay the mortgage and take care for people who depend on us. Oftentimes, we place these items before our needs. Yet we also partially hope that someone will wave a magic wand and make our happiness appear for us or, that somehow it will just be.

On one hand, nothing can exist without the belief and feeling that it can exist. Yet no one tells us how we get there. How do we follow our bliss? How do we get from one point to another? Faith and visualizing are key ingredients, but there also needs to be a commitment, which differs from faith in that it is a pledge, whereas faith is the expectation of the completeness of your desire. Action in the form of doing is essential, and in the form of undoing the negative thoughts and fears that keep you captive to a less than stellar existence.

Commitment is the conduit of faith in that it keeps you in faith, in the direction of your dreams. I almost trick myself into the pages of my manuscript, telling myself it is done, or the pages have been written before they are. My actions catch up to my faith, my commitment and my word, making it so.

Chapter 81

Full Circle

THERE ARE SMALL SYMBOLS AND SIGNS OF ENCOURAGEMENT that we are on the right path that are presented to us if we pay attention. Sometimes, when we make a responsible choice, versus the fun or easy choice, and let go of the beautiful object that we desire but do not need, we ensure that we can take care of the daily business of our lives. The item may return to you at a later date when you least expect it, and for a better price.

I had seen this beautiful, classy leopard print winter coat with a sort of metallic finish. I have a similar one in a brown and beige pattern. Both are from the same designer. I bought the brown version years ago and it is one of my favorite winter coats. A well-tailored coat can make you look good even if you are wearing something more casual underneath the coat. Also, a coat can be a fun fashion statement.

I saw the alternate version of the leopard pattern coat on sale and bought it impulsively. After a week, I returned the coat, since it was not significantly reduced. I had a similar version of the coat and I needed to be a little more fiscally responsible as I was in flux with my job. I am glad that I returned the coat, as I had a little falling out with one of my accounts. Unfortunately, the years of commuting to Orange County had worn me down and I decided to stay at a local client. It was one of those decisions that I was forced to make. If I did not feel pressured, I would have remained at the client in Orange County because it was familiar. I knew everyone, and I knew what to do and how to do it. In short, I knew how to be successful in that environment. However, sometimes we wish for change thinking that it will make us happier. I dreamt of having a day without a 3–4-hour daily commute, and imagined that I would be more productive and much thinner. Life is a series of choices and compromises that we make as the situations arise. We do not always know if we are making the best decision. It is almost as if we have blinders on and cannot fathom the full weight of our decision, as we are limited in the details and our reason can take us only so far.

So, although I would have preferred to stay where I was, I knew that stagnation was not a feasible option for me. One cannot keep up an unbalanced situation for too long. And so I chose the new client, who was local. By doing so, I unfortunately did not leave the former place the way I would have liked, and they refused to pay my final invoice. I decided that the lost money was collateral damage for wanting a better work life balance and made adjustments on my end to factor in the reduced money. Thus, I returned the coat.

Returning from a long weekend in Las Vegas to celebrate my boyfriend's birthday, we stopped at the outlet shops outside of the city. I do not do outlet shopping often since I do not like to hunt for a bargain. If I want something and can afford it, I just buy it then. I found a store that I like and was pleasantly shocked to see that the beautiful coat, that item I wanted, was on sale at 80% off.

I was grateful that there was one coat available in my size and without hesitation I grabbed the coat and paid for it at the register. While paying for the coat, I had a deep sense of contentment. I felt that I was rewarded for my responsible actions earlier in the year. As if this coat was a symbol that nothing you actually love or desire is ever lost. All things are possible. Once we let go of the fear and the doubt, good things can enter and even return to us. In fact, everything comes full circle, from desire to thought and belief, to letting go of the outcome, to attracting all of these actions represent a circle—a full circle of energy. I am grateful for this demonstration of manifestation.

As I trust that all will be well, I feel less need to control everything, or attempt to control everything. The company that I considered interviewing with is still a great company, but I changed my mind about pursuing a job there. It seems a high price to pay for security to make significantly less money and have caveats about how you will be paid, and to be assigned a job title. I take a risk in perhaps not always having the best account or knowing how long I will be with a client. I seek out my opportunities and decide my title now, so I should not have to settle for less pay, less reward, and a lesser title for the benefits of security. While thinking this way, I had an epiphany. If I try to control a perceived threat of stability, then I am assuming that I will not achieve my next goal of economic independence. I am working toward financial freedom, and perhaps placing energy in controlling a potential fear weakens my attraction point for the prosperity I already have and desire to enhance. Also, trying to protect yourself against future negative scenario planning—the "what if" dilemmas—is denying what is now. Now I am exceeding the prior expectations I had for myself, so why assume that I will not continue to grow, that I cannot exceed the current expectations? Why go backwards? As they say, do not look back, do not try to repeat the past whether in love or at work. Move forward and let go of the past to embrace what is appearing for you now.

After declining the interview, a small part of me doubted my decision. However, I know that is the voice of fear and judgment, a companion that I no longer choose to keep around. I can acknowledge the voice of my ego without indulging it. Replacing the doubt with the goals I have has helped diminish the fear and sense of regret I would otherwise carry around and beat myself up with.

That night I dreamt that I was on a train. As I walked from one side to another on the train, I fell, but someone was there to catch me. The person caught me so that I did not fall, and in doing so they embraced me and kissed my forehead. I felt safe and protected.

I believe that the dream was a symbolic message from my angels, informing me that I am on the right path and that they are here to protect and help me in a loving way. Since a picture is worth a thousand words, the images showed me that when I fall and stumble about, someone is there to catch me. It is true when they say we are loved, we are safe and surrounded by angels, for once again, on my life journey I was reminded of that fact. We need to pay attention to our dreams and the symbols that appear, because we are constantly being shown that we are not alone, that we are loved, and that all is well, for it is so.

Chapter 82

Paradise Lost

I
T IS INTERESTING TO NOTICE HOW THINGS UNRAVEL AND FALL
apart when transitioning from one state to another. I have noticed
that, as I end a phase, things go wrong, relationships that worked well
now end bitterly, it seems. The money increase changes to a decrease
in cash flow. The habits that were formed now seem overwhelming
or burdensome, a car crash occurs, signaling that change is imminent.

I used to panic when these things happened, but now I know that
it is just a representation that the changes I desire are coming to me.
If things were smooth and progressed easily, then there would be no
desire for the changes. One could stay in the status quo forever, and for
some that may be fine. Also, I noticed that things often dematerialize
in one area, so that they can materialize in another area, as Penny Peirce
states in her book *Frequency*. "There are a variety of frequency reasons
that things do not materialize when you want them to, such as using
too much willpower, not feeling the result as real in your body, or the

soul knowing something about a negative future impact of the result that wouldn't be on purpose for you."

Penny Pierce's book is brilliant, and explains how we have a "home frequency—which is the tone of your soul. By dissolving your shadows and not holding back the waves of energy that come and go through you, you've begun uncovering the you who's always been inside, the you made of diamond light and love."

My literature teacher Mr. Rourke was onto something when he became fascinated with Quantum Physics, for it seems that we are particles of energy attracting and repelling other particles of energy. We create our world and experiences.

Chapter 83

Chapter 83

A Quantum Leap of Faith

A Quantum Leap of Faith

As I approach the completion of my manuscript, I feel both anxiety and confidence. The awareness of the symbolism to my soul of keeping a promise to myself, for completing something that has been a dream is reason enough to continue on this journey.

I try not to think too far ahead of what needs to happen now and focus only on the immediate next step that I must complete. I am trying not to impose how things will happen just that it will. I am trying not to judge myself in this process.

It is easy to understand why many religions say that the root of all evil is in desire and specifically materialism. The drive for things and for possession is a restless and insatiable master. It is distracting and clutters and dulls your mind. The thirst one may have to own, to have things is also part of certain cultural norms, like owning a beautiful home with a nice yard in a good school district. It is unrealistic to say that you denounce all things unless you are that truly unique person who can live without attachments and brands.

I can see how one can be a slave to things, to a lifestyle or image one holds about themselves or wishes to become. It is also interesting to recognize how little we really need to be happy when the threat of things disappearing happens. Things can bring one awareness about the state of one's soul's evolution and the level of attachment we feel. Material items can be a good barometer of our compassion or lack thereof.

After work, I go for a walk outside. I always feel refreshed when in nature. I always tell myself, it is just a simple walk, not stressful. A leisurely stroll that is not physically demanding is nothing to worry about, helps get me out the door. No doubt the anxiety comes from a childhood of sports and competition.

Today, however, after a little bit of walking, my legs begin to run. Mentally I did not prepare for running, but my legs seem to desire to move faster—bypassing the mental trauma I sometimes go through to push myself to be active. As I run, I feel the movement happening without resistance. It is easy: there is no pain, no heavy feeling or stiff muscles, and even my breathing is easy and relaxed. Running has energized this seemingly empty vessel of a body, as if giving it an electric charge. I can feel a tingle of energy pulsing through my legs down to my toes, making me realize that I have been half dead. A body in motion stays in motion, a body at rest stays at rest unless acted upon by an outside force. The simple laws of physics. If you are sitting on the couch every day after work, watching TV shows of how other people lost weight, you will not become fit through the act of watching others.

My legs seem to want to carry me past where I am quickly. It is as if everything, including my body, is conspiring to move me toward completion. My dreams lately are telling me to finish, and that I am finished. After completing the run and still being able to breathe, I feel as if some of the cobwebs have cleared. The clutter of other people's dramas as they play out in front of my eyes lifts slightly, is swept aside like a curtain, held back by a tie, allowing for an unobstructed view outside the window of my soul. I need peace of mind and clarity to see, to write, to ponder and think. My thoughts and energy need to be clear in order for me to create. There can be no residual ringing of other people's voices or I cannot hear what I need to do next. It is as if the signal to my soul is drowned out by the noise of office politics, family drama or a friend's issues. Not to say that other people are not important but when creating for one's self, there needs to be focus which can only happen in a place of peace and relaxation.

We are easily distracted by the energy and problems of other people. When I get caught in a whirlwind of work, friend, or family drama, I stop focusing on what is important to me. I feel emotionally drained and am unable to concentrate. I feel stuffed with the energy and emotions of others. It is ironic how emotionally draining events and people can exhaust us, as if having completed a triathlon when all you did was talk and listen.

I forgot how exercise can help release that tension and clear the slate of the debris of others. Invigorated, I do errands and cook a healthy meal afterwards.

I even sit at the piano, my dear old friend, and read music and play. Again, I shock myself by concentrating for an uninterrupted 30 minutes to play the piano. I wish that I would not stop doing what I love when work gets busy and crazy. I wish that I could balance more of what is healthy and good for me while still working. Why do I allow stress to end my streak of running and ballet? It is as if I shut down everything except the work brain and sense of responsibility for my projects and basic needs.

I guess the answer to this question is twofold. On one hand, I need to place work in a new light, for it is not as important to me as it once was. I now value myself more. Therefore, I need to put my needs first while still respecting and accomplishing the goals of the organization I work for. On the other hand, discipline will help me maintain habits no matter what is going on inside or outside of me. The question I always ask myself is, why do I forget to do all the things that I know are so helpful to me during stressful times?

Chapter 84

Elusive Enlightenment

THIS MORNING AS I PREPARE TO DO MY ROUTINE OF WAKING UP and getting dressed for another day at my corporate job, I start to think about what it means to be enlightened. Whether it is achievable in a lifetime and whether it is achievable as a person living in the world, not as an ascetic tucked away in a monastery. The distance placed between me and my job when I close my eyes at night to fall asleep is much appreciated, as sleep is a significant buffer from the stress and dramas from work.

I ponder what enlightenment is and if enlightenment could be the realization that all is well, no matter what happens around or to you. The understanding that we are more than the physical body and more than the brain or socially constructed mind that programmed fear, desire, judgment, and objectives into our psyche. Is enlightenment, therefore, a sense of freedom experienced within the mind and spirit? A freedom that enables the feeling of limitlessness, peace and eternity, even though our physical existence is limited, and that the vagaries of one's life will leave you unaffected? Is it more a knowingness, an understanding of how the world works? Is enlightenment the understanding of the temporary nature of our human life, that commonality of all human experience and the eternal nature of our soul that should guide us to the highest state of compassion and peace?

Is enlightenment an ethereal thing, like the wind or the mist? Is it an image that is perceived to exist that few can see and internalize or even grasp, and if attained, is it a fleeting ideal, like a glimpse of a water sprite on a wave?

Chapter 85

Valentino

A S I REFLECT ON HOW I GOT HERE, MY UTOPIA, THE STATE OF freedom that I desired, I understand that one's sense of self-worth and self-love is a fragile state of being. It is not a linear undertaking—one cannot assume that one can move from point A to point B in equidistant increments of time and effort, even if for some that may be possible. For me, the journey is more like a walk along a mountain path. The path zigzags, has dead ends, stops and starts in incongruous places, has abrupt precipices that end suddenly, has peaks and valleys. Each sudden turn, each dark corner helps to reinforce the lessons of love already learned, confirming my understanding and testing my word to myself and others. Forcing me to have faith in myself and that all is well and will be well no matter what shows up in my life.

I completed the manuscript to share my ideas and thoughts with those who will gravitate to this collection of musings when they are ready for what it contains. I have learned to believe in myself and have faith in just me. Not my intelligence, not my education, not my skills or years at my job. I learned to believe in the essence of my soul, my authentic self. This book was drawn to me and out of me.

Before the closing of this book, I decided to go shopping for a Valentino gown or something exquisite. I remembered reading an article about a woman who bought a Vera Wang gown. She had shared that she was not yet married and wanted a beautiful gown, a distinctive dress and that most women buy their most expensive dress they will ever own for their wedding. The author decided that she wanted a beautiful evening dress now. She bought herself an elegant black evening dress from Vera Wang, and every once in a while, when home without a date, she would slip on the gown and feel amazing. I have always loved the idea of having an incredible designer dress that is not for a purpose or an event. Rather, that it can simply be worn to remind you of how beautiful you are. It seems like a romantic idea, and for my independent spirit it also seems like a symbol of freedom. I have forgotten the name of the author of the article, but not her message.

Chapter 86

Loving What is Not What Will Be

How many times have we told ourselves that we will be great when we lose weight, have a different haircut, or get a better paying job? I have constantly believed in the future outside of me and not appreciated what I am at the moment. I especially grapple with this conflict when it comes to the number on the scale and how I look in clothes.

I have learned that there is no shortcut to anything in your life, whether it is losing weight or feeling more secure within yourself. We may find temporary solutions that appear to fix the problem, but if we do not change the behavior and thoughts, the problem reappears and worsens. So, the battle of the bulge for me will only be won when I can make better and more consistent food choices. As easy as it is for me to be physically active, it's difficult for me to stay out of the drive-thru window and away from sugar.

Likewise, changing the thoughts and behaviors in other areas of my life is challenging work, to keep up healthier habits until they are natural and replace the old not-so-great ways. So as with everything, small but constant steps in the direction you want to go is the most effective way to get you to your end goal. As we are human, allowing yourself, forgiving yourself for indulging in the extra carbs or dessert or not exercising and reminding yourself that you can start all over is essential to completing. We are not perfect and for some, discipline comes in waves or spurts, and is not a steady state of action.

Through all of this, we must be kind and encouraging to ourselves. We should treat ourselves the way we would treat a good friend, we should champion our efforts as we would that of our favorite team at the playoffs. The compassion we show ourselves is more genuine and available for others when it is test driven by ourselves first, before sharing it with anyone.

With this sentiment, I know it is time to let go of the number on the scale and to embrace what I am at this very moment. To love not just my soul and spirit, but my human physical form, even if it is not cover girl ready, and to not berate myself for losing the battle of the bulge at this moment.

I am beautiful, damn it!

Now I just need my ego to accept this and stop torturing me with the reasons why I feel that I am not.

I am beautiful. So be it, so it is!

Chapter 87

Table for One

S HE LEAVES THE HAIR SALON AFTER BEING COIFFED AND MADE up with beautiful makeup. Everyone blows her air kisses and wishes her a good evening. She returns to her hotel room and catches her reflection in the mirror. She pauses for a moment and smiles. She is finally learning to like what she sees as she grows comfortable with who she is. So what if she is not thin like when she was in college? She loves herself now, even with a few extra pounds.

Her attention turns to her closet, where she takes out the garment bag containing the exquisite Valentino dress that she bought for herself. The secret is to make your dreams come true, no matter how big or small.

I always imagined myself in a beautiful evening gown, and created a reason for me to be in a gown by buying the garment long before an occasion was presented.

I decided that I wanted to wear my beautiful evening gown at a fabulous dinner. Instead of inviting others to join me, I created a date with myself, to see how far I have come. While on vacation in Paris, I put my theories to work. Testing my ability to enjoy a night out by myself and have a lovely time, to see how comfortable I am in my own skin, as the saying goes. I have always done dinner by myself—I have traveled and lived alone for a large portion of my life. Therefore, a few hours should not be an ordeal.

Tonight is that night. I have a date with myself and a chance to wear one of my couture dream gowns, since, of course, there is a substantial fashion bucket list. I unzip the garment bag and carefully take the dress off of the hanger and slip into the gown. Next I put on the earrings, ring, and diamond bracelet. No necklace is necessary as to not detract from the beauty and craftsmanship of the dress. I put on heels and grab a clutch with the essentials. A quick spray of perfume and I am out the door. Excitedly, I walk to the elevator and get a glimpse of myself in the mirrored hallways. As I enter the lobby, I am greeted by the concierge, the man who arranged for my transportation.

"Hello, Ms. Webster. How are you this evening?" asked the Concierge.

"I am well, thank you. How are you?"

"I am well, thank you for asking. Your car is waiting for you outside. If you follow me, I will take you there."

"Thank you so much," I offer in appreciation.

He escorts me to the car stationed in front of the hotel. He motions to the driver that the passenger has arrived. I discretely place a few euros into his hand and say thank you.

"It is my pleasure; enjoy your evening," he says with a smile.

The driver gets out of the car and introduces himself. He opens the car door for me and helps me get in. He pulls away and before I know it we are in front of the restaurant. "We're here," he announces.

He gets out, opens the door, and helps me to get out of the back seat. I flash him a grateful smile and give him a tip. He thanks me and places his card in my hand. "Please call me at this number when you are ready to be picked up. Enjoy your evening."

"Thank you so much" I reply.

In a beautiful classic Red Valentino gown with designer shoes and jewels, I feel that I look stunning. I carefully walk into the beautiful building and walk to the host's desk. The maître d' asks, "How many in your party?"

"One. A table for one, please," I confidently request.

The maître d' raises his eyebrow and says, "Of course. This way, chérie." He moves the chair at a quaint table for two. He removes the extra place setting and says, "Jacques will be with you shortly."

A tall, lanky, and handsome man saunters over to my table and introduces himself. "Welcome to Chez Alexandre. I am Jacques, and will be taking care of you this evening. May I offer you a glass of wine or champagne while you contemplate the menu?"

"Hi Jacques, a glass of champagne sounds heavenly, why not make it a whole bottle of Veuve Clicquot?" I request.

"Always a reliable choice. Are you celebrating something special, my dear?"

"Yes," I smile, "my book is being made into a movie."

"How lovely!"

"Yes, indeed, dreams and miracles do come true."

"Do you have someone to share your happiness with?" he asks.

"If you are referring to a man, no, I don't have the love of a good man," I explain. "That seemed a very tricky and challenging miracle to make happen. However, along the way I found another and even more beautiful miracle, I found how to love myself and respect myself and my secret to being happy. To be true to myself and honor and value myself and then I can honor and respect others and allow others to be who they are as they are now. I also learned that you are not weak when you ask for help and allow things to happen. That when things don't happen smoothly, they are not supposed to, and that is okay— oh, I apologize for the earful."

"Wow, good for you! That is truly a miracle!" he exclaims.

As Jacques walks away from the table, I'm left to contemplate if it was a good idea have a date by myself in such a romantic place on a Saturday night. A little voice inside—you know, that one that sounds like a reprimanding parent—says, *Foolish girl, what are you thinking, being here by yourself?* Then I stop, tell myself to cancel, clear, and upgrade my thoughts. I will not let fear terrorize me anymore. I laugh to myself and think, how brazen of me to defy the rules of single spinsterhood. Yet, if I had followed the rules, I would not have experienced all that I have, not have gained the insight I have. All is well in my sassy world.

I look around the room, trying to not look nervous or sad. I hold my head up high and represent myself, as Madam Alla would say referring to your presence while on stage. (Leave it to a prima ballerina to preach self-worth during ballet class.) I see people look over and whisper to their companions. Are they commenting on my beautiful dress, or clutch, or shoes? Probably not. They are probably feeling pity for me for being alone in such a beautiful place for lovers, or think that I am being stood up by my date. No doubt they imagine me suicidal and desperate by now.

I let them stare and gossip. I wonder about their lives. Are they happy? Do they feel loved and understood? What are the reasons they chose their partner: love, companionship, money, fear, biological clock, societal pressure, lack of choice?

Jacques returns to the table with the champagne and proceeds to open the bottle. The loud pop of a champagne bottle opening makes many people turn to look toward the noise and at my table.

He pours me a glass. I see he has another glass, probably out of habit, for a table for two. I ask him to pour a glass of champagne and to join me in a celebratory toast.

"Of course, chérie, it would be my pleasure."

As he raises his glass, I raise mine.

"What should we toast to, chérie?" he asks.

"Cheers to dreams and love: the only things worth living for, and they do come true."

"Salut," says Jacques.

"Salut!" I offer in response.

I sit there, peacefully happy, in my gorgeous couture gown. I am beaming from the inside out. I have finally found peace, self-love, and acceptance. I have left the desert of my life and found an oasis.

Jacques saunters away from my table. I overhear a table asking him why I am alone, what am I celebrating? For most people feel that a woman alone is nothing to celebrate. Jacques, replies, "On no, on the contraire, she has accomplished a great feat, success, and self-love. That is much to celebrate." The guests appear shocked, then look at me, then, in a most unexpected gesture, raise their wine glass toward me. I acknowledge their gesture while raising my glass of champagne toward them, bow my head slightly and smile.

I am at a table for one, but I am no less loved, no less special, no less beautiful because I do not have someone across from me to tell me so. Instead, I feel fierce, strong, and enchanting. Like a lioness, I have hunted, I have conquered. I have battle scars and can still see the beauty in life, in others, and in the power of love.

I am at a table for one and see that life is sweet.

May your own company be enchanting; may your reflection cause you to smile. May your thoughts be of peace, give you joy, and most of all, may you have courage to hold your head high when you are at a table for one.

Made in the USA
Las Vegas, NV
05 August 2021